PIECES OF ME

TICH BREWSTER

PIECES OF ME

Tich Brewster

This book is dedicated to Teresa Hughes, my soul sister and best friend, to all my readers, and anyone who has ever suffered depression.

Don't suffer alone, please talk to a friend, a counselor, or pastor.

ACKNOWLEDGMENTS

I want to thank all my readers for the continued support. You guys are awesome and mean the world to me. Big hugs and kisses to you all.

A big thank you to Teresa and Shalisha for standing by my side on this crazy journey. You two have supported me from the beginning. Love you girls to the moon and back.

Also, I want to thank Shalisha Cooper for helping me choose the names Kurt and Lee. I would also like to thank Jennifer Wedmore for helping me choose the names Brandt, Vince, and Alesandra.

When high school student, Makayla, finds herself spiraling down the rabbit hole of depression, feeling like there is no way out, she must make a conscious decision on whether she will allow her loved ones to help her fight the evil battles taking place within her mind.

Pain and shame eat away at me, like maggots consume rotten flesh...

Makayla

I mourn the girl I once was. Happiness no longer exists, and my life is in a downward spiral, filled with bad memories and regrets.

All because of one summer.

I slap a smile on my face and fake my way through each day, hoping life will be better, but when my mother falls into a coma, leaving my brother and I to fend for ourselves, I believe all hope is lost.

Eryc

She's not the same girl I once knew. The girl standing in front of me now is lonely, sad, and dare I say, broken.

No matter the time spent apart, or the damage done, I will be there for her when she needs me the most. Whatever demons she faces, I will help her fight them with a bright smile, vowing to help piece her life back together.

Nothing will remove me from her side. Not this time.

Will the traumas of their pasts and uncertainties of the future leave them far more broken than they were before...or will love prevail, creating a life worth living?

1

Makayla

Heaven and hell, do they exist? Are they more than just these old tales that have been told for centuries? Can one exist without the other, or are they like a packaged deal? I wish I knew the answers to these questions. The idea of being sentenced to an eternity in hell scares the crap out of me, and quite honestly, it is the only reason I have not killed myself.

Oh, the temptation is there. It is always there, taunting me with sweet relief. I struggle with the decision to end my life every single day, and at times it is almost too hard to resist. The promise of relieving myself from my own personal hell calls to me like a siren's song. I'm drowning in my own pain and no one else can see it.

The truth is, I don't want them to see it. I would be mortified if they knew what kind of person I truly am. Besides, if they found out, they would hate me. I cannot stomach the thought of my brother or my mother hating me.

It is so hard to keep the pain hidden.

Pain and shame eat away at me, like maggots eating away at rotten flesh. But despite how lost and alone I feel, I slap a smile on my face and fake my way through each day. So far, no one has noticed. If they have, they have not attempted to ask me what is wrong.

I'm not sure what hurts worse. My pain or the fact that no one seems to see that I am slowly falling apart. Can they not see me fading away into nothing?

My twin has not even felt my loneliness and depression. The fact that he cannot sense that I am falling apart at the seams makes me feel so alone and lost in this world. Why can't he feel my agony? This pain is truly the only thing that keeps me company and I hate it. I hate it with a passion.

I just want this suffering to end.

If I took a handful of pills and allowed the angel of death to take me, would anyone even notice? Would I be missed, or would it be business as usual?

Thaddeus might notice if I was no longer around.

Then again, he has been so busy with Heather, his on-again, off-again girlfriend, he most likely wouldn't even notice that my presence is no longer filling our mostly empty house. It's sad, really, because I have not had more than ten minutes of his time during the whole summer.

No one sees me anymore. It's like I'm just a ghost. My friends don't call, Thaddeus is busy with his girlfriend, and Eryc doesn't talk to me. Although, I can't say I blame him for that. I pretty much disowned him a few years ago so I could get in with the popular crowd. What a mistake that turned out to be.

I just want to die. The pain of living is a burden too great to bear.

Opening the cabinet door, I move my box of Claritin and pick up the bottle of Oxycodone. The prescription Thaddeus never finished taking after his biking accident. I could take the remaining pills and let oblivion welcome me with open arms. I know those little round white pills will kill the pain infecting my soul.

On the bottom shelf, right below the pills, is a tiny box of razors. A thought occurs to me. Taking a handful of pills is not a guarantee. There is always a chance of mom or Thaddeus finding me before my heart stops beating.

Turning the box of razors over and over in my hands, I contemplate removing a blade, digging it deep in my veins and slicing upward. Slicing my veins wide open is a guarantee of ending my suffering.

Deep down I know my mom and brother will be sad. They will grieve for weeks, months, maybe even a year, but they will eventually move on with their lives. There is no moving on for me, I struggle to find the strength just to crawl out of bed.

Death declares to be a friend of mine and promises to be the only solution to ridding myself of these demons. He stretches his hand out to me, daring me to take it and allow him to cleanse my infected soul.

I WAKE up to a fist banging on my bedroom door.

Bang. Bang. Bang.

"Makayla?"

My eyes blink rapidly as I try to bring moisture back to my dry orbs. Jeez, I feel like I've barely slept.

Bang. Bang. Bang.

"Get your butt out of bed. We're gonna be late!" I swear his voice gets louder with each word that comes from his mouth.

Late?

Ha, as if I care. My life has been a living nightmare for the past five weeks. Five weeks of pure hell. So, what if I'm late? Let me be late for school. Who gives a flying flip? Not me, that's for sure.

Bang. Bang.

"Makayla." Thaddeus grunts when I don't say anything. The doorknob jiggles and his heavy breathing comes through that wooden door, letting me know he is about two seconds away from losing his cool.

Rolling my eyes, I prop myself up on my elbows. "Alright, I'm up." If I am to get through this day, I will need a constant stream of caffeine flowing intravenously through my arm. I don't think one cup will do. "Can you fill my travel mug and toss a couple of Monsters into my bag?"

"Already done." The sound of his hand sliding down the door causes me to glance over. "Hurry, I don't want to be late." Thaddeus is a 4.0 student and has not missed a day of school, aside from that time in sixth grade when he had his tonsils removed.

Today is the first day of our senior year. I should be ecstatic but I'm not. In fact, I couldn't care less if I finished out the year and got my diploma. Life sucks, with a capital S.U.C.K.S.

Throwing the covers off, I head to the bathroom. I cringe when I catch sight of my reflection. The bags under my eyes give testimony to my sleep deprivation, and my hair looks like a monkey spent the evening rummaging through the curly strands. "Eww, I look like a frizzy-haired freak."

After wetting my hair in the sink, I pull it back into a messy bun. It's not what I would call pretty, but it'll do.

Then I apply some cream under my eyes, following it with concealer. Blending in the last of my make-up, I sigh at the sight I see in the mirror.

Sheesh, I still look like the walking dead. Story of my life.

Stuffing my cell phone in my back pocket, I rush out of the room. Thaddeus is waiting for me at the bottom of the stairs, arms crossed and boots tapping an annoying rhythm on the hardwood floor. "We have five minutes until final bell."

The look of irritation on his face hits me and I am instantly feeling guilty. My twin brother doesn't need to deal with my shortcomings. All I will ever do is bring him down, piss him off, or mess things up for him somewhere, or with someone else.

He should have left without me. Thaddeus does not need me to screw up his life any more than I already have. I'm a failure. Everything I touch turns to ash.

2

_____

Eryc

My auburn-haired beauty begins to fade as a bright light invades my vision. "Makayla?" I call out to her, but she just smiles. Then she disappears in a cloud of smoke, right before my eyes.

The light only grows brighter, annoying the crud out of me. A groan leaves my lips and I open my eyes, the sunlight blinding me instantly. "Ugh, why didn't I pull the curtains closed last night?" Then it hits me. Today is the first day of school and I don't think I set my alarm before going to bed last night. I am so exhausted. Honestly, I could really use another week of sleeping in before the school year begins. Rolling over, I peer at the clock. "Oh, crap."

Tossing the covers off, I jump from the bed, stubbing my big toe on the leg of the metal frame. Well, isn't this a wonderful start to my day? Injuring myself first thing and then being late on the first day of school. What a way to begin my senior year.

Bouncing on my right foot while holding my left, I breathe several slow breaths. When the pain eases, I rush toward the closet, riffling through what little is hanging on the rod. I had been so engrossed in my book last night that I forgot to wash clothes. This only makes me miss my mother more. Had she been here I would not have to worry about washing my clothes or setting my alarm for that matter.

Staring at the clothing hanging in the closet, I blow out a frustrated breath. The only thing clean is several well-worn T-shirts. "Just great."

Pulling a black shirt from the hanger, I slip it over my head and pray I have a decent pair of jeans that are clean. Opening the bottom drawer on the dresser reveals one pair of faded blue jeans and nothing else. Procrastination definitely came back to bite me in butt. Oh well, this will have to do.

I look back at the clock in my rush to the bathroom, 7:55AM.

"Crap. Crap. Crap." I have five minutes until the final

bell rings, that means I will have to speed brush my teeth and forget about brushing the mop on top of my head. Good thing my hair is short.

I break the world record brushing my teeth. Hoping they are clean enough, but I do make sure to scrape my tongue well. The last thing I want is to have funky breath on top of everything else. After wiping my mouth, I toss the hand towel in the vicinity of the counter and grab my keys and cell phone off the dresser.

Descending the stairs two at a time, I finger comb my hair. Thankfully, it's short enough to pull this off. It'll just leave me looking like a bad boy rocker. A pang of sadness overcomes me when my feet land on the last step and I take in my surroundings. It's strange not having my parents around. The house feels empty without them. I love them, but I'm also starting to love this newfound freedom. What I do miss is the smell of bacon and eggs accompanied by mom's singing first thing in the morning.

My parents moved to Dallas, Texas over the summer after dad was offered a pastoral job. It took some effort, but I finally convinced them I was quite capable of living on my own. Though I think the fact that Aunt Rene lives nearby was the selling point. I'm glad because it would have sucked to have to change schools in my senior year. Thanks, but no thanks. I prefer graduating as an EC Cardinal with the guys I have known since our elementary days.

The drive to EC High school is short since I only live three blocks away. I find a parking space toward the back of the lot and sigh in relief when I see eight other cars pulling into the parking lot behind me. Hitting the lock button on the key fob, I turn and bump into someone.

Before I can call out an apology, Chad Coleman, the quarterback, waves. "Hey, Delmonte."

Stuffing my keys in my pocket, I smile at the guy I had just bumped into. My teammate. "Hey, Coleman." Since I spent the summer in Dallas helping my parents move, I haven't seen my friends since the last week of school.

Chad waves at someone across the parking lot. "Missed you over the summer. Did your parents get settled in okay?"

This guy has been my best friend for as far back as I can remember. He has been there for me through the good, the bad, and the ugly. "Yeah, they did." A couple of girls run past us in their hurry to beat the bell. "They expect me to visit at least one weekend a month. I don't look forward to the five-hour drive between here and there."

Chad crinkles his brows. "Now, that's a long drive. I definitely don't envy you there."

Yeah, me either. "So, what'd I miss while I was gone?"

The carefree look on Chad's face falls and his mouth forms a tight line. He shakes his head slowly, looking almost sad. "Nothing much." A heavy sigh passes his lips, and he kicks at some rocks.

This reaction unsettles me, Chad is not the melancholy type. So, what isn't he telling me? "What happened while I was gone?" I press.

"Nothing." His tone is clipped, signaling that the conversation is over.

I open my mouth to speak but a loud whistle comes from up ahead. We both glance up at the shrill sound. Mr. Wilson, our principle, smooths his tie, glances at his watch, and points to the double doors. "You're late," he yells.

The look on the principle's face is enough to make me cringe. It's apparent that he isn't the slightest bit impressed with our tardiness. Chad and I pick up our pace, jogging toward the building.

I pause next to our principal. "Sorry, Mr. Wilson."

Mr. Wilson nods his head. "Nice to see you again, Eryc. Chad. Don't make a habit of being late."

I nod. "Yes, sir."

A slap to my shoulder draws my attention back to Chad. "Later, Delmonte."

"Later." I start forward but the sound of a motorcycle draws my attention behind me, to the parking lot.

My eyes follow the motorcycle, my heart rate spiking as I catch a glimpse of auburn curls blowing in the wind. It's Thaddeus Yasmeen's motorcycle and sitting behind him is Makayla. She has one arm wrapped around her brother's waist and the other is holding a travel mug.

I had caught a couple of glimpses of her last night when I got home, but other than that I hadn't seen her at all over the summer. My heart skips several beats. She has only gotten more beautiful. Since the day her family moved in next door, back when we were in preschool, I have loved that girl. The two of us were close. In middle school, we would stay up past our bedtime and talk via walkie talkies while staring at one another through our bedroom windows.

That all changed when we entered high school and she wanted to be part of the popular crowd. I suppose hanging out with the pastor's son wasn't the cool thing to do so she withdrew from our friendship, little by little. Sure, we still talked in passing and she was friendly, we just didn't hang out anymore.

Thaddeus, on the other hand, has been the single most popular person at EC from the very beginning. During our junior year, Makayla started hanging out with her brother and his friends, disowning me further. After that, I didn't even get a friendly wave from across the cafeteria. I miss our friendship. God, do I miss it.

Makayla slides off the bike, her auburn hair glinting in the sunlight. Both siblings are wearing biker boots and leather jackets. They begin walking toward the building, which happens to be directly toward me.

Though they are twins, they look nothing alike. Where Makayla has a mass of wavy auburn hair and green eyes, Thaddeus has golden-blonde hair and ice-blue eyes.

The tapping of a shoe pulls my eyes from Makayla. Coach Roberts, who happens to be passing by, raises a brow and points to the clock hanging on the wall.

Shoot, I'm already counted absent. Just great.

"So sorry," I call out as I head toward my classroom.

English IV is on the second floor, so I jog down the hall. Once I'm out of Coach Roberts's sight, I run up the stairs and to room 206. Every eye in the room shoots my way when I walk through the door. A few of the guys nod my way and a couple of the girls smile.

"Welcome to class, Mr. Delmonte." The graying English teacher hands me a thick textbook and several small literature books. "Please, try not to make this a habit."

"I won't, Mr. Green." I scan the room for an empty seat, there are two in the very back of the room. Naturally, I choose the one in the corner.

Just as Mr. Green is about to resume his instructions, the classroom door opens. I glance up to see who else is walking in late.

It's her and my heart melts at the sight of her.

3

Makayla

Mr. Wilson raises one brow as Thaddeus and I approach the building. That look of displeasure mixed with annoyance on his face sends a chill down my spine, and not a good one. This just proves that yet again, I'm a big fat disappointment to those around me.

Thaddeus jogs ahead of me and turns right at the first intersecting hallway. My first hour class is upstairs in room 206. English IV. I groan because English is the one class that I despise more than anything else. You would think since I speak English, I could pass this stupid class with an A, but unfortunately grammar is not my thing.

Mr. Green purses his lips when I open the door. "You're late, Miss Yasmeen."

Well, duh.

Since I don't want to get stuck in detention, I refrain from speaking the first thought that pops into my head. "I'm sorry, sir."

He turns to pick up a massive textbook and several smaller ones. Great, literature books. I glance down at the smaller book resting on top. *Wuthering Heights.* Really? Why can't we have something a little more modern? I would be more than happy to read a horror novel or a thriller.

Placing the books in my hands, he nods to the only empty seat in the classroom. "Take a seat, Miss Yasmeen."

I hate when teachers call me Miss Yasmeen. Do we really need to use proper titles? What is so wrong with calling me by my first name? Makayla sounds a thousand times better than Miss Yasmeen.

As I walk toward the empty desk, I can feel every eye on me. Why didn't I fake being sick this morning? This is the last place on earth I want to be.

When I glance up, John waggles his eyebrows and smirks at me. It's the smirk that gets to me. Oh, God, he knows. Suzy watches me then leans over to whisper in Tina's ear. Do they all know? This cannot be happening.

Bile rises in the back of my throat. I don't want to be here. What I want is to just go home and crawl back into my bed. With all these eyes on me, boring into my back, every inch of my skin crawls. The need to run out of here is strong, and it takes every ounce of strength I have to act like I'm not bothered by their prying eyes.

My heartrate is at an all-time high right, so much so that its pounding in my ears like a drum. Sucking in a deep breath, I let it out slowly in hopes of slowing my heartbeat and calming my nerves. It doesn't help. Nothing ever helps.

Mr. Green clears his throat. It's plain to see that he is getting impatient with me. Until I take a seat, he cannot continue with class.

Looking down at the empty desk, I'm not sure how long I have been standing here. Judging by the snickers around me, I would say I have been standing here like an idiot for quite a while. I drop my books on the desktop a little harder than I mean to. The sound echoes in the near-silent room.

As I sit, I notice Eryc. In my panic, I hadn't even seen him sitting there.

"Hey, Makayla." His eyes are kind, and his smile is the most beautiful and radiant I've ever seen from anyone.

I want to smile back but I can't. I can't even form a *Hey*, *Hi*, or *Hello*. All the whispering around me forces my lips into a tight line, and my brows furrow of their own accord.

Hurt flashes in his eyes before he turns away and I'm instantly sorry for my rude behavior. Though I never meant to be rude. It was not my intention to hurt his feelings. Eryc is the only one in this school that truly cares about me, well, other than my brother of course.

This is my life now. I am nothing but a loser. A big fat loser with absolutely no hope for the future. No matter what I do, it is never right. At least, not anymore. Not since this summer.

Just breathe, I tell myself.

Ignoring the stares, I take my seat and smooth the syllabus out in front of me. I try to focus on the words written on the blue sheet of paper, but my thoughts are elsewhere. I am wondering what the other kids are whispering about and what their notes say. Deep down I know they're gossiping about me.

My heart is pounding out of my chest because I *know* they are all talking about me. How do I know? I can see it in their eyes and feel it in their stare. They have all heard about what took place this summer and they're judging me without knowing the truth behind those tales.

Through all the chaos in my head I can feel *his* eyes on me, watching my every move, but for the life of me I can't turn to face him. There is no way I could handle judgement coming from the one person I used to trust more than anyone. If I look into those gorgeous brown eyes and see condemnation, I will lose it.

Eryc is the one person I cannot stand to receive judgement from. Are our lifestyles different? Yes, absolutely. He is a pastor's kid and lives a clean and wholesome life where I party, drink, and occasionally smoke pot. But if he knew the truth about me, he would hate me and that would kill what little of myself that remains.

The class seems to drag on forever. Mr. Green has gone over the syllabus and is discussing, in great detail, what literature books we will be reading throughout the school year. In addition to the stack of books we received this morning, we will also be reading Shakespeare. Yuck. Give me James Patterson any day, but Shakespeare, no thank you.

After the bell rings, I wait for all the other students to exit before I stand from my desk. Eryc is lingering by the door, and I wish he would just walk on like the others so I can get out of this room in peace.

His eyes search my face as I approach the door. "Makayla, are you feeling okay?"

I refuse to look directly into his eyes, so I stare at his hairline instead. "Um hum."

He reaches out to touch my arm and my whole body stiffens. My skin crawls where his fingers brush the flesh on my arm. Bile rises in the back of my throat and a high pitch ringing in my ears drowns out all noise.

His hand falls away, but he doesn't move. "Are you sure you're okay?"

"Yep, fine." I twist my body to squeeze past him. He doesn't move an inch to give me the room I need, so I use my shoulder to shove him out of the way. "See ya." My footsteps are quick and his are just as quick. Is he following me? Why would he be following me? Doesn't he have a class of his own to get to?

I jog down the stairs and follow the hallway around a curve to my next class, Calculus. Eryc is fast on my heels, and it irritates me that he refuses to give me what I need. Space. When I reach for the door, his hand comes up beside me to hold it open.

I glare at him over my shoulder. "Damnit, Eryc, just go away." On any other given day, I wouldn't dare use that language in front of him, but already my nerves are shot.

"Sorry, Makayla, no can do." He nods his head for me to enter. "We have Calculus together, it seems."

"Perfect," I mumble.

He blows out a puff of air that hits the back of my neck. Judging by the humph that follows, he is upset with me. I wish things were different between the two of us, but I can't go back and change the past. Besides, once he has gotten wind of what I've done this summer, he will surely hate me.

When the truth comes out, I will be unredeemable in his eyes.

And that, my friends, will kill me.

This class surprisingly goes by fast. Coach Roberts

wastes no time going over the syllabus and handing out our first assignment. Assignments on the first day are generally unwelcome but I'm thankful for the reprieve. It is keeping my mind busy and off the whispering going on around me.

As it turns out, Eryc's schedule mirrors mine. We have every single class together. If my life wasn't so jaded, I would be thankful to see his friendly face in every class. But it so happens that my life *is* jaded. I'm the tarnished goods that nobody wants.

I'm a nobody.

A loser.

Even my family would be better off without me.

THADDEUS SHUTS off the motorcycle and I slide off the bike. Mom's car is in the driveway. Such a rarity now days. I wonder if she will actually be home for dinner tonight or if she will be heading back to the office. It seems like she is always at work, I guess that's the way it is when your mom is the DA.

The sound of a car door draws my attention next door, toward Eryc's house. He looks at me over the top of his car but cuts his eyes away just as fast. Guilt washes over me because I know I treated him unfairly today and that is the reason behind his quick glance.

Eryc used to be my best friend. We shared secrets, hung out and played video games. All of that changed when I decided that being popular was more important than our friendship. In the beginning we were still friends, just not good friends. Then I threw it all away and for what? Pain and heartache? Because that's what being popular got me.

"Kids?" Mom's singsong voice comes from the kitchen.

Thaddeus grunts a, "Yeah," as he ascends the stairs, two at a time.

"Yes, mom. We're home." I set my travel mug on the end table. Mom heads down the hallway doing the moon-walk, her hosed feet glide easily on the hardwood floor. As she spins around, she lifts her arms and does some kind of weird Egyptian dance move. As crazy as my mother is, I wouldn't trade her for the world.

Mom smiles at me and it is the most beautiful thing in the world. She leans over and slips her high heels on, a sign that she is about to leave and head back to the office. Her arms wrap around me, and she kisses my cheek then rubs the lipstick residue off. "Honey, I've got to run back to the office. I put money on the counter for dinner."

As usual, mom will be at work. My mom is the DA and unfortunately, that means grueling hours at the office and little to no time at home with us. Why couldn't I just have a normal family? Instead, I got a dad who left us high and dry for his secretary and a mom who works overtime to keep our bills paid.

Mom kisses my cheek one more time then walks out the front door with promises to see us before we go to bed.

I step out on the front porch to watch her drive away. As I turn to walk back in the house, I see Eryc gathering the mail. He is standing on the curb in his faded blue jeans and a black T-shirt that accentuates his bulging biceps.

Nothing about him resembles a preacher's kid. Those clothes and that messy hair, mixed with his muscular build, give him a bad boy Rockstar kind of vibe. He is sexy as hell and all the girls fawn over him.

Taking a step back, I duck inside the house before he can spot me.

4

Eryc

Brenda waves at me as she drives past. I hate that Makayla's mom works so much. A girl needs her mother around, especially during her teenage years, or so I hear. The two of them should be bonding over clothes, coffee, and books. Brenda should be giving her daughter advice about dating and college.

I'm not suggesting that Brenda is a bad mother, she is a great woman, but Thaddeus and Makayla have basically raised themselves since we were in fourth grade. I am sure their mother's absence has taken a toll on them. It would have for me if I were in their shoes.

Tossing the mail on the kitchen counter, I stare at the tray of cookies that my aunt left. There is way more than I will be able to eat, so I pull a Ziploc baggie from the drawer and start shoving cookies inside. Chocolate chip is Makayla's favorite so I am hoping this little gift will get me back in her good graces.

Something big is going on with her and I want her to know that I am here for her, no judgements. Whatever she is going through, we can go through it together just like we used to. Hell, I would walk through fire for that girl.

Taking a bite of cookie, I wipe the chocolate from my lips and walk out the front door with my Ziploc bag of goodies. In a few long strides, I am standing in front of her house. The curtains are closed, and I hear rap music blaring from the other side of their front door.

I lift my hand to knock but the door swings open before my knuckles can reach the wood.

A blonde-haired girl looks at me with shock. "Eryc? What are you doing here?" Her words are not spoken with attitude, but it is clear she understands that I don't fit in with their crowd. I never have and never will.

"Hello, Heather. Is Makayla home?"

"Yeah," she looks around the door, probably at Thaddeus. Those two have been dating for almost a year now. Well, off and on.

Makayla's brother waltzes into view. "Eryc." Taking

Heather's hand, he leads her out, toward his bike. "Makayla's in the kitchen," he calls over his shoulder.

"Thanks." He doesn't say anything else, just a nod of acknowledgement before straddling his bike and taking off.

The rap music gets louder the closer I get to the kitchen. I'm not familiar with the song blasting through the speakers, the rap on my playlist is pretty limited. Classic Rock N' Roll and the newer country music with Jelly Roll are what take up my playlist.

Makayla is sitting on a barstool, her elbows on the island, and her head resting in her hands. The soft shaking of her shoulders signals that she is either giggling over something or crying. Judging by her slumped form and choice of music, I would say she is definitely crying.

I'm not quite sure how to approach her. Is there a right or wrong way to approach a crying girl? Should I just back away and go home? She didn't seem too thrilled about seeing me at school today. Will she even want me to ask her what's wrong? My feet remain rooted to the floor where the hardwood meets the tile of the kitchen.

A sniffle reaches my ears, and I can't stand it any longer. I rap my knuckles on the wall to gain her attention. Immediately, her back stiffens and she tries to discreetly wipe her nose on the collar of her shirt. A second later I hear rattling. It almost sounds like a bottle of pills. Maybe she's taking medication for something.

Swiping her arm over the countertop in front of her, she sweeps the contents of whatever made the rattling noise into her purse. Turning on her barstool, she meets my gaze. "Eryc?"

I nod like an idiot because my brain turns to mush when I see her tear-stained face.

"What are you doing here?" she asks, sounding shocked to see me standing in her house.

Why is it that my tongue has suddenly forgotten how to function? Seriously, I am an eighteen-year-old living on my own, and I can't even form a single word. Instead, I continue to look like a fool and just lift the bag of cookies I hold in my hand, as if cookies are the solution to her troubles.

Her gaze travels to the bag of treats and a small smile curves her lips. It's a smile but it doesn't reach her eyes. My best friend, the girl I have loved since the beginning of our friendship, is in pain. Not I-scraped-my-knee kind of pain, but heart-wrenching pain. Wiping at the remaining tears, she nods to the bag and asks, "Chocolate chip?"

Since my brain is still not functioning, I nod my head. She must think I'm a complete idiot by now. How could she not? But seeing those tear streaks on her cheeks and those puffy red eyes, her pain is breaking my heart. I wish, more than anything, that I could take away whatever is making her so sad and replace it with happiness.

Zipping her purse, she sets it aside and crosses the

distance. Peering at the bag, she holds out her hand. I pull the top open and place a cookie in her waiting palm. If I had to guess, I would say that it has been a while since Makayla has had a freshly baked cookie. Her eyes sparkle as she inhales the chocolaty scent before biting into the sweet, chewy goodness.

Chocolate stains the corner of her mouth so I reach out to wipe it away. The action causes her to immediately take a step back, her shoulders stiffen and her jaw clenches. What did I do that was so wrong?

All I wanted to do was wipe away the chocolate residue, not harm her. "Makayla?"

"I'm sorry." She takes another bite then goes to the coffee pot to brew a cup of java. "Would you like a cup of coffee?"

"Sure." I really don't feel like drinking coffee this late in the day, but if it'll buy me some time with her, I will drink it. While she brews our coffee, I slip onto a barstool and set the bag of cookies on the countertop.

The Keurig only takes seconds to spit a cup of coffee out. By the time I have myself situated, she is setting a cup in front of me and digging another cookie out of the bag, dipping it in her hot java.

"Mmm, these are so good." Licking her lips, she asks, "Did Rene make these?"

"Yes." Following her example, I take a cookie and dip it in my cup. This is not something I do with my cookies, I'm more of a milk dipper, but when that soft cookie crumbles into millions of mushy pieces when my lips close around it, I let out a satisfied moan. Now I understand her obsession with coffee and cookies. These are good. It's the perfect mix of both sweet and bitter.

We eat in silence, her music still blaring from the speakers hanging on the wall. There is no normalcy to our strange visit. Part of me wonders if she is mad at me for something, or if her heart has hardened toward me from the distance she put between us during our high school years. If there was a way to read her mind, I would. Unfortunately, I don't possess such a power.

When the last of the cookies have been eaten, I drink the remaining cookie-crumb infested coffee and stand. "Thanks." She doesn't say anything, just carries our cups to the sink. "I'll see you tomorrow."

"Yeah." Her back is still to me, and her shoulders are starting to slump again. I want to reach out to her. It is killing me to stand here and watch her look so defeated. "Goodnight, Eryc."

And just like that, I have been dismissed.

Conversation over.

Go home, Eryc.

5

I'm not sure what time I finally fall asleep. After reading and watching television in bed, I shut off the lights and glance at the clock. It's almost two in morning. Insomnia, the story of my life. I have a difficult time falling asleep and once my brain finally does settle down, it is usually a restless couple of hours before I am back up again.

That is where I'm at now, the restless part of sleep. Every whistle from the wind blowing outside, every creak of the floorboards in the hallway, the neighbor's dog that barks at anything that moves, including leaves blowing in the wind—every noise stirs my consciousness and I crack my eyes open, toss around, then close my eyes and go back to sleep only to repeat it a few minutes later.

That damn dog starts barking again as soon as my mind settles into sleep, and I open my eyes to glance at the clock, yet again. It's nearing four o'clock. Then I roll over and stare at the ceiling. It wouldn't matter if I slept in a soundproof room, my mind still would not shut off enough to give me peaceful rest.

The sound of a floorboard creaking outside my bedroom pulls my attention toward the door. Leaning up, I wait to see if my bedroom door will open. Maybe mom is finally home. She was supposed to be home before we went to bed, but she never came. I wait, anxiously, to see if she is out there, waiting for her to come in and check on me.

She doesn't.

Figuring its Thaddeus walking around, I lay back down and pull the covers up to my neck.

A couple seconds pass and the door cracks open. The light from the hallway spills into the room illuminating my visitor. Like I suspected, it's not mom, it's Thaddeus. But why is he standing in my doorway? He should be in bed or on his way back to bed, not lurking around like a creeper.

"Makayla?" he whispers. I don't say anything, I just lay here and watch him as he stands in the doorway raking his hand through his hair. Almost a minute goes by before he speaks again, this time his voice is a little louder. "Damnit, sis, wake up."

I don't tell him that I was already awake. Instead, I say, "I'm up." I prop myself up on my elbow and tilt the clock to see the time. It's just after four. "What are you doing up at this hour?"

Pushing the door open further, he steps fully into the room, hands in his pockets and rocking back and forth on his heels. This is odd behavior for Thaddeus. Words are not something the boy lacks and awkwardness is not something he is familiar with.

My pulse quickens and goosebumps form on my arms. His awkward behavior is a telltale sign of bad news. "Thaddeus?" Closing the distance to the bed, he sits down on the edge of the mattress. Silence hangs in the air and I worry if maybe he has found out my secret. "Thad?"

His sad eyes meet mine. "Sis, I need you to come downstairs. Like, right now."

Oh, God, he knows. That has to be why he is in here demanding I go downstairs. Did he tell mom? Is she down there waiting for me? The thought upsets my stomach. If mom knows the truth, she is going to kill me.

I swallow the lump in my throat. "Why do you need me downstairs at four in the morning?"

"Just get your butt out of bed and come downstairs." He stands and walks to the door. Resting a hand on the doorframe, he glances back at me. "Rene and Eryc are here."

Why is Eryc and his aunt here? I love Rene. Over these last few years, she has done what my own mother should've been doing. She has taken me shopping, given me the sex talk, helped me with homework, lectured me, and offered her motherly advice. But none of that explains why she is in my house at four in the morning.

Before I can ask why they are here, Thaddeus is gone. The air in the room seems to chill about ten degrees, or maybe it's the blood draining from my face and fear that causes my body to freeze.

Throwing the covers back, I slide my feet over the edge of the mattress and stand. The hardwood floor is cold to my bare feet, but I ignore the need to grab a pair of socks. Instead, I just head out the door.

The stairs creak and groan when I descend. Each step twists my gut with fear and anxiety. Halfway down the staircase, whispering meets my ears and I stop to listen. I hear Rene's voice, but I can't make out her words. A hair tickles my nose, and I'm suddenly reminded that my hair is a wild mass of frizzy curls. I try in vain to finger comb them into submission. After several failed attempts, I give up. Cupping my hands over my mouth, I blow a few breaths. Well, it's not minty fresh breath but at least it's not quite dragon breath either.

Thaddeus is whispering now. The only words I can

understand are *Why her?* Who is he talking about? I pray he isn't talking about me, especially with Rene and Eryc.

I crane my neck and strain to listen for my mom's voice, but hers isn't among them. What on earth is going on? Taking a deep breath, I descend the rest of the steps. When my feet land on the floor, all voices cease, and every eye turns my way.

What worries me isn't the tears streaming freely from my brother's eyes, or the red and puffy eyes of Rene. No, what pierces all the way to my soul is the sorrowful expression Eryc is wearing. The look on his face speaks volumes. Panic creeps up from my toes, travels up my body and sets its claws into the depths of my heart.

My breaths come in short pants, oxygen failing to enter my lungs. I have never hyperventilated before but I'm pretty sure this is what is happening to me. With no oxygen feeding my lung tissue, my chest burns, and my pants turn to gasps. Bending at the waist, I place my hands on my knees. The skin on my face is tingling, my vision is slightly blurry, and now I'm beginning to feel lightheaded.

Someone I love is hurt. I can feel it down in my bones.

Seeing how the only person missing from this room is my mom, dread overwhelms me. Something bad has happened to her, I can feel it. This cannot be my life. I can't live without my mother.

Pushing myself up from my knees, I start to sway. The room is spinning and nothing is in focus anymore. I think

I may get sick. Darkness closes in, dimming the light from my peripheral until all I see is a pinpoint of light. My legs are getting heavy, and I know I'm about to pass out and fall.

Though I can't see, I still feel the spinning sensation. It feels like I'm on a tilt-a-whirl and the ride is about to break and send me flying into oblivion.

Before I hit the ground, strong arms wrap around me and hug me close. I'm glad for that because I have no strength to save myself.

6

Eryc

I'm dreaming of Makayla, a normal occurrence for me. Dreaming of pushing her on a park swing as her laughter fills the air around us. She is happy and the sun glints off her auburn hair. Those green orbs sparkle when she glances over her shoulder.

This is my happy place.

My dream is interrupted when a hand grips my shoulder and shakes my body violently. Against my will, the dream vanishes like a cloud of smoke, and I crack open an eye to glare at the intruder. Aunt Rene is standing over me, gripping both of my shoulders and shaking me with all her might.

"I'm up, I'm up." I pry her hands off me. "Jeez, what is wrong with you?" Snatching my cell phone off the nightstand, I glance at the time.

3:55AM.

"Seriously? It's the middle of the night."

It is now that I notice my aunt's hands are shaking and she has taken to pacing back and forth next to my bed. "Eryc." She doesn't say anything else. This is unlike her, and that fact sets off my nerves. I sit up and reach for the lamp, pulling the chain. Yellow light illuminates the room. Her eyes are red and puffy, and her face is unusually pale.

"Aunt Rene?" I rub the sleep from my eyes and sit up straighter. "What's wrong?"

"It's Brenda." She chews on her thumbnail, a nervous habit of hers. "I think you should go next door with me. You need to be there for Makayla when I tell the twins."

Her words are like ice-cold water to my body. My mind is suddenly on high alert, and I rip the covers from my body, not caring that I am only in my boxers. Aunt Rene doesn't seem to notice my predicament, her eyes are staring blankly at the wall behind me.

I rush to pull on my discarded jeans from the floor at the foot of the bed, and then pull a fresh shirt from the closet.

She hasn't moved since I got off the bed, so I touch her lightly on the shoulder. "Aunt Rene?"

Shaking her head, she turns to me, looking at me with her sad eyes. "I'm really sorry for waking you up like this, in the middle of the night, to drag you next door."

I wave off her apology. Waking me was the right thing to do. If Makayla needs me then I will be there. Sleep be damned. "I'm glad you did. I wouldn't want them to go through this alone, especially Kay."

It doesn't take me long to slip on my shoes and slide my cell phone and keys into my pocket. Aunt Rene follows me down the stairs and out the front door. Locking the house behind me, we walk across the lawn toward Makayla's house. My aunt lifts her hand to knock on the heavy door. Thirty seconds pass and there is no answer. She knocks again with the same results. Then she places her finger on the doorbell and presses, not once or twice but repeatedly like a crazed maniac.

A light from the upstairs window illuminates the grass along the sidewalk. Through the small window in the top portion of the door I see Thaddeus walking down the stairs, rubbing his eyes. He peers out and his eyes grow wide when he sees the two of us standing on his front porch.

The deadbolt clicks and he opens the door. Thaddeus leans his head against the heavy wood with a yawn. "What are you two doing here at this hour?"

My aunt touches Thaddeus on the cheek. "Sweetheart, may we come in?"

I see it in his eyes, the wheels in his mind are turning. He straightens and steps aside. Looking around, his eyes scan the floor by the front door, the key hook on the wall, and finally land on the end table in the living room.

Is he looking for signs of his mother?

"What's wrong?" he asks.

Aunt Rene is wringing her hands in front of her. "Sweetheart, I need you to go get your sister."

Thaddeus shakes his head. "Tell me what's wrong."

"Sweetheart," my aunt says but Thaddeus stomps a foot, cutting her off.

"Just tell me." His eyes scan the key hook again. "It's about my mom, isn't it?" Thaddeus is very perceptive and my heart breaks for him.

Aunt Rene touches his arm in a show of affection. "There's been an accident. Your mother is in surgery as we speak." She grips his arm and pulls him in for a hug. "I need you to wake Makayla."

The color drains from his face and he walks backward, slowly. When his foot bumps against the banister, he turns and ascends the stairs two at a time.

I follow Rene into the living room and sit on the sofa. From here, I have a clear view of the banister in the entry-way. My heart aches because I know that Makayla's world is about to be flipped on its axis.

Several minutes pass and I am starting to wonder if I need to go up and assist Thaddeus, but then I hear his heavy footfalls. The weight of the world is sitting on his shoulders, and it shows in the worry lines on his forehead and the slump of his shoulders as he walks into the living room.

The sofa dips where he sits. Thaddeus rests his elbows on his knees and cradles his head in his hands. I've never seen him look so defeated. It's like he is a shell of the person he was just this afternoon.

I want to say something, anything, but what can I say. I have never had a parent in critical condition. These are circumstances I am not familiar with on a personal level, and I have no idea what he is feeling. Whatever I say will only go in one ear and out the other because I can't relate.

Aunt Rene kneels in front of Thaddeus and speaks to him in hushed tones, comforting him with her words of wisdom and love. She has experienced the loss of her father, so she understands the grief he is going through.

Thaddeus appears to be receptive to her words of encouragement. He is asking questions about the surgery and Brenda's chances of survival when soft thuds come from the entryway. They stop and I imagine Makayla standing just out of sight, listening to the whispers echoing from this room. I count to eight before her footsteps sound again.

I am watching, waiting for her to come into view. Her

bare foot is the first thing I see, her toenails are painted fuchsia. Inch by inch, the rest of her comes into view. Taking in the sight of my aunt and her brother, she sucks in a deep breath, but it's when her eyes lock on mine that all color drains from her face. Fear darkens the green of her eyes to the point they are nearly black.

Her shoulders rise and fall at a fast rate, and I fear she will hyperventilate and lose her balance. Scooting to the edge of the cushion, I am ready to stand and go to her aid should she need me.

Rise. Fall. Rise. Fall.

Her shoulders are moving at a faster pace now, and her face is growing deathly pale. Bending at the waist, Makayla braces herself with her hands on her knees and continues to breathe erratically.

Seeing the girl that was once my best friend, the girl that I have secretly loved since our cartoon days, suffering and in need, I stand. At the same time, she pushes herself up, but her body is not in control anymore.

Not willing to let her lose her balance and hurt herself, I quickly make my way to her side. In a few long and fast strides, I am standing next to her. I'm glad I acted because now her eyes are glazed over, and I can see that she is on the verge of losing consciousness.

Stepping around her, I spread my feet and ready myself for the added weight. Her body tilts and sways like a drunken loon and that's when I slip my arms around her and lift her body, cradling her against my chest.

"It's okay, angel," I whisper into her ear.

When I turn around, Thaddeus is standing next to my aunt. The worry lines on his forehead are deeper now. "Will she be okay?" he directs his question to my aunt but his gaze stays glued to his sister.

Carrying her into the living room, I lay her on the sofa and stroke her hair away from her face. I look up at my aunt, waiting for her answer.

"Yes, I think she'll be fine, Thaddeus. She just fainted." She touches his arm. "Can you get a cool rag for her face?" Shooing me out of her way, she pulls a penlight from her purse and kneels next to the sofa then lifts Makayla's eyelids and shines the light quickly across each eye.

Footsteps echo in the quiet house when Thaddeus runs from the room to fetch a cool rag. My eyes never stray from Makayla and my fingers continuously caress her forehead. Water runs in the distance then footsteps pound against the hardwood, growing louder until Thaddeus is standing next to me. He hands me the cool, wet rag and takes a seat next to Makayla's feet.

Placing the rag on Makayla's forehead, I stroke her cheek with my finger. This fainting spell of hers is odd. I don't think she has ever fainted before. Why now? We haven't even told her the news about her mother yet. It is odd but maybe she fainted because she sensed the worry in Thaddeus and the anxiety overwhelmed her.

Moving the cloth around on her face, I pray she will be okay. She needs her health and extra strength for herself and her brother as they deal with Brenda's critical condition.

When my fingers brush against her lips, her eyes crack open, and a groan rumbles out from her throat.

7

Makayla

The dull yellow light in this room is blinding and makes my eyes water. Closing them again, I groan at the thudding in the back of my skull. Sheesh, I feel like I have been hit by a Mac truck traveling at a high speed. Breathing in through my nose, I hold it and count to five before I release the air.

I do that four times and then open my eyes again. They flutter at first, blocking out most of the painful light. It doesn't take long until they adjust to the brightness, and I open them fully. What just happened, did I pass out?

Eryc's brown eyes are the first thing I see. Concern

shines bright in their brown depths, along with something that looks a lot like affection. That is the thing with Eryc, he is very compassionate. If you looked up compassionate, caring, or even loving in the dictionary, you would see his face printed on the pages as the definition. Okay, maybe not, but that is my opinion, at least.

The cushion shifts near my feet and I glance down. My brother is biting his lower lip and staring at me intently. I'm not sure I've seen him so concerned for my safety before. He's as white as a sheet and his blue eyes are more of a midnight color.

Rene enters the room with a glass in hand. It's when I see her that I remember the ill vibes I felt when I was descending the stairs. I remember getting the distinct feeling that someone I love is in danger. Blood rushes through my veins so fast that it's pulsing in my ears. Deep within my soul, I know this is about my mom. It's like my soul can feel her torment.

Nothing tragic can happen to my mom. Other than Thaddeus, she is all I have in this world. My dad is a loser who chose to abandon us for a cheap thrill with his secretary. We don't even have a way to contact him should we need to.

Dread washes over me and I allow my eyes to roam around the room, looking for any signs that mom came home during the night, but I don't see any. Oh God. I don't see mom's briefcase on the end table. I bolt upright, the cold, wet rag falling onto my lap and dampening my pajama bottoms. Craning my neck, I peer into the entry-way. Her shoes are not sitting next to the front door like they normally would be.

Those observations trigger emotions. Emotions that are already high, and a tear trickles from my eye. It slowly trails down my cheek, along my neck, and soaks into the collar of my shirt. The wetness is a testament to the tragedy I'm positive has happened to my mother. Our mother. I'm not going through this alone, Thaddeus is just as affected as I am.

"Drink this, sweetie." Rene presses a glass into my hand.

I don't need to peer inside the glass to know what is in it, I can smell the sweet fragrance of orange juice. Knots form in my stomach at the sugary aroma and I'm instantly nauseous. With a shake of my head, I gently shove the offending liquid away.

There's resistance as Rene presses the glass to my open palm. "Go ahead, Makayla," she urges. "You just fainted. This will do you some good."

Rene is a doctor so if she thinks I need the juice then I probably do. Raising the glass, I hold my breath and bring it up to my lips. If I don't breathe, the smell won't force my stomach to spew its contents. Right? At least I hope I'm right.

Tilting the glass, I take a small sip. The cold liquid

does the exact opposite of what I initially feared. The juice soothes the raging waves in my stomach and calms the storm. I take another sip, and another, until the glass is empty.

Handing the glass back to Rene, I scoot to the middle cushion so Eryc can sit next to me. I'm sure the hardwood is hard on the knees. "I think I'm fine now."

Eryc doesn't need to be told, he stands from the floor and sits next to me on the sofa. His leg firmly presses against mine.

"Why are you guys here?" I ask, looking at Rene. "Please don't say it's because of mom."

Thaddeus is sitting on the other side of me. He reaches over and takes my hand, sandwiching it between his calloused ones. I see it in his eyes. It is about mom. She's hurt or in danger and he is trying to console me before Rene delivers the devastating news.

"No." My voice is shaky and Thaddeus scoots closer, wrapping his arms around me and holding on tight.

I know his actions are meant to be comforting but it is anything but. Being trapped in his arms strips away my freedom. It is imprisoning me. I hate this feeling of being trapped in the vice of another's arms.

Eryc moves off the sofa and I follow his movements with my eyes only. A box of tissues is at the other end of the room, next to the television. He grabs it and comes back, kneeling in front of me. Setting the box on my lap, he cups my face, his thumb brushing away a lone tear that breaks free.

Caressing my jaw with his fingertips, he leans his forehead against mine. The pounding of my heart only increases the longer we sit in silence. It's slowly killing me. I open my mouth to speak and my bottom lip trembles. "Eryc, just tell me. Please," I whisper.

Tears blur Eryc's face. Blinking would clear my vision, but I can't bring myself to break eye contact, not yet. He is the only thing grounding me at the moment. I need this. Need him. Without him I have no doubt I would lose it. More so than I already am.

His nose presses into mine, his breath hot on my upper lip. "Kay."

Kay. It seems like a lifetime ago that he called me by that nickname.

A crease develops between his brows and his hands cup my face a little tighter. "It's your mom."

Tremors rack my body. You only get one mom and sadly I haven't had the pleasure of bonding with mine like a daughter should. Would I ever get that chance? Eryc's words echo over and over in my mind.

It's your mom.

Fear seeps into my bones like ice and a scream then rips loose from deep within my soul, tearing through me in a painful escape.

I don't know how long I have been screaming, but now

my throat is sore and scratchy. Thaddeus is standing across the room sobbing, and I am no longer sitting on the sofa. I am now sitting on Eryc's lap, his arms around me and he is rocking me back and forth.

This action is innocent and meant to comfort me, but it is having the opposite effect. My life has been a downward spiral for several weeks now and the simplest of touches make me want to puke. I pry his arms from me and push myself off his lap, sitting on the other side of the sofa.

Hurt flashes in his brown orbs. It's only there for a second before Eryc clears his emotions from his face, but I saw it and it makes me feel guilty for causing it.

Rene sits on the coffee table. She leans forward and takes my hand, rubbing circles on the back of it. "Sweetheart, your mom was in an accident. She was driving on I-44 when a drunk driver lost control and hit her car."

Acid burns the lining of my stomach and sends a fiery trail up my throat. There is no time to make a run for the bathroom. I push off the cushion and lean over the side of the sofa to let out the contents of my stomach on the plush white rug. If my world hadn't just been turned upside down, I might have died from embarrassment.

Sadly, my world hasn't only been flipped upside down, it is spiraling out of control. I can no longer tell up from down or left from right. Embarrassment doesn't even register on my radar. All I can focus on is this dooming void coming for me.

Lifting the collar of my shirt, I wipe my mouth clean.

Rene leans forward to peer into my eyes. "Your mom is in surgery as we speak. It's bad but you'll have me and Eryc to lean on while your mom heals."

I hear the words leaving her mouth, but my brain is not comprehending them. Robotically, I nod.

"You and Thaddeus get dressed and we'll drive you to the hospital." She points to the rug. "Don't worry about this, I'll take care of it."

The pulsing in my ears grows louder when I stand. With every beat of my heart the thundering pulse resonates in my ears. A hand takes mine and I look down. Thaddeus is holding onto me like a lifeline, I am his and he is mine. An urge to pull away overwhelms me, but in this moment, he needs me, and that trumps the need to preserve myself from human contact.

Silently we walk up the stairs, never breaking our connection.

We bypass his room and walk to mine. "What will we do if mom doesn't—"

"Don't even finish that sentence." Thaddeus pushes open my bedroom door, releasing my hand. "Mom will be fine." His words are reassuring but I can see it in his eyes. Even he doesn't believe his own words. "Get ready and I'll meet you downstairs."

I nod and watch him walk away.

THE HOSPITAL IS ONLY a fifteen-minute drive from my house. Though it's not far, tonight the drive seems to drag on forever. Minutes feel like hours. The longer I sit in this car, staring out the window, the more my imagination runs wild.

So far, my mind has conjured images of my mom with massive head wounds, broken and twisted limbs, missing appendages, and even a disfigured face—basically, every grotesque thing imaginable. As if picturing them once wasn't bad enough, my brain has these images playing on repeat in my mind and I can feel myself slowly going insane from the mental torment.

Thaddeus is sitting in the front passenger seat, rocking back and forth, and I catch his reflection in the window. He is chewing on his thumbnail, a habit he hasn't had since we were in elementary school. Watching him, I can see that the unknown is clawing at his nerves like it is mine. Grabbing the sleeve of his shirt, he wipes at his nose and continues torturing his thumbnail.

Eryc is sitting next to me, one arm resting on my shoulder, his fingers caressing my upper arm. His other hand is stretched across his stomach, holding mine where it rests on the seat between us. This guy is offering me his strength and comfort through touch. It is taking every ounce of strength not to jerk away.

I have ignored him for the last few years, all for my own selfish gain, but he is comforting me like nothing between us has changed. In my heart, I know I don't deserve it, but I'm thankful for his support. He is the glue holding me together.

Buildings pass by in a blur. The dotted lines on the highway merge into one solid yellow line as my gaze stays fixed. It's not cold out, but my body is chilled to the bone. My heart is hammering painfully in my chest the closer we get to the hospital.

Thump, thump. Thump, thump. Thump, thump.

Fear is an ugly thing. It is a cloaked demon, breaking my heart and soul, piece by piece. This demon of fear is willing me to fall into submission. My self-control is teetering on the edge of submitting to fear or remaining strong for mom and Thaddeus.

Through my torment, Eryc is my light in this raging storm. His light is giving me the tiniest bit of hope to hold onto, and it's that bit of hope that is keeping me from succumbing to fear.

I'm terrified of what will happen if my mom dies. Will her death be the one thing that will push me over the edge? It might. I'm already swimming in a black abyss, and I fear mom's death will be the thing that severs the last of my will, leaving me to drown in my own misery.

Restaurants and gas stations zip by, letting me know we are getting close to Tulsa Memorial. The hospital is just another mile up the road. I close my eyes and lean my forehead against the cool glass of the window. Butterflies swim in my belly, but it's not the good kind of butterflies. These butterflies are brought on by anxiety and fear.

A left turn brings us onto the hospital property. Rene follows the curve to the left and pulls up to the emergency doors. "Go on in. I'll park and meet you inside."

The sound of a car door opening and closing does nothing to stir me. Thaddeus is standing on the curb, his back to me. The bouncing of his leg is the only sign of his nervous tick. I hear Eryc encouraging me to exit the vehicle, but my body is rooted to the spot. I'm glued to the seat, so-to-speak.

Another door opens and closes, the car shifts when this person exits the vehicle. My mind is in shambles. I know I should get out and find my mom, but my body is unresponsive to the signals my brain gives. When my door opens, Eryc holds his hand out for me.

It baffles me, really, that he can continue to be nice to me when I have done nothing but ignore him for the better part of our high school years. I'm not sure I could respond the same way if it had been him ignoring me. Not to this level of kindness anyway. He will never know how much this means to me. This small act of kindness is what is standing between me and that bottle of Oxycodone and razors in my medicine cabinet at this very moment.

Thaddeus holds my left hand, Eryc my right. The three of us walk through the double doors. I know I look like an awful mess, wearing pajamas, flip-flops, and sporting a mass of wild curls frizzing out on the top of my head. My brother looks only slightly better with his ripped jeans and winkled shirt, which probably came out of his hamper.

Behind the glass window, a receptionist is typing on a computer. She glances up at us but furrows her brows as she once again focuses on the screen in front her.

I bend toward the small opening. "Excuse me, I'm here to see my mom."

The buttons on the keyboard click with each movement of her fingers.

The dark-haired receptionist doesn't acknowledge me, except to raise one finger to gesture for us to wait. Two nurses enter the reception area with electronic devices in hand. One of them flips through a filing cabinet and the other leans her hip on the counter as she waits for her co-worker.

Eryc knocks on the window and the redheaded nurse approaches. "Can I help you?"

"Yes, ma'am." Eryc steps toward the large window, bending down to the speaker hole in the glass. "We're here for Brenda Yasmeen, she was brought in earlier. She's in surgery."

Opening her device, she cradles it in one hand while typing with the other. A few clicks later she says, "Take the elevator down the hall," she points to our left, "up to the third floor. Follow the orange signs on the right, past the double doors, and the waiting room will be at the end of the hall."

"Thank you." Eryc takes my hand, again, and leads me to the elevators.

8

Eryc

Makayla walks beside me, zombielike, allowing me to guide her through the hospital. I'm not sure she is aware of much going on around her. Sure, she looks at the doctors and nurses we pass in the hallways, but her stare is blank and unfocused. It's like the lights are on but no one is home. I can only imagine how scared she must be.

Thaddeus is no longer walking beside his sister. Instead, he is following along behind us, his biker boots smacking the tile floor with each step he takes. Though he seems to be doing better than Makayla, but I think it's because he is trying to be strong for her.

The waiting room is mostly empty, there is only one other family in here. A man, a woman, and three small children. Several chairs and two small round tables are vacant on the other side of the room. I lead Makayla over to the first table. She picks up a magazine and thumbs through it, but her gaze is at the window in front of her and not on the magazine.

Thaddeus sits next to his sister and the legs of his chair scrape the tile as he scoots toward the table. I have no idea what to say to either of them. Small talk seems too insensitive considering their mom is critical, so I go with something more expected.

"Thaddeus, would you like me to give Heather a call?" I saw the two of them together at school today, and then again at their house after school, so it appears the two are still dating.

Tired and sad eyes peer up at me. Without saying a word, Thaddeus removes his cell phone from his back pocket and slides it across the table. I pick up the device and light up the screen. Heather's contact information is saved to his home page. Touching the image of her, I open the message tab and type a simple text.

> This is Eryc. Brenda is in surgery, she's critical. We're at Tulsa Memorial.

Pressing the off button on the side of his cell phone, I'm just about ready to hand him the device when the screen lights up with an incoming text. Out of curiosity, I glance at the name on the screen. It's Heather. Thaddeus is chewing his thumbnail, again, and staring at a spot on the floor, so I open the message.

HEATHER:
OMG. I'm on my way.

Leaving the text open, I hand Thaddeus the cell phone. He makes no move to grab his phone, so I slide it over to him and tap his arm. Thumbnail chewing ceases and Thaddeus looks over at me. I nod down at his cell phone and his eyes follow. After reading the text, he resumes chewing on his nail.

The magazine Makayla had been thumbing through hits the table with a thud. She rubs her face with both hands and lets out a long breath. Red tints her neck and face. I worry that she is stressing to the point of making herself sick.

"You okay?" I ask. Her chest expands in quick, short bursts. If she doesn't calm down, she will pass out again. Of that, I have no doubt. "Makayla?" When I say her name, I reach out to touch her knee.

That tiny bit of contact causes her to quickly scoot her chair back. Once she is on her feet, she runs from the room. Thaddeus watches her leave but makes no move to go after her. In her frame of mind, she shouldn't be alone, so I follow her. Since it's late, the halls are empty which makes it easier for her to run. I jog to keep up with her.

As she rounds the corner toward the elevator, a nurse is coming from the other direction and the two collide. The dark-haired nurse steadies Makayla and asks if she is alright, but Makayla continues around her like the two of them never crashed into one another. The nurse never smirks or remarks about Makayla's rude behavior. Actions such as this must be a common occurrence for the nurses.

To right the wrong, I call out an apology over my shoulder as I rush to catch up with Makayla. I want to get to her before the elevator takes her away. When I turn the corner, the elevator doors are beginning to close.

Shoot.

I lunge forward and catch the door with my hand, forcing it to reopen. The button for the first floor is lit so I lean against the steel wall, hands in my pockets, and watch the girl that is still my best friend. Her face is pale, and her breathing is labored.

Ding. Ding.

Two seconds after the ding, the steel doors open and Makayla dashes out. I'm fast on her heels. Almost to the door, a hand reaches out and stops me in my tracks. Heather.

She watches Makayla exit the sliding glass doors

before speaking. "Eryc, where is Thad? He isn't answering his phone."

"Third floor, just follow the orange signs to the right, past the double doors. He's in the waiting room at the end of the hall."

"Thanks." A wave of blonde hair wisps past my face when she turns around.

Panic settles in when I look out the doors and don't see Makayla. Where did she go? The sliding doors take forever to open and I'm ready to scream my frustration when they crack open enough for me to squeeze through.

Not a sign of her anywhere. The parking lot is void of activity as is the smoking area to my right. In her frame of mind, I worry she will aimlessly wander the streets and get hit by a car. I need to find her. Walking to the edge of the sidewalk, I scan the parking lot, looking for any sign of her, but find none.

Dread creeps up from my feet and fills me to my core. I cannot lose this girl.

Then I hear it. Retching. I follow the sidewalk around the side of the building and there, with her hands on her knees, is Makayla. She is leaning over between two bushes, gagging. Foul odor permeates the air around her, but I don't care. Standing beside her, I pull a few tissues from my back pocket and hand them to her.

"Please don't look." She wipes the bile from her mouth and blows her nose. "I'm a mess, just leave me alone."

"Not happening." For years, she has been pushing me out of her life. Today I refuse to be pushed. Let her harp or scream at me. I don't care. She is hurting and I am not going to stand by and watch her go through this alone.

When she folds the tissues into a tight square, I take them from her hand and stuff them back in my pocket. Then I pull her into my arms. Her body immediately goes stiff, but she allows me to cradle her here on the sidewalk. What in blazes has happened to her that would cause her to clam up every time I touch her? This reaction is the same I received when I brought her cookies earlier. It baffles me but I keep my questions to myself, she has enough on her mind.

Finally, she leans her forehead on my shoulder and cries. Not quietly. No, her crying is anything but quiet, it's loud, heartbreaking sobs.

Her hands fist my shirt, and she lets it all out until her voice is hoarse. When her body goes limp, I gently lower myself onto the sidewalk, bringing her down with me. Now her sobbing is quieter, and tremors rack her body as the tears run in a steady stream down her face. If I could take this pain from her, I would, in a heartbeat. But for now, I sit and allow her to cry and snot on my shoulder.

A doctor and nurse walk past us with curious expressions but say nothing. The nurse glances back when they pass and offers a sympathetic smile.

Using the collar of her shirt, Makayla wipes her face,

lets out a breath, and stands. Night air cools my skin where she had been, and I long to have her back. She is standing in front of me, waiting, so I push myself up and my knees pop and crackle as I do.

Motioning toward the entrance, I say, "Come on, let's go check on your mom."

9

Makayla

Walking toward the waiting room is a lot like a prisoner awaiting the jury's verdict. Sweat beads on my forehead and upper lip as my anxiety spikes up another five notches. Suspense increases my heartrate to the speed of a locomotive, and the oxygen around me seems too thin to inhale. I feel as if I am suffocating.

Just breathe, I tell myself.

An infomercial advertising a product that will cook potatoes in the microwave is playing on the television when we enter. The other family is now gone as is my twin. The only person occupying this room is Rene. She is sitting in a chair near the window and has her face buried in her hands. A pile of used tissues is in her lap, a testament that she has been ugly crying.

Images of my mother lying on a cold metal table in the morgue fill my mind and my knees go weak. Reaching out to a nearby chair, I steady myself. Needing to know, I open my mouth to speak but a croak is all that comes out.

Rene lifts her head, and her eyes go wide. She must be able to see the worry on my face. "Oh, sweetheart." She stands and crosses the room, taking both of my hands in hers. I'm lost for words, so I just stand here like a lost puppy in need of love. "Your mom came out of surgery a few minutes ago. She's in ICU."

She's in ICU.

Hearing those words, I lean my forehead against her shoulder and sob. My mom is in ICU, she is not dead. I cry until my nose is stuffy and my face is hot. Who would have thought I could have so many tears inside of me? Surely, I have cried a river in the last few hours. Where are they all coming from?

"Is she going to be okay?" Eryc asks the question I can't get to leave my lips.

My head is still resting on Rene's shoulder, but I see Eryc's black chucks as he moves next to me. He is standing to my right, rocking back and forth on his heels.

Rene rubs circles on my back with one hand and

strokes my hair with the other. "She's stable but they have her heavily sedated."

Pulling away from her, I furrow my brows. "If my mom is stable, why is she sedated?"

Rene is squeezing my hands. I know she is trying to comfort me, trying to keep me grounded, but all she is doing is freaking me out. Now, the image of my mom in a vegetative state is flooding my mind. "Honey, your mom is stable at the moment, but she did suffer internal bleeding. She had a laceration to her spleen and there was also some spinal cord damage which will require some therapy once she's healed. But right now, their main concern is her skull fracture which resulted in some bleeding on her brain."

Laceration on her spleen, spinal cord damage, skull fracture, and bleeding on her brain? All these words swim in loops in my head, my mind understands very little. For whatever reason, these words are not computing, probably because I'm stressed to the max. All I want to know, is if my mom will be okay.

Confusion must be evident on my face because Rene kisses my forehead and releases my hands. "Let's not focus on any of that right now. The doctors are going to take great care of her. Why don't you go see her? She's unconscious but she'll be able to hear you. I'm going to visit with the nurses and go over her chart."

Eryc steps forward, close enough that his arm brushes against mine. "Which room is she in?"

"Follow the hall back toward the elevator. The intersecting hallway, just before the elevators, is the one you want. Just follow the blue signs to the double doors. There's a doorbell, press that and they'll open the doors for you. Room 326."

Words are failing me. I must look like a crazed loon. Thank goodness Eryc is here to come to my rescue. He thanks his aunt then ushers me out of the room and down the hall toward my mom's ICU room.

Spleen laceration, spinal cord damage, skull fracture, therapy. The words are on a repeating loop. The colored signs on the wall that give direction don't register, I'm just robotically following Eryc. Closed patient doors taunt me with the possibility of my mom dying. To add to my agonizing torment, the sterile air around me is a reminder that people die every day, and their existence is wiped clean.

The buzz of the doorbell is what brings me out of my tormenting thoughts. A click sounds as the lock turns. "It's open," a voice comes through the intercom on the wall.

Eryc holds the door open for me.

A large circular desk is directly in front of us. Nurses sitting behind computers and monitors. One of the nurses wearing pink scrubs taps her pen on the countertop in front of her. "Who are you here for?" She must have been the one to speak into the intercom.

Eryc steps forward. "Brenda Yasmeen."

The nurse types on her computer then looks back at us. "Are you family?"

Eryc guides me forward to stand by his side. "Yes, ma'am."

She sizes us up, probably trying to determine whether we are being honest. Before she can say another word, Thaddeus exits a room at the end of the hall. He looks exhausted, like he is carrying the weight of the world on his shoulders.

Dark circles outline his eyes. "Sis." Wiping his nose on the back of his hand, he clears his throat before continuing. "Brace yourself, she looks pretty bad."

With nothing else to say, I watch my brother push through the double doors and out of sight. Part of me wants to go after him and comfort him, but I know he doesn't want me. Heather is the one he will want to console him. I glance in the direction of my mom's room. Nerves prickle my skin and goosebumps rise on the surface.

"Go ahead, Kay." Eryc urges me forward, guiding me down the hall to room 326. "I'll be right here. Take as long as you need, I'll find a chair or something to sit on if I need to."

Those four words *I'll be right here*, ease some of the

anxiety from my body. I'm not here alone. Eryc is here with me and will come to my aid should I need him. Again, I wonder how I got so lucky as to have him as a friend.

SUNLIGHT FILTERS in through the blinds and a yawn stretches my mouth wide. Time has completely slipped away from me, and I haven't even taken a moment to check on Eryc. It may sound strange, but I know he is still here. I can't explain it, but I can feel his presence.

Kissing my mom's hand, I stand and stretch my achy back. "I need to go home and rest, but I'll be back. I love you, mom." Despite what Rene said about my mom being able to hear me, I'm not sure if she actually can. Regardless, I've been speaking to her as if she does.

The door opens with a creak. Black chucks are the first thing I see as I peer out, my eyes travel the length of those long legs to his body and finally land on his face. Eryc is sitting in a hard-plastic chair, his head is leaning to one side, and he is sound asleep.

How did he manage to stay here overnight? Don't the nursing staff run visitors off after a certain period?

His body tilts to the left and then jerks back into its original position. With his neck resting on his shoulder, I'm sure he is uncomfortable. Jeez, now I feel like an idiot.

I should have sent him home hours ago. Instead, I self-ishly let him stay out here in the hallway while I sat beside my mom, watching her sleep, or whatever you call being heavily sedated.

Squatting down, I watch him sleep for a moment longer. It's strange, though his body is in the most uncomfortable position, his face is peaceful. A couple of seconds pass and he cracks his eyes open, blinking moisture into them. A smile lights his face. "Hey, how's your mom?"

Black and blue. Swollen. Broken. Deathly pale. Unrecognizable. All of those describe my mom perfectly, but I know that's not what Eryc is asking. "She looks bad but the last time the nurse came in to check her vitals, she said mom had made some minor improvements."

"That's good." He stands and offers me a hand.

I'm reluctant to take his hand, but I also don't want to offend him. He did sleep awkwardly in the hospital hallway just to be near incase I needed him. Slipping my hand into his, I allow him to pull me up. Exhaustion has finally won and forces a yawn from me. "Do you mind driving me home? I'm so tired."

Sitting next to my mom, I didn't close my eyes once. I was afraid that if I shut my eyes, she might open hers. She didn't. The nurse informed me that it would be another day or two before they take her off the medication that is keeping her knocked out.

Another yawn pries my lips apart. My body needs rest

and if I don't get home soon, I may pass out right here. Eryc gestures for me to follow him. We walk side-by-side toward the double doors. The nursing staff wave at me with sympathetic smiles on their faces.

Doctors pass us with electronic devices in hand. Visitors wonder the halls, looking for their loved ones.

When we arrive at the parking garage, I remember that we did not ride in Eryc's car last night, we rode in Rene's. I open my mouth to tell him we can call a cab and I'll pay for it when we get to my house, but as we walk through the parking garage, I see Eryc's car. "We didn't ride in your car last night. How did this get here?"

"No, we didn't." Eryc presses the key fob, and the doors unlock. "Aunt Rene arranged to have it brought in for me." I slide into the passenger seat when he opens the door for me. "Let's get you home, Kay."

10

Eryc

S ilence fills the atmosphere around us the entire fifteen-minute drive back to Makayla's house. I keep glancing at her, but I have no idea what to say. It's not like I can just make small talk about football or math. Talk about insensitive. As I gaze at her face, I notice dark bags that sag under each of her eyes, and the end of her nose is now red where she has blown it frequently this evening, or rather, morning.

Pulling into her driveway, I shut off the engine and just sit here, staring out the windshield. I open my mouth to speak but shut it immediately. She makes no move to exit the car, so I sit patiently and just wait. If she needs a moment of silence, then I will give it to her.

One minute turns into two, and two into three. No words have been uttered from either of us, the silence is deafening. The vehicle shakes from the bouncing of her leg. Makayla is lost in her own world of pain and sorrow, and there is nothing I can do to take that away from her. I wish I could just pull her into my arms and hold her, but the last thing I want to do is make her uncomfortable.

Time ticks by slower than molasses. Makayla continues to stare out of her window, her leg still bouncing, and now she is sniffling. I pull out the remaining tissues from my back pocket and hand them to her. It takes her a minute, but she accepts the tissues and wipes her nose. Without so much as a glance in my direction, she exits the car.

I hate seeing her so defeated.

Pulling the keys from the ignition, I chase after her. In the garage, the roar of a motorcycle sounds and then the overhead door rises. Thaddeus zooms out and down the road at a high speed, never acknowledging either of us as we stand in the yard and watch him race past. I pray he doesn't wreck and end up in a room next to his mother, or worse. I don't think Makayla could handle another tragedy right now.

Makayla looks at her empty hands, probably just now realizing her predicament. Last night we left in such a hurry that she didn't grab her purse which means she has no key to unlock the front door. A fresh tear falls down her cheek, and she wrings her hands in front of her. I open my mouth to tell her she can come over to my house until her brother returns home, when I notice the garage door is still open.

Taking her by the hand, I say, "Come on, Kay," as I tug her toward the garage.

At first, she hesitates but then she allows me to drag her inside the garage. Makayla's eyes are downcast, and her movements are more machinelike than human. Once we reach the door leading to the inside, I sigh in relief when I discover that Thaddeus had left in such a haste, he failed to pull the door closed.

Makayla is still robotically following me. Keeping my hold on her hand, I reach out and push the button on the wall to close the overhead door and tug Makayla inside the house. What lies on the other side of this door shocks me, and I consider taking her across the lawn to my house until I can get this mess cleaned up.

The kitchen is a complete disaster. It looks like a tornado swept through and destroyed everything in its wake. A large black trashcan has been kicked over, trash littering the floor. In the corner, the dining room table is overturned, and a crystal vase lay shattered in the midst.

Loud sobs come from the other room, and I follow the sound. As I come to the living room, I can't believe what

I'm seeing. Makayla should not have to deal with this right now, it's not fair to her.

My friend is standing amid more destruction, her hands covering her face as she rocks on her heel, sobbing uncontrollably. Judging by her posture and the sound of her sobs, I would say she is on the verge of a mental breakdown.

"Come on, Kay." I motion for her to come out of the living room.

Without hesitation, she steps out of the room to stand by my side. She doesn't say a word, but she does look at me with a sad smile on her lips. Moving past me, she ascends the stairs with slow, exhausted steps.

Stepping into the living room, I take in the extent of the damage. The expensive table lamp is on the floor at the other end of the room, shattered into a million pieces. Sharp glass litters the living room floor from lamps, dishes, and God only knows what. Both end tables are turned over and papers are strewn throughout the room.

This mess isn't something Makayla needs to stress over. While she is upstairs, I start picking up papers, stacking them on the entertainment stand. They appear to be legal papers for a case Brenda is working on. These are important so I place a nearby book on top to hold them in place.

This house is in such disarray that it will take me at least two hours to get it back into decent condition.

Turning the end tables over and putting them back into place, I set about cleaning the house. I pick up as much of the glass as I can and sweep up the rest.

Once I finish with the living room, I make my way to the kitchen and start with the trash littering the floor. This room seems to take longer to clean, probably because of the amount of garbage I have to pick up.

After I get everything back in order, I stand at the bottom of the staircase and debate on whether I should stay or go. We haven't been friends for so long, she may not even want me here. On the other hand, she has been my friend for much longer than not and I want to be in earshot should she need me.

So, I stay.

11

Makayla

Prunes. That's what my fingers and toes currently look like. Shriveled-up plums, or better known as prunes.

Seeing the destruction Thaddeus left behind had escalated my already pounding head, so when Eryc suggested I remove myself from the mess, I did. It took a great effort to climb the stairs, as I had no energy left in my body, but I made it. Instead of collapsing on my bed like I wanted to, I drew a hot bath to relax in.

I'm sure Eryc thinks I'm an ill-mannered brat, I never even looked back at him or excused myself. Like a rude and selfish child, I just left him standing there to stare at the chaos left behind by my irate brother.

Scooping up a handful of bubbles, I blow and watch them scatter in the air and float downward. The water is beginning to chill, which is a good indicator that I should get out. Blowing another handful of bubbles into the air, I pull the plug and reach for a towel.

As I dry off, I wonder if Eryc is still here. I can't imagine why he would stay. It's not like I have been friendly to him in a long time. What a fool I have been. Leave it to me to ruin everything good in my life. After I dress, I'll go downstairs to see if by chance he did stay.

I need to thank him for everything he has done for me. He didn't have to be there for me last night, or I guess I should say this morning, but he was. Without question, Eryc stood by my side in my time of need.

Wrapping my hair in a towel, I pick up my dirty clothes—the sterile hospital smell still clings to the fabric —and carry them to my bedroom, discarding them in the hamper. As I near the stairs, the smell of bacon wafts up from the stairway. An angry growl erupts from my stomach at the heavenly aroma.

I'm half expecting to see my mom standing at the stove when I enter the kitchen, but she's not here, Eryc is. My chest tightens at the thought that she may never be here again. I know I shouldn't be thinking like this but it's the truth. There is still a chance she won't pull through.

Pushing those taunting thoughts aside, I inhale through the nose and hold it for three beats before letting it out. Somewhat calmer, I lean against the doorframe and take in the scene in front of me.

Music plays from his cell phone. If I had to guess by the lyrics, the title is *Oh Lord*. Eryc flips a pancake then holds the spatula up like a microphone and continues to sing. His hips sway back and forth as his head bobs to the beat. Spinning on his heel, he belts out the lyrics but stops short, nearly dropping the plate, when he sees me standing in the doorway.

"Good grief, girl. Do you float on air or what?" Setting the plate on the counter, he clutches his chest. "I almost broke a plate and damn near wet my pants."

For the first time in what seems like forever, I laugh. Not a dainty laugh. No, this is loud and is followed by a snort. "Sorry, I didn't mean to scare you." The song playing from his phone is one I haven't heard before and I listen to a lot of music. "What are you listening to?"

Piling pancakes on the discarded plate, he gathers two more from the cabinet then carries them to the table. "That's NF."

Interesting, I have never heard of NF. Never in a million years would I have pegged Eryc as one to like rap music. How fascinating.

"Hum." You learn something new every day. "Well, I

like it." Pulling open the drawer, I gather silverware while he fills two mugs with coffee.

Sliding a mug toward me, he asks, "Do you want cream or sugar?"

Cream or sugar? Yuck, gag me with a spoon. I can't imagine contaminating my coffee with either of those items. Blech, thanks but no thanks. "No thanks. I drink my coffee black."

Eryc raises a brow. "A girl who drinks black coffee." He smiles like maybe he is impressed. "Now, that's interesting." Retrieving the skillet from the stove, he scoops eggs onto our plates along with two slices of bacon.

Bacon, eggs, and pancakes. I had no idea the boy could cook. Years ago, when we still hung out, he couldn't microwave a frozen dinner, and now he is cooking a full course breakfast. "Eryc, you didn't have to cook for me. I've been cooking for years. You know I could have managed on my own."

"Yes, I know you're quite capable of taking care of yourself." He pours milk into his mug then adds two teaspoons of sugar, stirring the contents until his coffee is a light latte color. "Kay, you're going through a hard time right now. I wasn't about to let you deal with life on your own. Besides, I'm happy to help."

Is my mom's tragedy the only reason he's here?

Flashbacks of him coming over with cookies float in

my thoughts. No, my mom is not the sole reason he is helping me.

Eryc still cares about our friendship.

That knowledge eases some of the pain tightening my chest. It allows me to relax my shoulders. He still wants to be my friend, and now I don't have to deal with this pain all by myself.

If only I could rid myself of the other pain infecting my soul.

12

Eryc

E dward and Bella. Makayla cannot stop talking about her favorite vampire movies. Honestly, I think this is her way of getting her mind off her mother. Which I'm okay with.

I gather up our dirty dishes and scrape them in the trash before filling the sink with soapy water. Truth be told, I have seen these movies a million times. Hell, I own all four books and the novella, but I listen to her like this is the first time I'm hearing of *Twilight*.

"So, do you believe in that kind of love? The kind that

binds your soul to another. The kind that makes you willingly put yourself in the line of fire to protect the one you love."

The unsureness in her voice raises the hairs on the back of my neck, but I can't explain why. Her simple question, brought on by talk of the movie series, seems like a normal discussion, yet I am detecting a hint of sadness in her tone of voice at the mention of love. Makayla is a girl, this should be a topic for her to gush over, not feel unsure about.

My stomach is twisting in knots over the tone of her voice. I glance over my shoulder and take in her posture. She is sitting on the kitchen island, kicking her feet back and forth, and looking down at her hands while chewing on her bottom lip.

Picking up the hand towel, I dry my hands and turn to face her. She angles her head, and her auburn curls fall in a curtain over her face, obstructing my view. Why is she so nervous? I don't get it.

Hoping to ease her nerves, I answer honestly. "Yes, Kay, I believe in that kind of love."

When she lifts her eyes to mine, I see fear hidden in their depths. "I want that. I want it so bad, to be loved and cherished above all else."

"You'll have it someday." I want to tell her that I have always loved and cherished her, but I don't want to spoil the moment, or ruin this rekindling of friendship we have so recently fallen into. It has been too long since she has opened up to me. To avoid blurting out my true feelings, I return to washing the dishes.

Silence fills the space around us while I finish the remaining dishes. Rinsing the last plate, I pull the stopper from the sink and turn to ask if she needs anything.

My eyes widen when I take in her appearance.

Eyes closed and body relaxing, exhaustion has finally won. Makayla's body starts to sway, and I wipe my soapy hands on my thighs. Not wanting her to fall off the countertop, I dash toward her and lift her against my chest.

The movement doesn't stir her, she is nothing but dead weight in my arms. Looking down at her, I study her features. Dark sunken eyes, pale skin, worry lines on her forehead, and creasing at the corners of her eyes. This has to be more than just worry for her mother. This kind of exhaustion comes from weeks of restless nights. But what is eating away at her?

Finding her room is easy, I spent most of our childhood up here building forts with her. It's true what they say about dead weight making a person heavier than what they truly are. Carrying her up the stairs is a challenge, a sheen of sweat coats my forehead.

Shoving the door open with my foot, I carry her to the bed. Blankets are twisted at the bottom of the mattress where she must have tossed them last night.

Settling her onto the bed, I pull the blanket up to her shoulders.

Lying this still, she reminds me of *Sleeping Beauty*.

My sleeping beauty.

Bang.

The pounding of my heart rings loudly in my ears.

What on God's green earth was that?

It sounded like the front door had been kicked in. Either it's a burglar who is brave enough to make this kind of racket in the daylight, or Thaddeus is home and taking out his frustration on the house, again.

Unaffected by the noises around her, Makayla lays undisturbed, snoring softly. I don't know how she can sleep through that. It even rattled the walls. Smoothing my finger down the bridge of her nose, I tiptoe from the room to investigate.

At the bottom of the stairs, propped against the wall, is the broom I used earlier to sweep the glass from the floor. The front door is wide open, and the doorknob is wedged into the sheetrock. With my back to the wall, I ease forward, grabbing the broom. It's not much of a weapon but it will have to do.

A thud sounds from the hallway, in the direction of the kitchen. I honestly hope this is not a burglar, I do not want to deal with that while Makayla lay helpless upstairs. Raising the broom handle up like a baseball bat, I tiptoe toward the sound of loud, unsteady footsteps. If this is indeed a burglar, they aren't afraid of being discovered.

Pressing my back against the wall, I inhale deeply. If by chance this is an intruder, I pray they do not have a gun because I don't stand a chance against a loaded weapon. Slowly, I peek around the doorjamb. The perpetrator is bent over with his head in the fridge.

Inching forward, I slide a knife out of the wooden block on the kitchen island and aim it at the trespasser. "Turn around, slowly."

On wobbly legs, the intruder stands and sways on his feet. Once that golden-blonde hair is in view, I sigh in relief. It's Thaddeus. Sliding the knife back into the block, I prop the broom on the edge of the kitchen island.

Thaddeus stumbles, catching himself on the door of the fridge and for a moment I fear he might pull it on top of himself. I guess I know where he took off to earlier. Judging by the looks of him, I would say he is drunker than a skunk.

"Thaddeus, are you okay?"

Slobber trails down his chin and he wipes it away with the back of his hand. "Yep. I'm just peachy." Glowering at me, he adds, "Why the hell are you still here?" His words are slurring together, and his focus is off.

Jeez, how much did he have to drink?

If looks could kill, I would be a dead man right now.

Ignoring his death glare, I cross my arms. "I didn't want to leave Makayla home alone."

At the mention of his sister, Thaddeus's glower falls away and his eyes mist over. Leaning his hip on the counter, his body sags. "That's good, she needs someone to keep watch over her." In the few hours after seeing his mother in the hospital, Thaddeus seems to have aged around his eyes. "Lord knows I've failed her."

What? Failed her?

This confession puzzles me. What could he have done that failed his sister? Grabbing a chair, I slide it toward him and motion for him to sit. "What do you mean, you failed her?"

Thaddeus sits in the chair, leaning back. "I didn't know." He shakes his head. "I went to her room to return her phone to her nightstand, and I found it. I was curious so I read it." The broom falls to the floor when his fist hits the countertop. "It's all my fault."

Dread creeps up my spine. What did he discover in Makayla's room, and is this the reason that she looks like she has not slept in decades? "What's all your fault?"

A shadow appears across the base of the island. I turn to see Makayla standing in the doorway, glaring at her twin. "You went snooping through my things?"

Thaddeus straightens and almost falls out of his chair. "It's not like that, sis."

Propping her fists on her hips, she nods toward the

front of the house. "I think it's time you showered and went to bed. Jeez, how much whiskey did you drink anyway? You reek."

The body language between the two of them confuses the crud out of me. She is clearly angry, and he looks like a mix of sorry, sad, and lost. I watch him stumble from the room, bumping his shoulder on the doorjamb on his way out of the kitchen.

13

Makayla

Nightmares consume me. This is the very reason I've been having a difficult time getting sleep at night. My body and mind are exhausted. I can hardly function anymore. For the last couple of weeks, I have been nothing more than a walking, talking zombie. Its moments such as this that the thoughts of suicide overwhelm me. No matter how hard I try, I cannot escape this continuous nightmare that has become my life. All I want is peace and freedom from these chains that bind me.

I hate reliving my nightmares in both my waking and dreaming hours. This burden is too much for me to bear. It chokes me with its evil hands and taunts me every minute of every hour of every day.

Standing in front of the medicine cabinet, I take the bottle of Oxycodone in my hand. The bottle is nearly full and offers promises of peace. God, I want peace. I want it so bad I can taste it. My fingertip rubs the edge of the bottlecap, going around and around the smooth plastic.

Voices travel up from the vents and meet my ears. Who in the world is in the house? Curious, I hide the bottle of Oxycodone behind my box of Claritin and make my way downstairs. Cars zooming down the road draws my attention to the front door, which is standing wide open. I ease it closed and notice the hole in the wall the size of the doorknob.

Thanks Thad.

Following the voices to the kitchen, I stand in the doorway quietly and listen. Thaddeus is clearly drunk. His words are slurring together like a drunken sailor. But the words coming from his mouth is like a punch to the gut. The only thing in my room that he could have read that would make him feel guilty, is my journal.

How dare he? That is my private thoughts meant for my eyes only. If I had wanted him to know my secrets, then I would have shared them with him. Anger consumes me at the thought of him snooping through my private journal entries.

Staring blankly at his hands, Thaddeus doesn't see me standing in the doorway eavesdropping. Fire is burning in my gut, searing through my veins. I take a step forward and Eryc turns his head, his eyes going wide when he sees me. The murderous anger must be evident on my face.

I need to shut up my brother before he spills my secret. "You went snooping through my things?"

Body stiffening, Thaddeus finally turns toward me. Panic flares in his eyes. "It's not like that, sis. I promise."

Muscles tightening in my arms, my hands form into fists. Settling my fists on my hips, I give a nod behind me, toward the front of the house. "I think it's time you showered and went to bed. Jeez, how much whiskey did you drink anyway? You reek."

Recognition sets in and his features soften. His eyes flick to Eryc and back to me as if he is begging me to confide in the two of them. Yeah, fat chance. Those were my private thoughts and were never meant for his eyes. The fact that he invaded my privacy irks my nerves in a way they have never been irked before.

My brother's eyes are sad, his expression is one of defeat. He is carrying the weight of my written words on his shoulders. That weight is not his to bear. It's mine and mine alone. I wish he had never seen my journal.

I step aside to allow him to pass. He stumbles into the doorjamb, cursing under his breath when his elbow hits the wood. Day drinking is not the norm for my twin, so the fact that he is drunker than a skunk worries me.

Waiting until his footsteps disappear up the stairs, I finally meet Eryc's gaze. "I'm sorry about that."

Studying me, he stands, shoving his hands into his pockets. "Don't worry about it." Rocking back on his heels, he asks, "Is there anything I can get you? Tea, water, hot chocolate?"

Hot chocolate. Yum. I point to the glass jar sitting on the countertop. "If you don't mind, I'll take a cup of hot chocolate with a peppermint stick."

The corners of his mouth tilt up until his eyes crinkle at the ends. "Still love peppermint in your cocoa, huh?"

A smile turns my mouth upward. "Yeah, it's the only way to drink hot chocolate."

"I agree."

"What?" I raise my brow. "You always gaged when I put peppermint in my hot chocolate. You said peppermint and hot cocoa do not go together."

Eryc crosses his arms over his chest. "Yeah, well, I changed my mind."

"Hum." We stare at each other for a moment, neither of us speaking. "I need to go check on Thad, he's pretty drunk."

Eryc nods but neither of us move. He continues to stare at me with questions brewing in his brown orbs. Uncomfortable with his scrutinizing gaze, I focus on my fuchsia painted toes. I know he wants me to elaborate on what Thaddeus hinted at, but there is no way in hell that is happening.

Black chucks step into my view, the toe of his shoe nearly touching my bare toes. Being this close to Eryc brings out two conflicting emotions within me. Comfort and fear. Part of me yearns to lean into his embrace and let all my worries fall away. The other part of me fears him, not because he has ever hurt me but because of what he is. A guy.

And then there is the fear of what he will think of me when he discovers my secret. Let's face it, now that Thaddeus knows, it will only be a matter of time before Eryc knows.

With a finger to my chin, Eryc tilts my head up until our eyes meet. "Kay, you want to explain why you shut up your brother?" A long pause causes goosebumps to prickle my skin. "Just why *does* he feel like he has failed you?"

Why can't he just leave this alone? This topic is not only painful, but it is downright humiliating. "No." I shake my head. "I do not want to discuss this." I never want to discuss this.

"But—"

I shake my head. "There are no buts, the answer is no. Drop it. Okay?"

Pursing his lips, he looks as if he is going to argue but then he shrugs his shoulders in defeat. "Okay."

Releasing a relieved breath, I say, "Just promise me you'll still be here when I come back down."

Stuffing his hands in his pockets, he says, "I'm not going anywhere, Kay."

If only I could believe that. Sure, he may still be here when I come back down, but I know the truth. As soon as he discovers who I really am and what I have done, he will run like the fires of hell are chasing after him. Fear of losing my only friend is what keeps my lips a locked vault.

Bolting from the room before my tears fall, I take the stairs two at a time. My limbs are shaky, and my stomach convulses with silent sobs. The walls I have taken great care in building are slowly crumbling underneath me. Pain slices my heart at the thought of Thaddeus knowing my secret. Is that the reason he is a drunken mess in the middle of the day? Is my secret, combined with mom's condition, what drove him to day drinking?

Awesome. I have ruined, not only my life, but my twin's as well. I have driven him to daytime drinking. If he ends up an alcoholic, it will be all my fault. Way to go, Makayla. More than ever, I wish the earth would open up and swallow me whole.

The sound of water running is briefly heard from the

bathroom at the end of the hall. I dash into my bedroom before Thaddeus can emerge and see the mess I have become. This is what I get for leaving my journal out in the open for anyone to see. A light rap of knuckles on the door brings me out of my thoughts.

"Yeah?" In hopes that he will not hear me and will continue to his room, my voice is nothing but a whisper.

No such luck. The door cracks open and Thaddeus pokes his head inside. "Look, sis, I'm so sorry for opening my big mouth to Eryc. I think the booze just got to my head."

Well, duh.

"Ya think?" Gripping the edge of the door, I yank it open. The sudden movement causes Thaddeus to sway. Pointing toward my nightstand where the journal lay, I say, "First off, *that* was none of your business." Crossing my arms, I square my shoulders and summon the strength to continue. "Secondly, you had no business hinting at my secrets to outsiders. What if I hadn't walked in when I did? You would have blabbed it all. How could you do that to me?"

Shoulders sagging, Thaddeus takes my hand and his eyes plead with mine. "I'm sorry, Makayla. I only read the first entry, but it was enough. You should hate me, I failed you, big time."

"You haven't failed me. The blame is not on you."

Squeezing my hand and blinking back his tears, he

repeats, "I'm so sorry. Sorry that I read your journal and sorry that I almost told Eryc, but most of all, I'm sorry I got you involved with Brandt."

Deep in my soul I want to say *it's okay, I forgive you,* but the words fail to leave my mouth. The silence brings mist to my eyes, and he drops my hand, exiting the room with a heavy sigh.

14

Eryc

Thoughts of how Thaddeus could have possibly failed Makayla leave me confused. At first, I thought he had been talking about leaving her alone at the hospital to deal with their mother's condition all by herself, but after the way she reacted, I'm not so sure.

What is she hiding and why does she feel the need to keep this from me? I wish she would trust me with her secrets like she used to. All I want is to be here for her. In every circumstance. If only she trusted me enough to be her rock.

Twisting the cap off the bottle of water, I tip it to my lips. Cool liquid quenches the dry ache in my throat and I sigh at the relief. My eyeballs feel like sandpaper from the lack of sleep, but I refuse to leave her until I'm sure she will be okay. Capping the bottle of water, I carry it to the living room and stretch out on the sofa. The textured ceiling draws my attention, and my eyes move back and forth over the wavy lines.

Soon my eyelids grow heavy. A yawn stretches my mouth wide. Thoughts of Makayla invade my mind. Happy thoughts, of a time when we were best friends and did everything together. Of days when we built forts in her bedroom, caught frogs out by the pond, chased fireflies in the dark, and shared secrets.

It doesn't take long for my memories to morph into dreams. Dreams with promises of everlasting love. Of Makayla smiling up at me, her ruby-red lips puckering for a kiss. Of her slender body pressed against mine and her auburn hair splayed across my pillow.

With my lips hovering above her, inching forward for a kiss, my cell phone rings, cutting through my dream. I groan at the interruption of a perfectly good dream. Glancing at the caller ID, *Aunt Rene* flashes on the screen.

Wiping sleep from my eyes, I swipe my finger across the screen to answer the call. "Aunt Rene, what's up?"

"Hey, honey, are you home?" The sound of a car door shutting comes through the line. "I'm off work and picking up food as we speak. I thought it would be nice if Thaddeus and Makayla didn't have to fret over dinner tonight."

Judging by the foreign language spoken in the background, my aunt is at the Chinese restaurant. I hope it's my favorite one on the corner of 129th East Avenue and 31st Street.

"Actually, I'm at Kay's," I confess. "I believe they're both upstairs sleeping."

"Oh, perfect." The foreign voices grow louder, and her muffled voice says a polite, "One moment, please."

"I'd love an orange chicken." I debate on whether to wake the others and ask if they have a preference, but knowing my aunt, she will pick up a nice variety. "Be sure to get plenty of egg rolls...please."

Laughter graces my ears. "Yes, yes. I'll get your egg rolls."

She's right, I do love egg rolls. I could eat them all day, every day.

"See y'all in a few," she says. With that, the phone line disconnects. Leaning over, I set my cell phone on the coffee table.

Sleeping on the sofa is killer on the neck. No amount of stretching will straighten the kink deep in my neck muscles. How long have I been sleeping anyway? Aunt Rene usually works until seven in the evening.

I glance at the clock on the wall. 7:15pm. "Damn, I slept the entire day away."

I should probably go wake the twins so they can get ready for my aunt's arrival.

Standing at the top of the stairs, I look from door to door. Who should I wake first? Thaddeus and I have never been great friends, so I don't feel comfortable enough to just walk into his room. Walking past his door, I continue down the hall and gently rap on Makayla's door. Fabric rustles on the other side, followed by the soft padding of her footsteps.

The door swings open and Makayla does her best to tame her frizzy curls with her fingers. It's a vain attempt but she's adorable. Because she's cute, I don't let on that the finger combing isn't working.

Letting out a puff of air, she spins around and snatches a hair tie off the dresser and twists the massive mane up into a knot. "I swear I'm going to shave my head someday."

Of their own accord, my fingers graze her cheek. "Don't do that. You're beautiful just the way you are."

Lines form between her brows. "If you had to mess with this," she points to her hair, "you'd understand. It's a pain in the butt to control."

"That may be, but it doesn't change the fact that you're beautiful." Rose tints her cheeks. That color looks good on her and butterflies soar in my belly knowing that I'm the cause of her blush.

Casting her eyes downward, she folds her hands in front of her, twisting them nervously. "Thanks."

"You're welcome." I tip her chin so she can see me. "Aunt Rene is on her way over with Chinese food."

In response, her stomach growls. Makayla presses her hand against it as if to shut it up. "That sounds good. Thank you." Glancing down at her wardrobe, she frowns. "I'll just change out of these pajamas and meet you downstairs."

"Okay."

As an afterthought, she adds, "I'll wake Thaddeus, unless you've already done that."

No, I have not.

"Nope, he's all yours."

Without another word, she grips the door and eases it closed, her eyes never leaving mine. The pain behind those eyes kills me. Every time. I want to take that pain from her, she is far too young to look so haunted.

15

Beautiful. Eryc thinks I'm beautiful? I wish I could be the person he wants me to be, but I can't. He will never understand, but I can never be good enough for him. Not as a friend and definitely not for anything more. I'm broken. There is nothing left but a thousand shattered pieces of me. Some days, I'm afraid I will never see the girl that I used to be.

I fear she is lost forever.

Opting for my *Forget Being a Princess, I Want to be a Vampire* shirt, I pull on my denim shorts and make my way to Thaddeus's room. I knock and give him a minute to announce his indecency.

When there is no response, I push the door open. "Thaddeus."

Jerking his head up from the pillow, Thaddeus falls off the bed with a thump. Curse words fly out of his mouth. Untangling from his blanket, he stands and glares at me. "What? Jeez, I think I broke my pinky finger."

His foul, sour whiskey breath makes me want to gag but I swallow it down as to not offend him. "Rene is on her way with Chinese food."

Thaddeus nods and picks up a shirt from the floor, slipping it over his head. I hope it's clean, or at least semi-clean. On the other hand, with his nasty dragon breath, no one will be able to discern whether his shirt has an odor.

Descending the stairs, I still expect to see my mom sitting on the sofa or hear her singing in the kitchen. My heart sinks when neither of those happen. She is not here. I knew she wouldn't be, but I still had to look for her. The pain that her absence causes, shreds my heart into a million pieces. One by one, those pieces of my heart float away to the ends of the earth, leaving a frigid void in the center of my chest.

I'm slowly losing pieces of myself and unlike Humpty Dumpty, no one can put me back together. This darkness is swimming in my veins and corroding my soul, luring me further away from life.

How much longer before I am lost forever?

Knock. Knock.

Before I can make my way around the kitchen island, the backdoor swings open. Boxes weigh down Rene's arms and a white plastic bag dangles from her fingertips. By the looks of it, she bought enough food to feed an army.

She kicks the door shut and carefully sets the boxes on the countertop. "Hey, sweetheart," she says as she looks up at me.

Sweet and spicy permeates the air, drawing me closer to the boxes lining the countertop. Sadly, I don't remember the last time I had food that smelled this wonderful, not counting Eryc's cooking this morning. My mom is usually working, and Thaddeus and I normally just order a pizza for dinner.

Eryc emerges from behind me and immediately pulls down plates and glasses from the cupboards. Thaddeus grabs a coke from the fridge, kisses Rene on the top of her head, and sits on a barstool across from me. Though I can smell toothpaste, sour whiskey still lingers on his breath.

Ugh, that's so gross.

I watch as everyone moves about, filling plates that are nearly overflowing with food. Dark liquid streams into a glass near me. The bubbles float to the top and pop, leaving splatters on the rim, much like the essence leaving my soul and splattering into oblivion.

Eryc's finger brushes against my hand and I automatically move back a step. It's a reflex and I don't mean anything by it but when I look at him, his eyes show the hurt that I caused. In true Eryc fashion, he is quick to cover that hurt with a smile.

Why must I be so damaged?

Ceramic scratches the granite countertop when he slides a plate toward me. "Here ya go, Kay."

Orange chicken, fried rice, broccoli, chow mein, and egg rolls cover the plate. The heavenly aroma wafts toward me and I inhale. It smells delicious and my mouth instantly waters. I can't even remember the last time I ate Chinese food. Two, three years ago maybe.

Picking up an egg roll and dipping it in the sauce from the orange chicken, I bite into it. Flavor burst on my tongue, orange mixed with vegetables from the egg roll, reminding me of happier times.

A time when I was carefree and enjoyed life.

TWO WEEKS. Two long and dreadful weeks since my mother had her car accident. The doctors still have her sedated due to the massive swelling in her brain. Most of what they say I don't understand, even when they try to explain the medical terms, I'm still at a loss. All I know is that the swelling in her brain has decreased but they need to see more improvement before they can ease up on the sedative.

During the day, while Eryc is at school, I stay at the hospital. The bruising on mom's face has faded to a dull yellow. I don't know what to say to her, so I just sit next to her bed and hold her hand. Sometimes I read to her and other times I just play music from my phone's playlist.

Our school counselor met with us the Monday following mom's accident and offered to have our school-work, along with power points, emailed to us each day so that Thaddeus and I can take the time we need to be here for our mom.

We print off our assignments, view the power points, and scan the completed paperwork so we can email it back to the school. It's fairly easy, and whatever I need help with, Eryc has been gracious enough to explain to me.

Yes, he has been by my side every single day since that horrible night. Thank God for that because he has been my anchor in this terrible storm.

Little by little, I have watched as Thaddeus slips deeper and deeper into depression. He doesn't look at me longer than necessary, and I think it's because every time he sees me, he can only see my secret. I know he thinks differently about me now that he knows.

My brother is never home when I am unless he is sitting in his room working on his homework. I know the reason for his elusiveness, he can't get past that massive secret of mine, and it is driving a wedge between us. Just like I knew it would. Just like I know it will between Eryc and me should he ever discover what I have been hiding.

Ding dong.

I glance at my cell phone. 5:30pm. Football practice is done for the day. Thaddeus blows out a puff of air, tosses his pencil on the table, and stalks from the kitchen. The creak of the front door testifies to its need of some WD-40. There is a moment of silence, then footsteps echo through the hallway.

Eryc emerges with two plastic bags in hand. "It's nothing fancy, just tacos and burritos." He sets the bags on the kitchen island and arranges the food in neat stacks on the countertop.

This has become the norm. Eryc delivering food every day after football practice and cleaning up before heading home in the evening. I have come to depend on him, probably more than I should.

Once mom is released and back home, his time here will decrease, or it will cease all together.

I don't think I will ever be ready for that to happen. Now that I have had Eryc back in my life, I can't imagine not having him around.

Abandoning my homework, I join Thaddeus and Eryc

at the island. Axe body wash greets my nose when I sit on the barstool next to Eryc. After each practice, he smells heavily of this soap, and I happen to enjoy this particular scent on him.

Eryc slides a nacho cheese taco toward me. He knows me well. I love the nacho cheese tacos. Comfortable silence surrounds us, apart from taco shells crunching and Coke fizzing. It's nice being here with the two men in my life.

It's moments such as these when my life feels somewhat normal. Sour cream coats the corner of my mouth as I take a bite. Poking my tongue out, I quickly swipe it away before either of them can see.

The rage in my stomach eases as I finish my first taco, I hadn't even realized how hungry I was until the first bite of food hit my stomach. I reach for a second taco when the doorbell chimes.

Both guys glance toward the hallway but neither of them move. Unwrapping the taco, I stand and make my way toward the front door, munching on the crunchy awesomeness as I go.

Knock, knock. Knock, knock.

Ding dong. Ding dong.

Jeez, anxious much?

"I'm coming, sheesh." Unlocking the door, I swing it open. My half-eaten taco hits the floor, splattering lettuce, tomatoes, meat, and sour cream on the welcome mat.

My worst nightmare is standing on the other side, hands in his pockets and wearing a dangerous grin.

Brandt.

"Hey, Makayla." He leans a hip on the doorframe. "I haven't seen you at school lately. What's up, sweet thang?"

"Um." I squat down before his hand can touch me and start scooping spilled taco into the wrapper. Pieces of lettuce remain on the mat along with some smeared sour cream. I will have to scrub that later.

When I stand, he takes a step forward, crossing the threshold. "I've missed you." Lifting his hand, he brushes a finger along my jaw. "Where have you been?"

"Here." If he doesn't already know about my mom's accident, I sure as hell don't plan on informing him. "You need to leave."

Heavy footsteps thud on the hardwood floor, growing louder with each step. Before I can look to see who is behind me, a hand grips my arm, dragging me backward.

Thaddeus jambs his finger in Brandt's chest. "What are you doing here?"

"Dude, chill." Brandt brushes Thaddeus's hand away. "I was just talking to Makayla."

Thaddeus takes a step forward and Brandt takes a step back. "Well, she's not talking at the moment."

"Dude, what is wrong with you?" Brandt looks mildly wounded.

Red creeps up my brother's neck, I can't see from my

position, but I would guess that redness settles in his cheeks as well. His spine straightens and his fists clench. Oh man, he's angry. Extremely angry.

Taking another step forward, Thaddeus jams his finger in Brandt's chest, again. Hard. "Just leave."

"And if I don't?"

Thaddeus's shoulders square and his feet brace for a fight. "Leave or I will make you leave."

"Makayla?" Brandt calls my name, but my focus is on the back of my brother's neck where the red is deepening. I don't answer. "Makayla, for crying out loud, get your lunatic of a brother off me."

A shove to Brandt's chest pushes him down the porch steps and Thaddeus slams the door, locking the deadbolt faster than lightning.

16

Eryc

Thaddeus leans sideways to see down the hallway. Eyes wide and a scowl on his face, he stands and marches toward the front door.

What was that about?

I stand to follow after him. Brandt is caressing Makayla's cheek and Thaddeus jerks her behind him with enough force she stumbles. His actions baffle me because I don't understand why he would behave so irrational.

Thaddeus jams his finger into Brandt's chest. "What are you doing here?"

"Dude, chill." Brandt brushes the offending hand away. "I was just talking to Makayla."

Moving to stand next to Makayla, I notice she is fisting her hands to the point they are stark white.

What am I missing here?

Thaddeus takes a step forward, forcing Brandt to take a step back. "Well, she's not talking at the moment."

Brandt looks wounded but there is something in his eyes that betray his wounded expression. "Dude, what is wrong with you?"

At Brandt's words, red tints Thaddeus's neck and his shoulders stiffen. Makayla's brother is angry, that much is apparent. "Just leave."

"And if I don't?"

Judging by Thaddeus's posture, I would say he is two seconds away from decking Brandt square in the jaw. "Leave or I will make you leave."

"Makayla?" Brandt calls out but her focus is on her brother. She is completely ignoring the guy who was just caressing her cheek like a lover. "Makayla, for crying out loud, get your lunatic of a brother off me."

A puff of air leaves Thaddeus before he shoves Brandt in the chest, pushing him over the edge of the porch. As soon as Brandt tumbles down the steps with a grunt, Thaddeus slams the door and locks the deadbolt in record time.

Spinning on his heel, Thaddeus gazes at Makayla with concern. "You okay?"

She nods her head, but her eyes are downcast.

Starting for the stairs, Thaddeus looks back, meeting my gaze. "I'm leaving. He," he points at the door, where Brandt was just standing, "is not allowed to talk to her."

Confusion settles over me. Not allowed to talk to Makayla? Why not? I feel like I have just entered the *Twilight Zone*. What in the world is going on and why isn't Thaddeus giving any explanations?

"Okay." I want to ask why, but the hard lines marring his forehead and the set of his shoulders quiet the questions brewing in my brain.

Crinkling paper draws my attention to Makayla's hands. Unfurling her hand, the taco wrapper sits in a tight ball with taco remains spilling from its creases. It's now that I see her tear-streaked face and trembling form.

Something isn't right. What happened between her and Brandt?

"Kay?" I take her trembling hands in mine. She makes a mewling sound in the back of her throat and her body stiffens. Then before I can inquire, she's gone, running up the stairs two at a time. This reaction hits me in the gut. She is shutting me out and I don't know why.

What just happened?

Thaddeus jogs down the stairs, keys jingling from his fingers. "Stay and keep an eye on her until I get back."

Like I would leave her home alone after what I just witnessed. "Will do."

The sour cream and bits of lettuce on the welcome mat catch my eye. This must be why she had a squished taco in her hand, apparently, she had dropped it. I get a wet rag and a plastic bag then set about cleaning the welcome mat. There are a few grease spots that will most likely not come out, but I will do my best.

While scrubbing the mat, I cast a few glances over at the staircase, hoping to see Makayla descending, but there is no sign of her. When I'm done, I rinse the rag in the sink then set it on the washing machine to dry. When I come back to the entry room, there is still no sign of Makayla. No noise of any kind to indicate that she is still here.

Obviously, she needs a minute to collect herself, so I will leave her be. Sitting on the bottom step, I lean back against the wall and wait. However long it takes for her to collect herself, I will remain here.

17

Makayla

I have been sitting on my bed for the last three hours, staring at the *Divergent* poster that is pinned to the wall. In some ways, Eryc has become my Four. I would not have survived these last two weeks without him. It may sound odd, but his presence alone gives me the strength to just be. With him in my life, my pain is somewhat bearable. Suicide has not had a stronghold on my thoughts in several days.

Don't get me wrong, those thoughts creep in but they do not weigh me down like they once did. Well, that was until Brandt showed up and stirred the pot. Now every ounce of self-loathing I had shoved away is brimming on the surface again. Thanks a lot universe. I really appreciate that. For the last three hours, I have been sitting here reliving my summer.

Reliving my worst nightmare.

Will there ever be a day when I feel normal again? Will this pain ever go away? Or will I just rot away like a corpse, and never find true happiness again?

The muscle in my palm begins to cramp and I loosen my grip on the taco-filled wrapper. Lettuce falls from my open hand, landing on the plush carpet. I dash the tears from my cheeks with my free hand and stand.

"I wonder if Eryc is still here or if he decided to get as far away from my craziness as possible." My words echo in the stillness of my room.

I wouldn't blame him if he left and never came back. A guy like him doesn't need a broken fruitcake like me.

Tossing the mangled taco in the trash, I brush my hands on my jeans and head for the stairs. I am so busy glancing over the railing to see if Eryc is in the living room that I don't see him on the bottom step, propped against the wall, sound asleep.

Until it's too late.

My foot catches under his bent leg and I fall forward, landing on my hands and knees.

Oh, God. How embarrassing. Please open a hole under me

and let oblivion take me into the darkness, never to be seen again.

"Kay, are you alright?" Fabric rustles as he stands.

Embarrassment overwhelms me and I imagine it coats my face a bright crimson. I feel like an idiot, and I can't bear to lift my head to see his face. When his black chucks stop inches from my hands, I groan. Shutting my eyes tight, I pray for time to rewind.

When I open my eyes again, his chucks are still in place but along with those, his knees are also in my view. He's squatting next to me and his calloused hand cups my face. "Kay, please look at me."

I shake my head. There is no way I can face him after my klutzy tumble.

"Kay?" he urges. His fingers shift, sliding along my cheek to the underside of my chin. Gently, he lifts my head. "Are you okay?"

Tears well up in my eyes, my pride is wounded. I try to keep my voice from trembling, but I fail miserably. "I'm okay."

"You fell, pretty hard. Are you sure you're okay?" He looks me over as if he suspects I'm lying. Which I am, my knees are aching but it's nothing I can't handle. "Come on, we can finish dinner. The tacos may be a little soggy by now, but the burritos should be fine."

His goofy expression brings a smile to my face. "Nothing like a soggy taco." Taking his offered hand, I allow him to pull me to my feet. On the way to the kitchen, I look around for Thaddeus.

As if reading my mind, Eryc says, "He hasn't come back yet."

Most likely out drinking himself into a coma. Does he not see that I'm hanging on by a thread here? His drinking escapades only add to my guilt and turmoil. "He's probably out drowning in a bottle of Jack Daniels."

Eryc's gaze softens. "I'm sorry." Wrapping his arm around me, he gives me a half hug before pulling out a chair at the kitchen table. "I'll bring the food over. Do you want Coke or tea?"

The kindness he continually shows me is astounding. He has never shown his frustrations or abandoned me when I have freak-out moments and draw into myself. "Tea, thanks."

He smiles then leaves to gather the food and drinks. When he returns to the table we eat in silence. It's a comfortable silence and we pass a smile here and there as we eat. Two tacos and a burrito later, a metallic taste coats my tongue and the back of my throat. My breathing comes in quick pants and saliva fills my mouth.

Eryc jumps from his chair and grabs the trashcan, setting it in front of me. "Jeez, Kay, are you sure you're okay?" He squats to peer into my eyes. "Did you hit your head when you fell?"

"No." I inhale and hold it.

One. Two. Three. Four. Five.

Releasing the breath, I repeat the action. The raging storm brewing in the pit of my stomach begins to ebb away after the fourth breath I release. "I'm okay. Maybe I caught a cold or something from the hospital."

Heat soaks into my forehead where he touches it with the back of his hand. "You're not warm." He stands, pacing. "What can I do for you?"

"Nothing." I sit up now that the sourness has dissipated. "Honestly, I just want to lay down on the sofa and watch TV."

"Okay." He grabs the trashcan and follows me into the living room.

I have no idea what that spell was, but I seem to be feeling better, just tired and achy.

Eryc retrieves the remote from the entertainment stand. "What do you feel like watching?"

"You pick." In truth, I'm not going to make it through a movie, I just don't want to be home alone. He skims trough the new releases on Netflix, finally deciding on *The Notebook*.

I raise my brows.

"What?" He shrugs his shoulders. "I can't enjoy a good love story because I'm a guy? Please."

"I didn't say that." Okay, I didn't say it, but I was definitely thinking it.

He presses play and I lean back, watching a movie that I have seen more times than I can count.

18

Eryc

Ten minutes into the movie and Makayla is sound asleep, softly snoring from her end of the sofa. Legs curled against her body, she takes up no more room than the one little cushion she's lying on. Deciding to let her enter that deep-sleep stage before moving her, I continue watching the movie. I have probably seen *The Notebook* a hundred times, but it never gets old.

Shuffling and whimpering draws me out of my movie trance, and I cast my gaze to the other end of the sofa.

Makayla tucks her head to her knees, quietly whimpering like she is having a nightmare. My brows furrow and I wonder if she does this often.

Her body jerks and she turns her head, covering her face with her hands. "Stop. Please."

I lean over and gently shake her. "Kay."

Her body goes completely still, and I think she is waking up. Then I hear her sniffle. Perching myself on the floor, next to her, I move her hands away from her face and see the tears free-falling from her eyes. She's not awake, but she is in fact crying in her sleep.

"Kay," I say a little louder.

"Please, don't—" her voice is but a whisper and I almost don't hear her.

"Kay?" I shake her again when she doesn't wake.

Suddenly, her eyes open wide in panic. I have never seen her this distraught, and I don't know what to do to help her. Is she having a night terror? I don't know the first thing about those but I'm pretty sure that is when the sleeping person screams in their sleep and she isn't screaming, she is just crying.

The sound of the front door opening and closing echoes throughout the house. Two soft thuds, where Thaddeus's boots land on the hardwood floor, follow the sound of the door. Makayla scoots to the other end of the sofa, the end I just vacated, and tucks her legs under her chin, rocking back and forth.

Thaddeus storms into the room but stops short upon seeing Makayla curled in on herself. "What the hell happened here?" he yells at me as he crouches in front of his sister. "Hey, sis, you okay?"

Makayla glances from her brother to me and back again. Standing on the cushion, she steps over the arm of the sofa and runs up the stairs.

Thaddeus stands and glares at me. "What the hell did you do to her?" He advances on me. I take two steps back. "Don't think I won't kick you where the sun doesn't shine."

It's now that I notice the bloodstains on his swollen knuckles. Looks like he has already been in a fight tonight, no doubt due to the amount of alcohol he drank. The boy reeks of whiskey and I hold my breath to keep from gagging.

Flinging his arm toward the stairs to point where his sister ran off, he yells, "Why is she crying?"

Taking another step back to inhale a breath of fresh air, I answer his question. "I have no idea why she's crying. She fell asleep watching a movie and starting whimpering in her sleep. When I woke her, she freaked out. That's it. I have no clue why."

Thaddeus stumbles forward, jamming his finger into my chest. "You better be telling me the truth, preacher's kid."

I ignore the jab to my father's profession. "What

happened with you tonight?" I point at his bruising hands.

Snickering, he flops down on the sofa, kicking his feet up on the coffee table. "Just a little payback to a prick, is all."

"You should put some ice on that," I say.

Cackling, he leans back, resting his arms behind his head. "Pretty damn sure I'm grown enough to take care of myself."

"Fair enough." I sit on the edge of the coffee table. "Care to explain what happened to Kay? Does she have episodes like that often?"

He runs his hands over his face and blows out a breath. "Not my story to tell."

What?

I didn't ask for personal information, so-to-speak, I just want to know if she has nightmares often. Instead of pursuing the issue, I say, "Okay."

I study Thaddeus for a moment. His left eye is starting to swell and darken. Who did he get in a fight with? Brandt? Today has been the strangest day ever, starting with Brandt's appearance that led to Makayla's meltdown, then her nightmare that turned into a freak out, and now Thaddeus's battered knuckles.

Deciding to wait until tomorrow to question Makayla, I slip my shoes on and start for the door. "Tell Kay that I'll stop by before school tomorrow."

The only response he gives me is a grunt.

Standing at the threshold, I look at the staircase one last time before shutting the door behind me. I will get to the bottom of her meltdown and nightmare if it's the last thing I do.

As promised, I stop by Makayla's the next morning. The front door opens, and she stands on the other side with her hair wrapped up in a towel. Smiling, I hand her a plate full of blueberry muffins that I baked first thing this morning.

Makayla has three weaknesses. Those weaknesses match mine, or rather, mine match hers because they quickly became my favorites when we were apart as a way of feeling close to her. Those weaknesses are chocolate chip cookies, peppermint infused hot chocolate, and blueberry muffins.

"Thanks." She picks up a muffin and bites into it before taking the plate. "Oh my God, that is so good."

I smile.

Raising a brow, she asks, "Did you make these?"

"Yep." My smile grows bigger when she takes another bite and rolls her eyes in pure bliss. "I gotta go before I'm late. I have practice this afternoon and then work, but I'll stop by afterward."

"Okay, thanks again. These are fantastic."

I bite my lip to keep from smiling any wider. The last thing I want to do is scare her off.

Getting into the car, I wave before backing out and driving to school. When I arrive, I'm not the only one showing up at the last minute. I gather my bookbag from the backseat and run toward the building.

The halls are full of students rushing to get to their first period classes. Weaving through the hoard of bodies, I rush upstairs and to my classroom. I hate being here while Makayla is at home, but I know that she will be heading to the hospital in an hour to spend the day with her mom.

Class is boring and my thoughts are on Makayla the majority of the time. I'm thankful we are just going over Shakespeare today, I have already read this and will be able to get my assignment done without complications.

My classes seem to go by rather quickly and I make sure to pay extra attention in Calculus incase Makayla needs any help with it later.

Now that the final bell has signaled the end of the school day, I dash out of the class and to my locker. I gather what books I need and place them in my bookbag and then head out to my car to exchange this bag with my gym bag.

The football field is lined with guys from the team. They're all doing leg exercises when I arrive. Chad fist bumps me when I fall in line beside him to do high knees. I should have warmed up first, but I was already running late to practice because I took the time to text Makayla.

She didn't respond, of course, and I stood out by my car for five minutes, like a lovesick fool, waiting for a response.

Coach has us do several leg exercises and then we hit the weight room. Lifting is one of my favorite things and it definitely helps to relieve some of the tension and pent-up stress I have been carrying around.

Thirty minutes in the weight room doesn't feel like enough time. Yet, it also feels like too much time away from Makayla. After a quick shower, I towel dry my hair, not bothering to comb it, and get dressed. Just as I reach for my shoes, I hear shouting at the other end of the locker room.

Leaving my shoes on the bench, I jog toward the commotion. As I come around the corner, I see Chad shouting at Brandt and then he shoves him into a locker. Brandt has a sneer on his face as he swings his fist at Chad.

This is the second time in less than twenty-four hours that I've seen Brandt evoke anger in someone.

Chad knees Brandt in the groin and swipes his feet out from under him, knocking him to the ground. Gripping Brandt's shirt in his fist, Chad punches him twice with his free hand. "Don't you ever talk smack about that girl again. You hear me?"

What the hell did I just walk into? "Chad?" My best friend doesn't acknowledge me. "What's going on?"

Gripping the collar of Brandt's shirt with both hands now, Chad lifts him up and then shoves him down to the tile floor. Standing, Chad shoves people out of his way then glances at me before stating, "Keep that SOB away from Makayla."

Chad is the second person to tell me that.

I jog to catch up with him and tug his arm. "What do you mean?"

"Just keep him away."

Chad starts to walk off, but I halt him by stepping in his path. "Seriously, tell me what this is all about."

I would really like to know what has Thaddeus and Chad all uptight about Brandt, and what it has to do with Makayla.

Chad is breathing heavily, his hands fist at his sides. "Look, this is a discussion you will need to have with her."

"I'm asking you," I plead. "Thaddeus isn't talking, and Makayla shuts down on me."

Chad runs a hand down his face then locks eyes with me. "Look, this summer something happened between the two of them. I didn't witness it. I only heard the idiot and his friends bragging about it." He glares back at Brandt, who is now wiping his bloody nose on a towel.

"That's all you're getting from me. Ask her, it's her story to tell."

With that, he stalks out of the locker room, and I'm left wondering what in the world happened while I was away this summer.

Makayla is my best friend and if this prick hurt her in any way, I will knock him into next week.

19

Makayla

Bile rises in the back of my throat. The nurse's voice drones on and on while my eyes scan the room for the nearest trashcan. My name leaves her lips, but I can't respond because sour liquid is rushing up my esophagus like hot lava. I reach the metal can just in time to release the hot, bitter liquid that spews from my mouth, coating the small can in a sheen of yellow.

Tissues are shoved into my hands as the nurse moves past me. Water runs and a door opens. When my stomach ceases its convulsions, Nurse Kelly wipes my face with a cool rag. "You alright, hun?"

I nod because I don't have the energy to speak. White fabric moves behind Nurse Kelly, and I lean over to see Dr. Harmon making notes on his electronic device. His gaze meets mine, studying my flushed face.

"I understand you spend your days here with your mother." I nod, though he didn't phrase it as a question. "Maybe you should go home and rest. Your body is most likely worn out due to stress. Take some over the counter sleep aid if you need to because you need your rest."

Latex stretches and snaps when Nurse Kelly removes her gloves. Her warm hands take hold of mine, those honey eyes capturing my gaze. "I'll call if there's any change, I promise. Right now, your mother looks good, and she's made some small improvements. Trust me, she's doing well, considering." Smiling at me, the nurse adds, "You should follow the doctor's instructions and get some sleep."

I know they're right. You don't have to be in the medical field to know sleep is important. My body is beyond exhausted. I can't even remember the last time I slept for more than two hours at a time. "Okay." The words that leave my mouth are rough, a result from the bile burning my throat.

Giving mom's toes a gentle squeeze, I gather my things. Leaving her is always hard, I long for her chirpy self to wake up and hug me. I need her. My life has been turned upside-down and flipped inside-out. I need my mother in my life and I'm desperate for her comforting embrace.

Several people crowd around the elevator, so I pass by keeping my head down. The waiting room around the corner has a pot of coffee brewed. It's dark and smells extra strong. Filling a Styrofoam cup to the brim, I sip the scalding java. Muscles in my belly instantly quiver in protest and I find this reaction odd because coffee is an old friend of mine. Why would my body detest its deliciousness?

Maybe that was just a fluke. Deciding to try this again, I take another sip. This time is no better than the first, the bitter liquid upsets my stomach and I have to hold my breath to calm the raging storm taking place in my intestines.

"Ugh." Dumping the java down the drain, I toss the cup in the trash and head back toward the elevator. Maybe it's just the brand of coffee this hospital serves that isn't agreeing with me.

Who knows.

VOICES STIR ME FROM SLEEP. Stretching my arms over my head, my spine snaps, crackles, and pops. A quick look at my phone indicates its 5:25pm. I have been out for nearly two hours, yet I feel like I haven't slept at all.

No surprise there, as this has been my pattern since July.

"You cannot continue down this path, Thaddeus. It's a dangerous one." Rene sighs. "Honey, I'm just worried about you."

"Don't." Boots stomp on the hardwood floor.

I sit up in time to see Thaddeus storm past. "Thad?"

Coming to a stop, he takes a step back, peering into the living room. "I'm just going outside, I'm not leaving." His lips press together and form a hard line. "Yet," he mumbles.

Up until our mom had her accident, Thaddeus and I were close. Now? Now, we are nothing more than two people residing in the same house. Being his twin, I can sense his emotions. They are dark, almost as dark as mine. Where I have Eryc to turn to when my darkness threatens to overtake me, Thaddeus has shut out his girl-friend and has been slowly distancing himself from me, preferring the company of his good ol' friend, Jack Daniels, instead.

I'm worried that he will get himself killed driving under the influence. If I lose him, I'm sure even Eryc wouldn't be able to pull me out of my sea of blackness. One foot in the entry and one foot still in the living room, I debate whether I should go after my brother. My soul cries out to him but if I step foot outside, he will most likely bail.

"Kay?" Eryc's voice startles me out of my thoughts. He is standing at the end of the hallway with his hip leaning against the doorframe to the kitchen. A smile turns up the corners of his mouth. Pushing off the frame, he waltzes toward me. His steps sure and steady, unlike the pulsing of my heart.

Toe-to-toe, Eryc gazes at me like I'm his most prized possession. With each exhalation, the scent of Coke surfs the waves of his breath.

When did I become so attached to Eryc that even the scent of his warm breath calms the war raging in my heart and mind? Just being in his presence eases my fears and brings me a sliver of peace.

"How are you feeling today?" He brushes a lock of hair behind my ear. "You were looking a little on the green side last night." Feeling my forehead with the back of his hand, he says, "At least you don't have a fever."

"I haven't been sleeping well." Remembering Dr. Harmon's words from earlier, I repeat them to Eryc. "My body is just exhausted from lack of sleep and worry. I'll be fine."

Taking my hand, Eryc leads me back to the sofa. "Well then, no caffeine for you tonight."

Is he serious? That eliminates not just coffee and soda but tea as well.

Seeing the horrified expression on my face, he chuckles. "Don't worry, Kay. There's orange juice in the fridge.

Oh, Rene brought over some pizza. I figured we could have a movie night. That is, if you're up for it."

Juice? What am I, a two-year-old? "Movie night is fine, but I require Coke. I could handle tea, but I much prefer a Coke."

"You're stubborn, you know that?" Tapping the end of my nose, he motions for me to sit. "I'll bring the pizza boxes in." He points to a stack of movies on the coffee table. "You pick the movie." Halfway out of the room, he adds, "And I may share a Coke with you."

Share? Oh no, I'll be drinking the whole can.

Digging through the movies, I see that Eryc bought several chick flicks and a couple of action movies. I'm not so much in the mood for any romantic movies but I do see an action film that catches my interest.

Popping the movie in the DVD player, I sit back on the sofa and wait for Eryc to come back with the pizza and Coke. I hope that boy is smart enough to bring two Cokes because I sure as hell will not be sharing mine.

Eryc enters the room, followed by Rene, and guess what? The boy was not smart. There is only one Coke in his hand. I giggle because as soon as that can of soda is handed to me, I will not share a single drop of that delicious brown liquid.

Setting the boxes on the coffee table, Eryc glances at me and smirks. "You have plans on devouring my Coke, don't you?"

The boy knows me well. "Yep."

He smiles and shakes his head. "I guess that means I need to go back for another can."

"Uh huh, because you know I don't share." I take the can from his hand and pop the tab, taking a rather large gulp.

20

Eryc

End credits roll for *Captain America* and Thaddeus finally strolls back into the house. Makayla starts to stand but I touch her knee, signaling for her to stay. When Thaddeus is ready to talk, he will make his way into the living room with the rest of us. The worry in her eyes is enough to split my heart in two. If I could take her pain and suffering away, I would do it in a heartbeat.

When the legs of a barstool scrap the kitchen floor, Makayla's shoulders relax. Sighing, she pulls her feet under her and angels her body so that we are sitting side-by-side. This is the first time she has sat this close to me. Every other time we have watched television, she has sat at the other end of the sofa. But now? Now, she is resting her head on my shoulder, her hand slipping behind my elbow and her fingers curling around my arm.

Her body feels good pressed against mine. I yearn to wrap my arm around her and hold her close, but I don't want to ruin what little trust she is gaining in me. Quiet footsteps pad across the hardwood and Thaddeus emerges in the living room, barefoot and holding a plate of leftover fish.

Makayla pats the cushion next to her, inviting her brother to sit beside her. No sooner does he sit down; Makayla's fingers tighten around my arm and her body goes rigid.

"Kay?" I ask. "What's wrong?"

When she releases me and bolts upright, I notice her greenish complexion. That's not a good sign. I sit forward and rub circles on her back in hopes of soothing her, but it doesn't appear to be having the effect I had hoped for.

Pressing a hand to her stomach and one to her mouth, she shoots off the sofa and flees as fast as her feet will carry her.

With a mouth full of fish, Thaddeus gives me a questioning look. "What was that about?"

I shrug my shoulders and take off after Makayla. Her retching can be heard long before I turn the corner toward the bathroom. The door is ajar, so I ease it open to find Makayla kneeling on the tile, heaving into the porcelain bowl.

Rene enters behind me with a worried look on her face. She steps around me to get a cloth and runs it under cold water. I gather Makayla's hair and hold it above her head with one hand and massage her neck with the other. She heaves a couple more times and then leans back, resting her weight against my legs.

"I wish you hadn't seen that." Covering her face with both hands, she lowers her head and groans. "I'm beyond embarrassed."

My aunt squats down next to her and gently pries Makayla's hands away from her face. "No need to be embarrassed, sweetheart." Taking the cool rag, Aunt Rene pats Makayla's red, blotchy face.

After a few moments, Makayla relaxes further into me. Her breathing starts to slow down. When my aunt removes the rag, I can see that her natural peachy color is beginning to return to her face. August is not flu season, so I wonder what is causing her to be so sick. This seems like something more than just lack of sleep, I fear she is coming down with some kind of virus.

When she gathers enough strength, I help her to stand.

Thaddeus is standing in the hallway, peering through

the bathroom door with a look of concern. "Sis, you okay?"

"Yeah, I'm fine." But the moment she takes a step toward her brother, she quickly covers her nose and mouth. Glancing down at the plate in his hand, she shoves him away from the door.

Confused, Thaddeus raises a brow. "What was that for?"

Backing up, Makayla says, "That fish smell...I just... can't."

Thaddeus looks as confused as I feel. The fish he is eating isn't bad, it smells rather delicious. In fact, it's making me hungry, and I just ate four slices of pepperoni pizza. Maybe her stomach is just weak due to her exhaustion. Who knows.

Aunt Rene looks from one twin to the other. "Makayla, are you sure you're feeling alright?"

She nods but continues to hold her nose. "Yeah, I just haven't been sleeping well."

Aunt Rene examines Makayla's eyes and feels the sides of her neck. I'm not sure what she's feeling for, but this is something she does to me when I'm sick. "And how long have you been sick?"

Makayla scrunches her nose in thought. "Just for a couple days. Mom's doctor thinks the stress has exhausted me."

My aunt glances at me with a raised brow but

continues to question Makayla. "Well, you're not feverish. How often are you getting sick to your stomach?" She gazes at Thaddeus and his plate of fish, then returns her attention back to Makayla. "Are there triggers, certain scents that upset your stomach?"

Makayla looks around at all of us, fidgeting with the hem of her shirt. "I guess. That fish makes me gag, as does the sterile hospital smell." She pauses and looks up at the ceiling. "Oh, and coffee. I couldn't stomach the coffee at the hospital today."

My aunt glances at me, then at Thaddeus, before meeting Makayla's gaze. "Honey, when was your last period?"

Eyes wide, Makayla looks at me, red tinting her cheeks. "Rene, seriously? Eryc is standing right here."

"Wait, are you suggesting?" Thaddeus leans against the wall with a thud and mouth agape. "Do you mean that this could be—" He looks at his sister with a horrified expression. "Sis?"

Thaddeus seems to have put some puzzle pieces together, but I'm still confused as to what is happening right now. I have no idea what her period has to do with her sensitive stomach to her brother's plate of fish, or her exhaustion in general.

"I really wish somebody would tell me what's going on." I glance at Makayla, my aunt, and then at Thaddeus. "I hate being left in the dark. If there's something I can do to help then I—" As if a light bulb turns on, it suddenly dawns on me what my aunt is asking.

Aunt Rene is an OBGYN, she takes care of pregnant woman every day. Looking at Makayla's horrified eyes, I would guess there is a possibility that she could be pregnant. I slowly back out of the room. This is not a topic that should be discussed in my presence. I'm not even sure why my aunt brought it up with Thaddeus and me in the room.

Makayla watches me back away with wide frightened eyes. She's embarrassed and maybe even ashamed, if her expression is anything to go by.

21

Makayla

Oh. My. Word.

I cannot believe Rene just asked me that question in front of Eryc of all people. Asking me in front of Thaddeus was bad enough, but with Eryc in the room? I'm mortified. No, I am beyond mortified. Please, God, let lightning strike me down so I don't have to face either of them. After tonight I will never be able to look Eryc in the face again.

Thanks, universe, for taking away the one good thing in my life right now. The one good thing that I just got back might I add.

To my relief, Eryc walks out before Rene can discuss my sex life. Like that is anyone's business. Thank goodness, he took it upon himself to vanish, otherwise I would most likely go postal. Sheesh, I cannot believe how this evening is turning out.

Thaddeus continues to stare at me with a mix of concern and anger. I know he wants me to confide my deepest, darkest secrets but there is no way in hell that is happening. My business is mine and mine alone.

Rene tucks a strand of hair behind my ear. "Makayla, is there a chance you could be pregnant?"

I shake my head.

No way. Absolutely not.

She bites her lip as she studies my face. "So, there is absolutely no chance at all that you could be pregnant?"

Thaddeus clears his throat and turns an icy glare toward me. Just when I think my life couldn't get any worse, the universe decides to spit in my face.

Holding up my thumb and index finger to indicate that there is a very small chance, I say, "It's slightly possible."

Rene looks at me with sympathy. "I'm going to run down the street to pick up a pregnancy test, I'll be right back." She exits the room and a few seconds later I hear the front door open and close.

I lower myself down and sit with my back against the bathtub. Wrapping my arms around my legs, I rest my head on my knees. Fear snakes around my neck, choking me. Which only serves to make me feel nauseous all over again.

As if my life wasn't screwed up enough, now I have to deal with this little mishap. What the ever-loving hell am I supposed to do now? A baby? No. There is no way I can be pregnant. I have no boyfriend, no job, and I'm living in a sea of ever-increasing darkness.

I. Do. Not. Want. A. Baby.

If by some small chance I *am* pregnant, I could never be a good mother to it. For crying out loud, I'm only eighteen years old. This is not how my life was supposed to turn out. Senior year is supposed to be filled with fun, laughter, a little mischief, and dating the hottest guy in school. Yet here I sit, drowning in my misery and the universe is sitting back cackling at my sorrow.

His shadow has not moved an inch since Rene left for the store. I don't have the courage to look up into my brother's eyes. Disappointment. Disgust. Which of those will shine in the blue pools of his eyes? Probably a good mix of disappointment and disgust.

I would rather not see the evidence of my failure written on my twin's face.

Burying my face between my knees, I wrap my arms around my legs and let the tears fall. The sound of bare feet padding across the tile is the only indicator that my brother is entering the bathroom. He's close, I can feel him hovering over me. Silence fills the room as neither of us is willing to talk about the subject at hand. His knees pop when he squats down next to me. He's so close that his leg rests against mine.

Seconds turn to minutes. Eryc has not made an appearance in the doorway to check on me and I wonder if he is still here. It's highly possible that he is disgusted with me and went home. I mean, why wouldn't he? Being a preacher's kid, he probably thinks I am just a heathen on my way to hell and wants nothing to do with me.

Story of my life.

"You need to talk to them."

At those words, I finally turn and glare at my brother. "No."

His nostrils flare. "You need help and I'm in no position to offer you any. This is tearing me up as much as it is you. You need their help and their support."

Just as I open my mouth to tell him to get lost, Rene saunters into the room with a brown bag in hand. "Thaddeus." She steps aside and gestures for him to exit the bathroom.

He stands and obeys. Before the door closes, he peers back at me. "Please, Makayla."

His plea is for me to confide in Rene but I'm not ready to divulge that information to anyone. Doing so would mean confessing my failure. The last thing I want to do is drive a wedge between Eryc and me, and confiding my secrets to him would do just that.

Locking the door, Rene removes the box from the bag and hands it to me.

Oh, God, is this really happening?

Pulling the white stick out of the box, I carefully follow the instructions. Rene sits on the edge of the tub and holds my hand while I wait for the results to appear. "Whatever that test reveals, you are not in this alone. You have Eryc, Thaddeus, me, and your mother. You will never have to do this on your own."

Dread builds up in my core. She has no clue what I have done, she wouldn't be offering me her support if she knew the truth. What did I ever do to deserve such bad luck? I don't walk under ladders, and I haven't cracked any mirrors. Ever. Fear seeps into my pores and soaks into my veins, coating my soul with blackness. My heart constricts and I choke on a sob.

I cannot do this. With or without support from Rene and my mom, I cannot do this. Please let me rewind time and go back to correct my mistakes.

"It should be ready." Rene squeezes my hand, encouraging me to peek at the stick lying on the counter.

Letting out a long breath, I pick up the white stick. Two pink lines stare back at me. Positive.

I'm pregnant.

The quiet sobs I have been trying to rein in rush out

with the force of thunder. Agonizing pain rips through me and the stick slips between my fingers, clanging against the tile. Anguish unlike any I have ever experienced before severs my heart in two, causing it to skip a beat.

"No," I whisper.

Rene reaches around me to pick up the discarded stick. After a quick glance, she places it in the trash. "You can do this, sweetheart. I will be with you every step of the way."

"No."

Rene's eyes go wide. It's plain to see that she is clearly shocked by my outburst. Giving my hand a gentle tug, she says, "Honey, it will be okay."

Jerking my hand free, I glare at her. "No, it won't." When she opens her mouth, I raise my voice. "You have no idea what I'm going through and I don't need, nor want, you to help guide me through this pregnancy."

She sucks in a breath. I have hurt her feelings and the look on her face pierces my heart. Pain racks my body like a knife twisting in my gut. The only woman who has ever put me above all else is the one I'm lashing out at.

One more thing to add to my ever-growing list of failures.

Blinking back her tears, Rene stands. She stares at a spot on the wall behind me. "I'll let you process this. When you're ready to talk, I'll be in the living room."

When the door closes, I let the tears fall. As if my life

didn't suck enough, now this. What did I ever do to deserve this hell that is my life? Is there any hope for me? Does God even exist? If he does, he sure has a way of allowing disaster to crush his so-called perfect creation.

A sob rattles my chest, rising until it escapes my lips in a loud strangled cry. Slapping my hand over my mouth, I try to stifle the horrid sound but it's not enough. My heartbroken cry emerges from my nostrils, and I fall to my knees, resting my forehead on the cold tile floor.

My life is going to hell in a handbasket and there is nothing I can do about it.

I'M NOT sure how long I've been in here crying. Minutes? Hours? It's possible I have been in here for hours though I don't think it has been quite that long. All I know is that my throat is dry and scratchy from all the sobbing I have done. Swallowing is awkward, it feels like I have cotton stuck in my throat.

As I lift my head, I notice the tiny puddles of tears that rest on the tile before me. A clear indicator to my current state of misery. I should feel ashamed for my breakdown, but I feel nothing. I'm just numb.

Shadows move back and forth from the crease under the door, reminding me of the fact that Eryc is here, or at least he was. I have no idea if he stayed or left. I can't imagine why he would have stayed but if he did, then he was a witness to my major meltdown. Well, if he didn't think I was crazy before, I'm sure he does now.

Pushing up from the floor, I get a glimpse of myself in the mirror and grimace at my reflection. My hair is frizzing out around my face, my eyes are bloodshot, and red splotches cover my cheeks and neck. In short, I look like the walking dead. Well, minus the rotten teeth and decomposing skin.

Knock, knock.

Startled, I gasp. Taking a step forward, I place my hand on the doorknob but refrain from turning it. I don't want to open the door for fear that Eryc might be on the other side. The last thing I want is for him to see me in my current state of distress. One look at me, and he will surely be running for the hills.

Knock, knock.

"Just open the door, Makayla."

At the sound of my brother's voice, I rest my forehead on the wooden door. "Just leave me alone, Thad."

"No can do. Open up." His fingers drum on the door, vibrating the wood under my palm.

My brother is stubborn, I may as well open the door and face the music. Chances are, Rene has told Eryc by now anyway. Either he is still here, or my friend was so disgusted with me that he left. I'm not sure which I'm hoping for at this point.

Breathing in through my nose, I release it through my mouth and turn the knob, pulling the door open. Lifting my gaze, I find Eryc leaning against the wall opposite me. Concern softens his features. There is absolutely no condemnation in his eyes. Thank God.

Standing right in front of me, chewing on his thumbnail and worry lines creasing his forehead, my brother says, "Okay, sis, spill it."

Staring down at his bare feet, I whisper, "It was positive."

"It's time to let him in on this little secret." Thaddeus jerks his thumb behind him, indicating that he means Eryc.

I tilt my head. "I'm pretty sure he knows by now."

Thaddeus's lips harden into a tight line. "No. It's time for you to confide in him about that damn journal and what transpired over the summer."

"No."

My brother's hand slams on the sheetrock next to the door. "You need to tell him," he yells.

The tone of his voice brings a new set of tears to my eyes. My brother never yells at me. "No, I don't, and you need to butt out and leave this alone. It is none of your business."

Pointing his finger in my face, he opens his mouth to speak but before he can get a word out, I cut him off.

"You do not get to order me around, Thad. You have

no idea what I'm going through." I ball up my fist and punch him in the chest, something I have never done before. His eyes widen but he makes no move to chew me out for it. "Just leave me alone, Thaddeus Wyatt Yasmeen."

He lifts a brow, probably because I just used his full name. "Look, sis, I may not totally understand how you feel, but don't you dare for one minute think I don't see the damage it has done to you. This is bigger than you and you need their support." When I shake my head, and refuse to spill my secrets, Thaddeus slams his hand on the wall, again. This time not only do I jump but so does Eryc. "Damnit, sis, if you don't tell him, I will."

A threat? My brother is threatening to share my secret with the world. Okay, maybe not with the world but with Rene and Eryc. Still, it is not his secret to share, and I don't appreciate him taking this into his own hands.

Anger rises in me, and I slam my own hand on the sheetrock. "No."

Nostrils flaring, Thaddeus points his finger in my face. "You are in no position to make demands. You need help and by God I will see to it that you get it."

"I don't need help. What I need is for you to get out of my face."

Reaching into his pocket, Thaddeus pulls out his old prescription for Oxycodone that I had hidden in my medicine cabinet upstairs, along with my box of razors.

Embarrassment washes over me. I close my eyes.

Taking a step back, I can't believe he went snooping through my bathroom. "Why were you snooping around in my bathroom, Thad?"

"Snooping? HA!" He holds up the drugs and razors. "I ran out of Claritin and thought I'd just grab one from your medicine cabinet." Closing his eyes and taking a deep breath, he gazes at me with concern and anger. "How long have you had my old pain meds?"

"A while."

"Those will not take your pain away and they damn sure won't make your problems go away." Thaddeus turns my hands over, inspecting my wrists. "Are you cutting?"

"No, those razors are just a backup incase the Oxycodone doesn't do the job." That's a lie but I refuse to let him know this secret as well. After he told me that he had only read the first journal entry, I took my notebook and hid it in a box in the back of my closet.

Eryc gasps at my confession and I glance over Thaddeus's shoulder to meet Eryc's stare. Pain and concern are evident on his face but there is no sign of disgust. At least not yet.

At my confession, anger flashes in Thaddeus's icy-blue eyes and he throws the contents on the floor at my feet and again points his finger in my face. "You *will* tell him. If I were you, I'd get started before I bring down your journal. And I am bringing down your journal."

"Don't you dare." But really, he has no idea that I hid it or where to look, so I have nothing to worry about.

Thaddeus's grip on me is firm yet gentle. "Sis, you're in trouble." He points to the two items at my feet, the items that I had hidden for that moment when I finally found the courage to end my life. "Tonight, we bring your secrets out into the open. I'll be damned if I sit back and watch you continue to deteriorate."

"Kay?" Eryc's voice wavers and I force myself to meet his gaze. He looks from me to the pills and razors then back to me. "Please talk to me."

Thaddeus squeezes my hand. "I'll be back with your journal."

It's over. There is no point in hiding anymore. If I don't confess, Thaddeus will tear the house apart searching for my journal, so I nod. Confession time has arrived, whether I'm ready or not. The fact is, if I don't let Eryc in on my secret, then Thaddeus will tell him everything, journal or no journal.

I release a breath and tell my brother where to find my journal. "It's in my closet in that box where I keep my photo albums."

Letting out another breath, I motion for Eryc to follow me back to the living room. Fear makes me nauseous with every step I take. I am so scared that after I divulge all my secrets Eryc will not want to be my friend any longer.

I fear that he will avoid me like the plague.

When we enter the living room, Rene is sitting on the sofa. She smiles when she sees me and pats the cushion next to her. Feeling guilty for the way I treated her earlier, I apologize. Waving off the apology, she pulls me into her side and hugs me.

Eryc sits on the coffee table in front of me, his knees touching mine. Cupping my face in his hands, he peers into my eyes. "Please talk to me."

Bare footsteps slap on the hardwood floor and Thaddeus hands me the notebook. My journal. With fresh tears flooding my eyes and clouding my vision, I hand my notebook to Eryc. "It's all in there." I stand because I can't be near him while he reads my deepest, darkest secrets. "But I can't watch you read it."

22

Eryc

I'm not sure what to expect from Makayla's journal but her and Thaddeus want me to read it. So here I am, sitting on the coffee table with her journal in hand. Its awkward opening Makayla's notebook to read her private thoughts. This is like an invasion of privacy, but they want me to read the words written within so that is exactly what I am doing.

Exhaling a long breath, I open the notebook and begin reading Makayla's private moments.

*July 4*th

I've never been one to keep a diary. Writing about yourself in a notebook for your eyes only just seems juvenile. It seems silly. But here I am, writing in this stupid notebook, getting ready to bear my soul.

Tonight, started out fabulous. Thaddeus and I met up with Heather at Lake Keystone. A bunch of us were there. Brandt was there.

Brandt. I've had a crush on him since Freshman year, so I was ecstatic to see him at the party. This was going to be a fantastic night. Or so I had hoped.

Brandt brought the fireworks, Kurt brought the alcohol, and someone else brought the pot.

I'm not sure how much I drank, but I do know there was some Jack Daniels involved. Sometime during the night, Thaddeus and Heather disappeared. Most likely to make out. To my delight, Brandt came to sit with me on the tailgate of Kurt's truck.

I was like "Brandt-freaking-Taylor is talking to me". This was my dream come true.

Or not.

Never in a million years would I have thought this, but Brandt turned out to be my nightmare from hell.

He convinced me to sit in his car so we could talk in peace without having to yell above the music and fireworks. And of course, I went because my biggest crush wanted to talk to me. There was no way I couldn't not go.

We talked, and we shared a joint.

I don't remember how we got there, but we ended up on the

other side of the lake, away from our friends. It was just us and an open field. He started kissing me. I admit, I loved it...until he slipped his hand under my shirt.

I asked him to stop because I wasn't ready for a step like that, I mean, we weren't even dating yet. Instead of stopping he only progressed. This was way out of my league. What he was doing made me uncomfortable. I asked him again to stop but he ignored me, and soon I resorted to begging. I even managed to get out of his hold and was able to get out of the car.

Brandt got out after me and apologized profusely. I accepted the apology. We sat on the hood of his car and continued to talk. As soon as I started to feel comfortable again and began to relax, he leaned over toward me and started kissing me again.

It was okay until he started kissing me roughly. At that point, I asked him to stop but he just raised my shirt like I hadn't spoken.

I pushed against his chest and asked him to take me back to the party.

Do you know what his response was? He said, "Come on, baby." Licking and kissing my neck, he acted like I was playing a game with him. "You know you want me."

No, Brandt, if I had wanted you then I wouldn't have asked you to stop. So, I threatened to scream. You know what he said?

"Go ahead and scream, no one can hear you." Really, Brandt? You're a real gem, you know that?

I have never felt more humiliated in my life. At that point, I knew there was nothing I could do to stop this madness. My phone was inside his car. Getting to it was impossible since he had me pinned down to the hood. So, I did the only thing I could, I stared at the moon and let him pull my pants down and have his way with me.

When he was done, he refastened my pants, thanked me, and then he kissed my cheek. What? Who does that? Apparently, Brandt does. After that he drove us back to the party. In front of everyone, he draped his arm over my shoulder. He acted like we were now a couple and carried on like nothing had happened.

Thaddeus never noticed the tear streaks on my face. That's okay, I didn't want him to see my pain anyway. I don't want my brother to know because Thad would kill him if he found out.

Home sweet home.

You would think I'd feel safe here, but I don't. My heart was shattered tonight. My spirit is now broken. The first thing I did was run to the shower to wash Brandt's scent off me. No amount of scrubbing helped. Even as I write this, I can still smell him on me.

What did I just read? Seriously, what-the-ever-loving-frack is this? Brandt Taylor, a rapist? I think I'm going to be sick.

I turn the page.

July 7th

Kurt called Thaddeus to invite us over for another party.

Honestly, I didn't want to go. What if Brandt would be there.
Thaddeus was stoked and Heather wanted me there, so I
agreed. I mean, we've been partying together since Freshman
year, if I bailed it would look weird.

Oklahoma summers are summers from hell. The heat is
enough to melt the makeup right off your face. Heather helped
me decide on an outfit suitable for this 110° weather.

As usual, Kurt's house was packed. Heather took me by the
arm and headed straight for the backyard. The pool was full of
splashing teens, beer cans littered the poolside, and the patio
had been cleared of outdoor furniture to make room for
dancing.

Justin Timberland blasted from the speakers. Nothing can
get me moving quite like JT, that's for sure. Heather and I
danced for several songs, and I felt normal.

Normal! Brandt, you may not realize this but that night,
three nights ago, you ruined me.

And apparently that dreaded night was just the beginning.

Tonight, when you stepped out into the backyard, your
eyes instantly zeroed in on me dancing with Heather. Out of
the corner of my eye, I watched you grab a beer from the ice
chest and then you came toward me. I tried to ignore you,
hoping you'd get the hint and walk away. You didn't. You came
up behind me and tugged my back flush against your front and
started dancing with me.

Eventually, Thaddeus dragged Heather away and your
arm snaked around my waist, turning me to face you. You held

me like you owned me. Let's get this straight, Brandt, you do not own me.

Beionnce played and you swayed our bodies to the beat. You told me how much you enjoyed our night together and how you've thought about me nonstop since then. You told me how pretty I am. You even said that you wish you could marry me. Really, Brandt? Marriage? You don't know me from Adam.

You're quite the charmer, I'll give you that.

I must have drunk more alcohol than I realized because, like a numskull, I followed you into the house. You, Lee, and Vince talked me into playing a game of pool downstairs in the game room. Lee suggested I get the break shot and I surprised myself when two solids fell into pockets at opposite corners of the table.

Just when I started to fully relax, you were behind me, grabbing my butt. You said, "Damn, girl, you look sexy as hell in these shorts."

When I set the cue stick down and started to walk away, you apologized. You begged me to stay. To assure you got your way, you told me that I made you feel alive. That you couldn't survive this life without me. Playing on my emotions, you informed me of your mother's verbal abuse and your father's physical abuse.

I felt horrible for you, and you saw it written all over my face. Then, to push me right over the edge, you said, "Makayla, you're my safe haven. The only thing in this world that makes me feel whole."

*YOU MADE ME FEEL GUILTY FOR WANTING TO
LEAVE.*

*It was that guilt weighing on me that overrode my rational
thinking. Like a dimwitted fool, I stayed. You draped your arm
over my shoulder and smiled. Then, like before, you started
kissing my neck.*

*At this point, I knew where this was leading, so I did what I
needed to in order to NOT feel. I found a focal point, a poster of
dogs playing pool, and zoned out while you bent me over the
pool table and took what you wanted from me.*

*When it was over and I was pulling up my pants, I noticed
that Lee and Vince were still in the room, watching. Is this
what you guys get off on, watching a girl being taken advantage of? And yes, I realize that I didn't fight you off, Brandt, but
you have to understand that in this situation when I felt guilty,
felt sorry for you, I just gave in to what I knew you wanted,
myself be damned.*

God, what is wrong with me?

I close the notebook. There's no way I can read any
more. This is sick. It's beyond sick. Lee and Vince are just
as guilty as Brandt for this crime. You do not make a girl
feel obligated to have sex with you. Unless she declares
that she wants to have sex with you, you don't take it.
Lying beneath you, unresponsive, is not a yes. In my book
that is rape.

The contents in my stomach churn, threatening to
make an appearance on the living room floor. I do not

understand this kind of evil. Standing from the coffee table, I take to pacing. Inhaling a deep breath, I open the notebook and turn the page.

July 8th

Same crap, different day.

Next page is the same and so are the two afterward.

July 15th

I hate my life.

There is a whole two weeks between this entry and the next.

July 29th

Why doesn't this end? Yeah, I know what you're thinking. I keep bringing this upon myself by attending these parties. I have the choice to say no, to get away. It's not that easy when Brandt constantly makes me feel guilty for his parents' abusive behavior.

Brandt, why do you keep pressuring me into having sex with you? I know you can see that I'm just a shell of the girl I used to be.

The next entry is nearly a week before the first day of school. This is the reason Makayla has been withdrawn. I'm not sure how much more of this I can read. I already want to kill Brandt.

August 5th

Vince, why did you watch and do nothing? You just sat there, watching with wild fascination.

Brandt, why did you feel the need to share me? After you

were done, you rolled off me and stroked my hair. You shushed me and said, "Makayla, you're amazing." You sang along to a Bryan Adams song, still stroking my hair, while Lee had a turn.

I guess the question I should be asking is, why in the world am I still going to these stupid parties?

I'm so screwed up.

Thad, I love you. Never doubt that. You are my only solid rock. Please don't hate me. I know you're going to be mad, but please forgive me. I just can't take it anymore. I need to find peace.

What does that mean?

I still have that bottle of Oxycodone that was prescribed to you when you had your motorcycle accident, the one you never finished taking. I'm going to swallow the entire bottle and step into the shower to await the darkness. I'm ready for the angel of death to take me home.

Please tell Eryc that I'm sorry for being a selfish brat word to him these last few years.

Mom, I'm sorry. I just can't deal with my fractured life anymore. Please know that I love you.

A freaking suicide note, is that what this is? That explains the pills and razors Thaddeus threw on the floor earlier.

August 6th

Well, as you can see, I chickened out. The reason? Hell.

I'm not a religious person but I did go to Sunday school as a kid and heard the whole fire and brimstone teaching.

When I dumped the Oxycodone in my hand I thought about hell. I wondered if suicide was a direct pass into hell. You know, like a 'go to hell, go directly to hell, do not pass go, do not collect two hundred dollars'. If hell is real, I don't want to burn for eternity.

Thank God. I can't imagine a life without Makayla in it.

August 10th

Well, I'm still here. I haven't partied since that night a week ago. I still look longingly at the bottle of pills and my box of razors, but the idea of hell still scares the ever-living-hell out of me.

I hated going to school today. Everyone stared at me and whispered when I entered the room.

Then there was Eryc. He was the only one that didn't whisper behind my back. Some might say I'm being paranoid, but I can't shake the feeling that they're all laughing at me, calling me a whore behind my back. Being at school is like being tossed in a shark tank with an opened wound.

23

Makayla

Watching Eryc pace while reading my private entries is making me dizzy. On top of that, his facial expression is giving nothing away. Is he angry with me? Disgusted with me? Not knowing what he is thinking is slowly eating away at me. He is my one true friend and I do not want to lose that.

Not counting my mom and Thaddeus, Eryc is the one good thing in my life.

Closing the notebook, Eryc tosses it onto the coffee

table and rakes his hands through his hair. "I don't even know what to say, Kay."

Rene has been watching her nephew this whole time, wearing a curious expression. Now that the notebook has been tossed aside, she picks it up and starts thumbing through it. It doesn't take her long to get the gist of what is written on the pages. Once she's read that first entry, she tosses it back onto the coffee table.

I knew it, Eryc hates me now. He has not looked at me since closing the journal. It will once again be bye-bye friendship and hello loneliness. "You hate me now, don't you?"

Swiveling on his heel, Eryc gives me a look of disbelief and then rushes to my side. By now, I'm sitting back on the sofa, holding Rene's hand. Pushing the notebook out of his way, he sits on the coffee table and takes both my hands in his. I fix my gaze on his large hands, calloused over from years of weightlifting and football playing.

"Look at me, Kay."

I obey and am surprised by the compassion I see shining back at me.

"I could never hate you." Pointing toward the notebook that is now teetering on the edge of the coffee table, he says, "That was not your fault. Don't you dare believe otherwise. What Brandt did was wrong on so many levels."

Relief washes over me. My friend is not going to abandon me. Until now, I'm not sure I realized how much I have come to depend on him. A sob breaks free, and Eryc gathers me into his arms. All my pent-up emotions rise to the surface. I cry, releasing all the anger, shame, and humiliating pain I have been carrying since July 4th.

The sound of a motorcycle racing down the road brings on a new set of guilty tears. My brother is hurting, and I haven't been there for him. My brother appears tough on surface, but I sense the pain he is hiding. The pain he has been drowning in whiskey for the past few weeks. How could I have been so absorbed in my own suffering to be blind to the depth of his?

"Shhh, I've got you, Kay." Eryc scoots forward and wraps his arms around me, rubbing circles on my back with just enough pressure to soothe. "I'm here." Kissing the top of my head, he rocks us back and forth. "I'm not going anywhere. You don't have to do this alone."

Something about his words bring comfort to me. An indescribable peace begins to wash over me, silencing my sobs. Now that my secrets have been revealed, the weight on my shoulders has been lifted. I relax in his arms and welcome the all-consuming darkness, also known as sleep.

OPENING MY EYES, I blink rapidly to bring moisture back to them. It's dark outside and I'm lying on the sofa with a blanket draped over me. Beneath my head is a leg and I roll over to see Eryc asleep, sitting up and his neck dangling off to the side in an awkward position.

That neck-breaking position is going to leave him with a major crick. After everything he has done for me since mom's accident, I cannot allow him to suffer from a stiff, sore neck in the morning. Sliding my legs off the side of the sofa, I start to rise but his arm snakes around me, holding me in place.

"Don't." When I look at him again, he smiles groggily. "Stay."

What? Did Eryc just ask me to stay on the sofa and sleep next to him? "Stay?" I ask, wanting clarification.

Conflicting emotions rage war in my mind, tightening the muscle in my chest known as my heart. Part of me wants to move to the opposite side of the sofa and get some distance between us. Being sexually abused takes its toll on a person and there are times that a single touch sparks fear in me. But the other part of me, the part that longs for Eryc's touch, is screaming for release. Screaming for me to trust and allow him to comfort me.

Liquid warmth heats my body from within as his arm tightens a little more. "Yes." He smiles down at me. "Stay here with me."

What I am about to say goes way out of my comfort

zone, but Eryc is my one true and best friend. A friend that has never taken advantage of me or abused me in any way. I have known him my entire life. He is safe, he is gentle, and he is the kindest soul I have ever met.

Sucking in a deep breath, I count to ten and then release it. "Okay."

His smile grows wider.

"But only if you lay on this sofa next to me." Raising a brow, he shakes his head and opens his mouth to object, but I cut him off. "You're going to get the worst crick in your neck if you continue sleeping like that."

Those brown eyes of his darken. It looks as if I may have offended him, which was not my intent. His eyes rove to a spot above me. Apparently, these new feelings I am experiencing are one sided. It looks as though he doesn't like me the way that I like him.

Pain pierces my heart and my gut twists into a knot. The intensity of it overwhelms me and tears begin to blur my vision. I want to take back my words, but I can't. There is no taking back what I've spoken, my words are now hanging in the air between us.

Removing his arm from my side, he shifts his body until he successfully removes himself from under my head. My aching heart breaks into tiny pieces and the built-up tears slide down my cheeks before I can stop them. Humiliated and dying inside, I stand and rush from the room.

"Makayla." His voice is soft and comforting. It causes me to stop but I can't look at him. The soles of his chucks thud on the hardwood with each step he takes. In a few beats, he is standing behind me and I can feel the warmth radiating from the closeness of his body.

The hairs at my nape move when he exhales.

24

Eryc

Her request is innocent. I know she doesn't mean anything by it, but after everything I read in her journal, I'm not sure that her suggestion is a good idea. When I asked her to stay with me, I meant for us to stay the way we were with plenty of space between our bodies.

The words penned in that notebook, in her beautiful handwriting and splotched by her tears, haunt me. And the last thing I want to do is lie next to her in an intimate way and cause her any more pain, or to have her wake up in a panic because she has forgotten that I'm lying next to her.

Carefully, I scoot myself out from under her head. Rounding the coffee table, I stride to the window and brush the curtain aside. Streetlights illuminate the paved roads. A dog sniffs the mailbox across the road, then runs down the sidewalk and out of sight. Shadows dance on the street from the tree limbs blowing in the breeze.

She has no idea what she is asking. Aside from my worry about how lying next to her will affect her, what if Thaddeus walks in and sees us. That boy will go postal on me. Or maybe, he wouldn't. Maybe he would understand that Makayla and I have been friends for our entire lives and that she is safe with me.

When she sniffles, I realize that I've given her the wrong impression. The words that came from my mouth was not received correctly. That I have hurt her feelings. She must think I hate her, but nothing could be further from the truth. I love her, more than just a friend. Because of my love for her, I want to protect her.

Her bare feet thud on the hardwood floor as she runs from the room.

"Makayla." Dropping the curtain, I quickly make my way toward her.

Her shoulders slump and her head droops, causing her hair to drape around her face. "I'm sorry. I didn't mean to suggest—" Her words are cut off by a sob.

Gripping her shoulders, I gently turn her until she is facing me. Her head is still down so I place my finger under her chin to guide her head upward until she is looking at me. Tears are streaming down her cheeks in a steady flow.

The sight of her so broken kills me. A pain stabs my heart, like a knife, slicing downward and severing the organ in half.

"You misunderstood me." I cup her cheek and caress her smooth skin with my thumb. Her eyes close at my touch. "My reservation has nothing to do with my feelings toward you but rather the trauma that you've endured." More tears fall, coating my fingers. "Kay, the last thing I want to do is cause you any more pain than you have already suffered."

Squeezing her eyes shut, she nods her head. "Okay." She looks defeated, like I have stolen all the joy from her life.

Kissing her forehead, I wrap an arm around her and guide her back to the living room. "Come on, I'll get some blankets and pillows from the closet and make us a pallet on the floor."

With wide, puffy eyes, she looks at me. "So, you'll stay?"

The fear I see hidden in the depths of her green eyes, tugs on my heartstrings. I tap her nose with a finger. "Of course, I'll stay."

A hint of a smile graces her lips. "Thank you, Eryc. Thank you for everything."

"Hey," I cup her face with both of my hands. "You don't need to thank me. You are my best friend, there's nothing I wouldn't do for you. I hope you know that."

"I do." Makayla sniffles. "You're a good man, Eryc." Her hands cover mine, her skin soft like velvet. "You're the bestest friend a girl could ever ask for."

I laugh at her use of bestest. "I'm pretty sure that isn't really a word."

"It is, trust me." She smiles. "I mean it. You are the best."

For her I will always be the best I can be. She is the only girl I have ever cared enough for to be the best friend that she describes me as. I kiss her forehead, again, lingering a little longer than necessary. "I'll be right back."

"Okay."

Heading to the hall closet, I gather three blankets and two pillows. When I enter the living room, Makayla is sitting on the edge of the coffee table, her leg bouncing manically. She stands and holds out her hands.

There is no way I'm going to let her help me spread out these blankets, so I hand her the two pillows and a couple of pillowcases. She gives me a curious look but takes them and begins tugging the pillowcases on the large, fluffy pillows.

I spread the thickest blanket down and unfold the

other two, placing one on each side of the makeshift bed. Makayla tosses the pillows down and looks at me expectantly.

"Pick a side," I say.

While she gets comfortable, I remove my shoes then settle in next to her, careful to tuck her blanket under her and create enough space between us that we are not in each other's personal space.

She is facing me and biting her bottom lip, a clear sign that she is nervous. Placing my hand on her shoulder, I say, "Go to sleep, Kay. I'm not going anywhere."

With the confirmation of my words, she closes her eyes and soon her breathing evens out and I know that she has finally allowed sleep to take her under.

25

Makayla

The creak of the backdoor echoes in the all-too-silent house and I hold my breath as I listen. Most likely it's just Thaddeus and not someone breaking and entering. At least I'm hoping that is the case, otherwise we are royally screwed.

Keys jingle, hit the floor, then jingle again before landing on the hallway table. Yep, it's Thaddeus and he is being clumsy which means he is probably drunk off his rocker. Judging by how slowly he is walking, I'm guessing he is trying to tiptoe but failing miserably because his thick boots thud heavily on the hardwood floor with each step he takes.

Peering over Eryc's sleeping form, I watch my brother fumble with his boots.

Lifting his foot, he tries to untie the laces but stumbles, hops a few steps, and falls into the wall. Cursing and swaying, he walks the two feet to the staircase and sits, or rather falls, onto the bottom step.

Once he gains his balance, he sets to work on untying his boots. It's clear that the feat isn't easy for him. A few more whispered curse words tumble out of his mouth. When he stands, his body sways. He takes a wobbly step up the stairs, clutching the banister like a man in need of a cane. Before he can manage to get himself up one more stair, I call out to him.

"Thad?" I try to keep my voice low as to not wake Eryc.

Whipping his head around, he looks toward the living room. He must be having difficulty seeing in the dark because he cups his hands around his eyes like he is looking through a window. "Makayla?" At least his voice is almost a whisper and not loud enough to wake the dead.

"I'm in the living room, Thad, on the floor." Eryc shifts but soft snores continue to fall from his lips. I lower my voice, so I don't disturb him further. "I was worried about you. Where were you?"

Thaddeus squats next to me. "Don't worry about me. I'm good."

I hate when he behaves this way. Of course, I'm going to worry about him, he is my brother, my twin. He must know that I can feel his pain. We are linked like only twins can be. I just wish he would trust me enough to let me help him. "Thad, seriously?"

His lips form a hard, tight line. "Leave me be, Makayla." Then, as if to soften the blow of his harsh words, he touches my cheek and smiles. "Don't worry about me. It's time to take care of yourself. Get some rest."

My brother is so irritating.

I don't want to rest because I'm worried that he is drinking himself into an early grave. "I can't rest when you're out there giving yourself alcohol poisoning and killing your liver."

A puff of air blows from his mouth and the sour scent of whiskey hits my nostrils. The smell enough to turn my stomach. Seeing me scrunch my nose in distaste, he turns his head in what I can only assume is embarrassment. "Makayla," his eyes meet mine again. "You're not my mother."

I take his hand and squeeze. "No, I'm not, but right now you are the only family I have. The only blood I can lean on. I need you. I need my brother, Thad."

Sadness fills his face. He plops down on his butt. When he shuts his eyes, a tear slowly trails down his cheek. "Makayla, I'm so sorry that I got you mixed up with that crowd. I never should have introduced you to Brandt and his goonies."

The pain in his voice brings fresh tears to my eyes. He shouldn't be apologizing to me. It was not his stupidity that hurt me, it was Brandt and *his* stupidity. My brother is not responsible for the actions of those blazing idiots.

Placing my finger over his lips, I stop his heart wrenching apology. "Look, Thad, I don't blame you. Yes, those bloomin' idiots hurt me. Yes, I have had a difficult time dealing with what they did to me. Yes, I fell into a dark place where death looked like my only option. But I never once blamed you. You did nothing wrong. The only ones responsible are the ones that participated and let it happen."

Those words taste like acid in my mouth. Yes, I believe that Brandt, Vince, and Lee are the ones responsible, but I also feel like I'm to blame. I could have fought harder. Instead of agreeing to go to those parties, night after night, I could have stayed home. Hell, I could have told someone about the things they did to me.

I'm to blame for not doing anything to prevent Brandt from taking advantage of me. But that blame is not for Thaddeus. He did nothing wrong. There was no way he could have known the damage his friends had done to me.

Every day since that first incident, I took great care to plaster a smile on my face so no one could see the hell I was living in. Tears start freefalling down Thaddeus's face.

His shoulders shake with the heartbreaking sobs. Laying down beside me, Thaddeus lets out all the pain and hurt he has been keeping locked away.

I feel Eryc stirring behind me, but I ignore him. My brother needs me right now, so I pull him close and comfort him.

Eryc places a soft kiss to the back of my head, giving me much needed support, while I do the same for my brother. I could not have asked for a better friend than Eryc. He gives me strength and courage just by being by my side.

I stroke Thaddeus's hair while his cries echo throughout the house. Those pain filled wails mirror what I have been battling internally since July. It absolutely kills me that my brother is hurting this badly over a situation he had no control over.

After what feels like hours but was probably only minutes, Thaddeus quiets his sobbing and sits up. Pulling his shirt over his head, he uses it to wipe his face and then blows his snotty nose on it.

Bending over, he kisses my forehead then nods toward Eryc. "He's good for you, sis. You seem peaceful with him around. That makes my heart happy."

"Yes." I peek behind me, at Eryc. His eyes are closed but I know he isn't sleeping. It seems that the words my brother just spoke resonate with Eryc because I catch the smile on his face. "He's the best. With him here, I have actually been able to sleep soundly."

"That's good."

Looking back at my brother, I add, "Instead of the nightmares that have been plaguing me for weeks, I was actually having a peaceful dream for once."

A smile breaks out on Thaddeus's face. "Maybe he's your guardian angel, or knight in shining armor, or something to that effect." Brushing hair off my forehead, my brother leans forward and kisses me between my eyebrows. "Get some sleep, sis. I love you."

"I love you too." I point toward the staircase. "Try not to fall down the stairs, I'd hate to see you break your neck in a drunken fall."

"I'll do my best." Standing, he leaves the room on unsteady feet.

26

Eryc

I hate that I am lying here awake, eavesdropping on their conversation. To give them the illusion of privacy, I do my best to appear to be asleep. When Thaddeus leaves and I can no longer hear his footsteps above us, I lean up on my elbow, resting my head in my hand. "Your brother loves you very much."

She rolls over, facing me. "Yeah, I know. I love that knucklehead just as much." Biting her bottom lip, Makayla scrunches her face like she's thinking of how to phrase her next words. "Um, how much of that conversation did you pay attention to?"

I shrug a shoulder. "Oh, not much."

Makayla rolls her eyes. "You are such a liar."

Guilty.

I never could lie to her. This girl has always been able to read my face like an open book. So, I smile at her and brush a wild lock of hair out of her face. "Yes, I am." My hand has not moved from her hair and my thumb gently caresses the tip of her ear. "I'm your knight in shining armor, huh?"

Makayla's eyes squeeze shut. A groan rumbles out of her. I picture pink tinting her cheeks a lovely rose color. It's too dark for me to see if she is blushing though. Yet I've seen it enough times I can imagine it.

I chuckle.

She is adorable when she's embarrassed.

"Oh, come on," I say. "It's not that bad."

Peeking at me with one eye, then the other, she seems to size me up. Maybe she is looking to see if Thaddeus's statement about me being her *knight in shining armor* was offensive to me. It wasn't.

"No, I suppose not." Pushing herself up, she reaches over and snags the television remote off the coffee table. "Do you mind if I turn on the TV? I'm not really tired anymore."

There is no way I can fall back to sleep either. My mind is wide awake now. "Go ahead, I'm not really tired either."

A click of the remote brings the television to life. The screen lights up to reveal one of those god-awful infomercials. I hate those stupid things, who in their right mind watches these long tedious infomercials with overpriced crap? Not me, that's for sure.

A man who is probably in his early thirties, is animatedly talking about this hair color product that is covering his graying head.

My brows furrow. I have my doubts about his graying hair since he looks too young to have any. He is demonstrating the product, which looks like a spray can. Really? What is this, and are people actually going to believe this load of horse pucky?

Shaking my head at this nonsense, I stand. "Do you still like popcorn with lots of butter and salt?"

Using the coffee table to push herself up off the floor, Makayla sits on the sofa. "Yes, of course." Snagging the square pillow from the other end of the sofa, she throws it at me. It misses me and lands next to my feet.

Seeing her like this, playful and with a smile on her face, is the best thing I have witnessed in a good long while. To play along, I dramatically fall to the ground clutching my chest. My reaction causes her to laugh out loud. That laugh is a beautiful sound that I could listen to all day.

A shift in the light coming from the television draws her attention to the screen and I use this opportunity to pick up the pillow and toss it back at her. She laughs some more and then hugs the pillow to her chest.

"I'll be right back with your popcorn."

"Okie dokie." She curls her feet under her and begins flipping through channels in her search for something to watch.

I search the cabinets for the air popper. Makayla has never liked microwavable popcorn. Says it's not crisp enough. Seriously, I don't see what the big deal is. The only popcorn I keep at home is microwavable, it's less of a hassle, but I will never serve her something she doesn't want.

The popper is in the cupboard next to the stove. It doesn't take long to get it set up. While the kernels are warming up, I pull two Cokes from the fridge. The smell of popcorn fills the room and my mouth waters. I'm not sure how long it's been since I have eaten any, probably the last time I went to the movies, which was four or five months ago.

Unplugging the popper, I add the melted butter to the bowl along with salt. I'm not sure how much salt to add so I carry the shaker along with the bowl and drinks back to the living room.

As I come around the corner to the living room, I notice two things. One, Makayla is sitting ramrod straight, and two, her face is fiery red. The sight of her and the thickness of the atmosphere sends shivers down my spine.

I want to go to her, to comfort her, but my gut tightens with a warning. So instead of going to her, I stay put and watch her struggle. Her fist tightens, and her body shakes with nervousness or anger, I'm not sure which.

In a flash, she rears her arm back and chucks the television remote. The hard piece of plastic sails through the air, right toward me. I'm not sure why she aimed it in my direction. I lean to the side just in time to miss being hit in the face.

The remote hits the wall behind me. Glancing down, I see the back of the remote next to my foot, the pad of buttons not far from me, and the black piece of plastic is in two pieces next to the wall.

"I'm sorry." Those words are so soft-spoken I barely hear them. Makayla doesn't look at me, her eyes are on the floor. I take a step toward her, but she stands quickly and runs from the room, dashing out the front door like the fires of hell are chasing after her.

It's only now that I glance at the television and see what has upset her. What I see sets my blood to boiling. No wonder she ran out of the room like a bat out of hell. Her own personal hell was being flaunted right in front of her eyes.

The scene playing on the television shows a girl sprawled out on the grass with ripped clothing, a cut on her upper lip, bruises forming around her eyes, and her pants around her ankles. There are two men standing

above her, laughing, and passing a bottle of whiskey back
and forth.

Setting the popcorn and drinks on the coffee table, I
push the off button on the television then pull the curtain
back to see Makayla pacing on the porch.

How in God's name am I supposed to handle this?

This is not familiar territory for me. Do I go to her and
comfort her or do I stay put and wait for her to return? My
stomach is in knots with worry. Makayla stops pacing and
leans against the railing of the porch, resting on her arms
with her head hanging down.

Throwing all caution to the wind, I decide to just go
out to her. What is the worst she can do, send me home?
She can sure try. I'm not going anywhere until I know she
is okay. Let her hate me, I don't care.

Stepping out onto the front porch, I join her, leaning
my hip against the railing. "Kay?"

Her breathing hitches at my voice but she doesn't look
at me.

"You alright?" I don't know why I ask. It's a stupid
question and I immediately feel like an idiot for asking.

*Couldn't I have thought of something better to say than
that? Jeez, I'm such a moron.*

"Yeah." Her shoulders slump further, and I know she
is lying. "No." Wiping her eyes with the collar of her shirt,
she continues. "Will these feelings ever go away? Every
time I turn around there is something to remind me of

what Brandt did to me." She sniffles. "It's like the harder I try to forget, the more I'm reminded of it."

Makayla is hurting and I don't know how to make it better. It doesn't matter what I say, I'm afraid whatever leaves my mouth will set her afire. So, I settle for a simple truth. "Have you tried forgiveness?"

She sucks in a breath, the air hissing through her teeth. Pushing away from the railing, she spins around to face me. Eyes hard as stone, she jams a finger into my chest. "Are you flippin' kidding me, Eryc?" Pushing her finger harder into my chest, she advances on me until my back is arching over the railing. "This isn't church, don't push that load of crap down my throat. That monster does not deserve my forgiveness. What he deserves is a life sentence in hell."

I can't argue with her there. Brandt does deserve life in hell for his transgressions but that is not for us to determine. Ultimately, God is the only one with the authority to sentence Brandt to such a fate. But forgiving Brandt wasn't what I was referring to, she needs to forgive herself before she can begin to heal.

"I was raped. How am I supposed to forgive that?" Taking a step away from me, she gazes off into the distance. A grunt leaves her throat before she speaks again. "You know what? I'm tired after all." Walking to the front door, she stops on the threshold. "Stay. Go. I really don't care." With that, she disappears into the house, slamming the door behind her.

"Well, that went well," I whisper into the night. Not sure whether she locked the door, I turn the knob.

It opens with a slight creak. Fighting against the urge to go inside and keep watch, I reach inside and lock the knob before shutting it and heading across the yard in nothing but my socks. I will see her tomorrow when she has had time to cool down.

I will wait until then to get my shoes.

PLOPPING DOWN ON MY SOFA, I slam my hand against the cushion. I hate that Makayla is suffering and there is nothing I can do to ease her pain. God, why did I have to go to Dallas for the summer? It's not like my parents needed me to help them move. I should have stayed and protected her.

Christian values aside, I would have beaten the snot out of that crazy fool for assaulting her. I still may beat the crap out of him the next time I see him. Oh sure, if I had beat him up, then people would have talked bad about me because I'm a preacher's son.

People always pick on me because of what my father is. They would have taken my actions and used them as an opportunity to quote scripture to me. Saying something along the lines of, *"What about turning the other cheek?"*

Turning the other cheek?

Ha. Truth be told, that particular Bible verse is referring to religious persecution and not protecting yourself against predators. Turning the other cheek? No, I would have beaten his sorry ass if I had been here.

My hands tighten into fists just thinking about it. I'm itching to punch him in the throat. Give him a taste of his own medicine. It's a good thing we're not in school right now because I'm afraid I would knock him to the ground and bash his head into the locker-room tiles.

Even as my brain rambles on, I know the truth. My being here during the summer would not have made a difference. Makayla would have still hung out with the popular crowd, and I would have still hung out with my less than popular friends.

I'm not sure how long I have been sitting on the sofa, contemplating what-ifs, but when my eyes become too heavy to keep open, I pull my socks off and toss them in the laundry room then head toward my bedroom.

With heavy lids and a deep yawn, I slip under the covers and immediately fall asleep.

Dreams of running a touchdown on the field and Makayla cheering for me in the stands morph into something much darker.

In place of my happy fantasy, I am suddenly left with

images that my brain conjures of Makayla and Brandt. The words I have read in her journal play on a loop in my dreams and I feel myself tossing and turning. Occasionally, I open my eyes, breathing heavily and my blood boiling with anger.

Now, I am staring at the popcorn ceiling. My eyes are as dry as the Sahara Desert and blinking is almost painful. The sun is up and beaming through the window, streaking across my neck and chest. Thank God it's Saturday, because there is no way I can stand spending the day in school. My body is worn out and my brain is fried.

The sound of a fist pounding on the front door startles me. I jump out of bed, worrying that it is about Makayla. My sweet girl has been through enough, I hope she is alright. Plush carpet squishes between my toes as I jog down the hallway toward the door. The pounding grows louder with each hit of the fist.

Unlocking the deadbolt, I swing open the heavy wooden door to find Thaddeus with a scowl on his face and his fist up, ready to pound into the door for the umpteenth time.

Crossing his arms over his chest and widening his stance, he yells, "What in the hell happened last night?" He doesn't give me time to answer his question. "I woke up this morning to my TV remote smashed to smithereens, popcorn spilled all over the kitchen floor, and a glass shattered in the sink."

"What?" I knew Makayla was upset when I left but I had no idea she went on a crazy popcorn throwing spree.

Thaddeus shifts and before I realize what he is doing, a hand shoves against my chest and I stumble backward, hitting my shoulder on the doorframe. "I swear to God, if you hurt her in any way, I will wring your neck like a soggy dishrag."

He thinks I'm responsible for Makayla's outburst? Yeah, not by a long shot. I thought he knew me better than that. Gaining my composure, I step aside and wave him in. Thaddeus's eyebrow raises and the scowl he wore when I opened the door is still in place. He is still suspicious, but he walks over the threshold to hear what I have to say.

Shutting the door behind me, I take a seat on the sofa and motion for him to join me. He is hesitant at first but sits on the edge of the coffee table directly in front of me.

"Look, I'm not the source of Kay's anger." *She needs to see a counselor* is what I want to say but don't. "After you went up to bed, we were both wide awake and decided to watch a movie. I left her to surf the channels while I made her popcorn. When I came back into the room, I nearly lost an eye due to the flying remote."

Thaddeus leans forward, lines crease his forehead. "How in the world does that explain the destruction left in my house?"

Leaning forward, I rest my arms on my knees. "Thaddeus, I know we've never been good friends, but I thought you knew me well enough to know that I would never hurt Kay. I'd die before I let her get hurt."

Our faces are close enough I can feel his puff of air when he exhales. "Then explain."

Scrubbing my hands over my face, I lean back. "I have no idea what movie she stumbled across but when I got back to the living room, she was livid. The scene was of a girl lying on the ground with ripped clothing and two men standing over her, laughing. It was apparent that they'd sexually assaulted her."

Thaddeus runs a hand through his hair and lets out a long whistle. "Well, holy shit." Standing, he takes to pacing and chewing on his thumbnail. "You know, I hate Brandt Taylor." Ceasing his pacing, he looks at me. "I could kill that sorry boneheaded SOB for what he did to her. I wish it had never happened."

"That makes two of us." I stand and stuff my hands in my pockets. "Sadly, though, it did happen and now it's up to us to help her recover."

Thaddeus nods in agreement. When he looks up at me, his face is one of misery. Maybe it will be all up to me to help Makayla recovery from her tragedy. Thaddeus reaches in his front pocket and pulls out his keys.

Nodding to the keys in his hand, I ask, "What time are you supposed to be at the hospital?"

Thaddeus is staring at his keys like they hold the answers to the universe. "I'm meeting with mom's doctors in twenty minutes." He tosses the keys up in the air and catches them. "After seeing the mess Makayla left behind, I didn't want to wake her up and endure her wrath."

"Smart move." I give Thaddeus a half smile. "She needs her rest. I know she hasn't been getting enough."

Thaddeus doesn't speak but rather grunts his agreement.

"Don't worry about Kay, I'll shower really quick and then head back over."

Thaddeus tosses his keys again before turning his blue eyes in my direction. "You're good for my sister, don't piss her off and mess things up."

Like he needs to tell me that. I would rather chew my leg off than sever this newly formed friendship. "I don't plan on it."

His eyes soften and he nods before spinning on his heel and walking out the door.

FRESHLY SHOWERED, I grab my keys from the hook in the kitchen and leave through the back door. Dew from the grass causes wet spots to form on the toe of my shoes as I walk across our yards. Makayla's car is sitting in the driveway and a black cat is perched on the hood. As I pass in front of her car the cat's ears pull back and he slants his eyes at me.

"Relax, kitty, I'm not here for you." The cat mewls, stands, and turns in two complete circles, then sneezes before resting his head on his paws.

Attached to the side of the garage door is a padlock opener. Sliding the cover upward, I press in the four-number code and the door slides up. Once I am inside, I press the button on the wall to close the door and I enter the house through the kitchen.

Just as I suspected, Thaddeus did not clean up the mess Makayla made last night.

Popcorn not only covers the floor, but it is also on the countertop and island. This room looks like a tornado came through and scattered fluffy kernels in its wake. The plastic bowl is under the table, upside down. "Okay, it looks like I will be cleaning up this mess before I do anything else."

Retrieving the broom from the pantry, I set about sweeping the floor.

27

Makayla

Warm water beats on my neck and shoulders, releasing some of the tension from my achy muscles. Whoever came up with the term, morning sickness, was obviously not a woman who has gone through a pregnancy like mine. I cannot even count the number of times I have hugged the toilet since Eryc left last night. It's a constant make-you-feel-green nausea.

I am so ready for this icky feeling to go away so I can feel human again.

Leaning forward to allow the water to wash over my

face, I groan at the thought of sitting in the hospital all day. To be honest, I'm not sure I will be able to stand that horrid sterile scent that overwhelms my nose every time I walk through the doors. I love my mom, don't get me wrong, but my stomach cannot handle any additional dry heaving. My abdominal muscles already feel like they have been through a meat grinder.

What was once a nice steamy-hot shower is now cooling to a slightly chilly temperature. I reach out to turn the handle fully to hot but it's already there.

"Seriously?"

Honestly, I'm not sure how long I have been in the shower, I know I stepped in right after I heard Thaddeus slip out the backdoor. That could have been half an hour ago for all I know.

Speaking of Thaddeus slipping out the backdoor, I knew he was on his way to Eryc's house to chew him out for my temper tantrum last night. I should have told him that Eryc had nothing to do with my childish behavior, but I just didn't want to face my brother and own up to my tantrum. It was a stupid move, I know. Hopefully Eryc will overlook my idiocy and forgive me for allowing my brother to storm over there all hot tempered.

Shutting off the facet, I grab my towel off the hook and step onto the cushy mat to dry off. Pulling my *Twenty One Pilots* T-shirt over my head, I slip into my jeans and open the bathroom door.

The instant I step over the threshold, a sweet maple fragrance wafts toward me. Surprisingly, this is one scent that does not cause my stomach to twist in knots. In fact, my tummy rumbles at the promise of sweet, yummy goodness.

A laugh escapes me. "Eryc has got to be here because my brother cannot cook to save his life."

Jogging down the stairs, my mouth waters more the closer I get to the maple goodness. I'm wearing socks so my footsteps land silently on the hardwood floor. Eryc is standing next to the sink with his back to me. Two plates have been laid on the table, each with two pancakes.

Eryc turns around with a coffee cup in each hand. When his eyes land on me, he sucks in a breath and takes a step back. "Oh, you scared me." Crossing the distance, he hands me a steaming cup. "How are you feeling this morning?"

I'm not sure what it is about Eryc, but I find that I rather enjoy when he asks how I'm feeling. Had it been Thaddeus that asked, I would have rolled my eyes and grumbled an answer. "I'm feeling better now, just a little tired." He raises his eyebrow in question, so I explain. "I didn't sleep well after I went up to bed. I've been a little on the sick side."

"Ah." Pulling out a chair, he motions for me to sit, so I do.

Looking around, I see that my mess from last night has

been cleaned up. I know Thaddeus did not clean it and now I feel ashamed because I know that Eryc took the time to clean up after me. I take a deep breath and apologize. "Eryc, I'm really sorry about last night. I had a sucky attitude, and I shouldn't have blown up at you like that."

"No worries, Kay." He tucks a stray strand of hair behind my ear. "There is absolutely no reason for you to apologize for that outburst." He pulls out the chair beside me and sits. "You suffered a traumatic ordeal. For you to feel overwhelmed at what you saw on TV is perfectly normal and understandable."

"I love you." As soon as the words leave my mouth, I squeeze my eyes shut and groan. "That is not what I meant. I mean...it is...but it's not...ugh. Never mind, just forget I said anything."

Eryc raises one brow, a glint of humor in his brown eyes. "I understand what you mean." He sips his coffee, those beautiful brown orbs never looking away from me. Pointing to the cup in my hand, he asks, "Is there anything I can get you? Creamer, or something?"

Looking down at the dark liquid in my cup, I cringe inwardly. I love coffee, a lot, but the last few times I tried to drink it, bile rose in my throat. Eryc pushes his chair back and stands so I say, "No. This is fine, I'm just nervous about putting anything in my mouth considering—" I point to my stomach to indicate the pregnancy and the morning sickness that goes along with it.

Understanding shines in his eyes and he shoves his hands in his front pockets. "Would you like a glass of milk instead?"

No, I would like to sit down and enjoy a cup of coffee without retching.

"No, thank you."

He sits back down but watches me like I'm a fragile doll. It is both endearing and annoying. In hopes of getting him to relax and enjoy his breakfast, I take a sip of the steaming coffee. The soft velvety liquid fills my mouth and for the first time in a while, it doesn't upset my stomach. Surprisingly, the smooth java settles well, and I roll my eyes back at the heavenly taste.

"What is this? This isn't mom's coffee." Tipping the cup to my lips, I take another sip. The warm java glides down my esophagus like silk then settles in my stomach. "This is fabulous."

A laugh tumbles out of Eryc. That laugh earns him a smack on the arm which only causes him to laugh more. "It's gourmet." He is still chuckling when he brings his cup up to his lips. After a couple of healthy drinks from his steaming cup, he says, "I buy from this gourmet company that uses Ganoderma extract in their coffee. I love the stuff."

Tapping my nails on the ceramic, I ask, "What in the world is Ganoderma?"

The smile that spreads on his face is absolutely wicked. "I'll tell you later."

Suddenly afraid that this Ganoderma product is going to grow teeth and eat me, I set my cup down and push it away.

He pushes it back toward me with a chuckle. "Relax, Kay, Ganoderma is just a mushroom."

I frown at my cup of coffee. Mushroom? I hate mushrooms with a passion. In fact, I have one word for them. Fungus. And who in their right mind eats fungus? Looks like Eryc does. Well, he drinks it anyway.

There is a war taking place in my mind. Part of me wants nothing to do with his fungus infested coffee and the other part of me wants more of that delicious java. It doesn't take long for the coffee-loving part of me to win, and I sit back and enjoy the heavenly drink once more.

Eryc watches my every move with a look of satisfaction on his face.

My insides twitch with a feeling I have never experienced before. Our relationship is different from what it used to be. I'm not sure what exactly has changed between us, but he looks at me like I am precious.

I now feel closer to him than I have ever felt to anyone, including my twin brother.

"What?" he asks. "Do I have something on my face?" He swipes a hand across his mouth.

"Nope."

Pointing his fork at me, he nods to my untouched plate. "You should eat before it gets cold."

How did I get so lucky as to have Eryc as my best friend?

Surprise, surprise. Rene wants to see me today to do an official pregnancy test and whatever else that is involved in a prenatal visit. Since her schedule is pretty full, she is squeezing me in during her break.

The ride to Rene's clinic is a quiet one. I'm not sure how I'm supposed to act, and I think Eryc feels the same way. He glances at me every so often, his eyes full of kindness and maybe a hint of pity.

Tulsa Memorial hospital comes into view and my mind wonders over to my mother. I need to visit her sometime today. She is conscious now and I am not there with her. Which makes me feel like a bad daughter.

Guilt eats at my heart, and I begin to feel like a failure for not being a good child. The woman that gave birth to me, the one who suffered sleepless nights when Thaddeus and I were babies, is helpless in that hospital bed and I have been at home like a shellfish brat. The last thing I want is for her to feel like I have abandoned her, just like my father did to us all those years ago.

Turning into the hospital parking lot, Eryc follows the

lane that leads toward the back of the building, where the clinics are. Nerves twist my stomach like a wet dishrag and moisture collects on my palms. I'm not sure I want to go in there. Can I just rewind time and stay in the comfort of my bed?

The car veers into a parking space, between two minivans. Minivans. Ick, there is no way in hades I will ever be caught dead behind the wheel of one of those horrid monsters.

Rough, calloused fingers graze my wrist and I look over at Eryc.

He smiles and says, "Come on, Kay. It'll be okay, I'm right here. I'm not going anywhere."

Words fail to form in my mouth, so I nod and unbuckle my seatbelt. Before I can grab my purse from the floorboard, he is already out of the car and opening my door. He holds out his hand and helps me out of the car. It is still awkward when he, or Thaddeus, touch me, but Eryc pays close attention to my reactions and pulls back when he sees me struggling. Because of his attentiveness, I am slowly reacquainting myself with a man's touch.

The moment those sliding glass doors open, my nostrils are assaulted with sterile air that immediately leaves my nasal passages dry. Taking a deep breath to calm my nerves, I cross the threshold and follow Eryc down the hall to Rene's clinic.

The waiting room is full of expecting mothers with

large round bellies. Some of these women have toddlers bouncing on their laps and I cringe inwardly at the thought of motherhood.

A baby is not something I look forward to. Babies are supposed to be a happy season in a woman's life, one she can share with her husband. My pregnancy is not a happy one, nor is it wanted.

A gentle tug on my hand draws my attention down to the one gripping mine and my gaze travels up his arm, settling on his brown eyes. Eryc nods toward the check-in window. "You'll be fine, I'm right here with you. I'll never abandon you."

A petite woman looks up from her computer screen, her fingers still tapping on the keyboard. The moment she sees us, her lips turn up in a huge smile. "Hi, sweetie." She glances down at the screen, taps a couple more keys, then looks back up. "Your aunt is with a patient, but she said to go on back to her office and she'll see you shortly."

Eryc smiles at the receptionist. "Thanks, Mel."

"No problem, sugar." Mel smiles and gives me a friendly wave before giving the screen her full attention.

I hesitate for a heartbeat but then allow Eryc to lead me through the door separating the waiting room from the hallway that is full of exam rooms. The carpet is snot-green and ugly as sin but so cushiony, putting a comfortable barrier between my feet and the hard-concrete floor beneath.

Passing the last door on this hall, we turn to the right and the hallway ends with one final door. Rene's personal office. A low buzzing sound rings in my ears and my lungs constrict. I don't want to be here. I would rather face a den of lions than sit in this room.

Eryc releases my hand and points to one of the chairs against the wall. "Kay, sit down and relax. Everything will be fine."

Relax?

Everything will be fine?

Easy for him to say, he is not the one carrying a monster child in his belly. And how do I explain my ill feelings toward my own unborn child to the preacher's kid standing next to me? He will never understand why I can't keep this baby. Keeping the baby means a constant reminder of Brandt and all the pain and humiliation he caused me.

Just as I open my mouth to voice my fears, and most likely humiliate myself, the door opens and Rene walks in wearing a white lab coat. "Good, you're here." Stepping further into the room, she gives me a hug and a kiss on the cheek. "How are you doing, sweetie?"

"Um." I look at Eryc and then back at Rene. "I'm okay, I guess."

"You'll be just fine." Rene pats my arm like I'm a two-year-old.

What is it with these two? I am not fine. I won't be fine.

Ever. I'm stuck in this life trying to get by one day at a time.

Rene nods toward the door. "Come with me and we'll get started."

I stop at the threshold and look back at Eryc. He crosses the distance and tucks a strand of hair behind my ear. "I'll say these words a thousand times if I have to. I'm not going anywhere." His hand is still touching my ear and he leans in close enough I can feel his breath on my cheek. "I'll be here for you until the day I die."

Those ten words are all it takes to calm the raging storm within me. Letting out a breath, I nod. He is here and will not abandon me when I need him most.

Eryc is my rock.

28

Eryc

Makayla releases a breath, and her shoulders visibly relax at the mention of me being here for her until the day I die. She may not know this but when she gets nervous, her face heats up and turns bright red. Even the tips of her ears are crimson and hot to the touch. If I could stay with her during her exam, I would, but Aunt Rene explained to me last night that the exam is personal and involves next to no clothing.

"I'll be right here," I say again. I'll repeat those words to her for eternity if need be. The last thing I want is for her to feel alone and lost in this world. My girl has felt lost and alone for far too long as it is. Never again will I allow her to go through this life alone.

Her eyelids flutter shut, and her body relaxes further. The red in her face lightens and the worry lines smooth out. Makayla is the prettiest girl alive, even with red blotches marring her beautiful face. I'm pretty sure I am falling in love with her. I have always loved her, we have been friends our entire lives, but this is something else altogether. This feeling is soul deep. I would walk through fire for her, hell I would take a bullet for her.

Makayla takes a deep breath, blows it out slowly, and turns to follow my aunt out of the room. She is scared but my aunt will comfort her. Those two are pretty close, they are close enough for Makayla to occasionally call her Aunt Rene or Momma Rene.

The door clicks shut and now I sit in the all-too-silent room. Voices drift in from under the door. Two nurses out in the hallway are chatting about their weekend plans. I pull my cell phone out of my back pocket and open my messages. There are five missed texts from my football buddies. All of them asking if I will be at practice this afternoon. I don't miss many practices but the last two I missed so I could be with Makayla.

I open a group text so I can message everyone with one simple text.

> Yes, I plan on being there. Unless there's an emergency.

They are sick of hearing this excuse, I know they are. Since Brenda's accident, I have used this excuse on occasion to get out of fifth and sixth hour classes, as well as the last couple football practices. It will eventually backfire on me and get me kicked off the football team, but honestly, I would gladly give up football for Makayla. Football is just a sport and is easily replaceable in my life, Makayla is not.

Sixty seconds pass before my phone vibrates with a reply.

CHAD

> Be there, man. We need you to get your head in the game if we're going to win against Union on Friday night. Besides, Coach said for you to get your ass on the field this afternoon or you're out.

I knew this was coming, and frankly, I don't blame Coach. He needs a team that is there, and on their game, not a no-show, scatter-brained dimwit like I have been here lately. The last thing I want to do is let my team down, but my number one priority is Makayla, everything thing else in this life can, and will, take a back seat.

Tossing my cell phone on my aunt's desk, I pick up a magazine. The cover is of a pregnant woman with both hands resting on her round belly and the caption reads

Rockin' Your Baby Bump. I open the magazine and flip through the pages. Nothing within interests me, it is full of toys, foods, stylish maternity clothes, and an article on breast feeding.

Blowing out a puff of air, I toss the magazine back in the basket on the end of my aunt's desk. "I wonder how long this will take." Sitting here with nothing but my thoughts will slowly drive me insane.

Time seems to pass by at a snail's pace. I dig through the pile of magazines, again, but they are all the same. What to wear, what to expect during each trimester, what to pack for the hospital, and how to breast feed. All things that do not interest me in the least. Giving up on reading material, I begin pacing the office. Thoughts of this week's game run through my mind.

Union is a big school, and their team is one of the best in Tulsa. Beating them will take practice and dedication. Since I have no idea how long Makayla will be in the exam room, I run through the plays in my head. Just as I get lost in my thoughts, my cell phone chimes with a text.

I pick the device up from the corner of my aunt's desk and check the incoming message. There isn't one. My last message was from the guys on the team. The chime sounds again, and I realize it's not coming from my cell phone. Searching my aunt's desk for a cell, I carefully lift papers and look behind a file rack, but I don't find a phone anywhere.

"Huh." My eyes roam around the office, looking for any signs of the tiny device but I'm not seeing any. Then it sounds again, and my eyes follow the noise to my left. Makayla's purse is sitting on one of the chairs. I hadn't even noticed that she had left it behind.

Not wanting to invade Makayla's privacy, I continue my pacing and leave her purse untouched. My thoughts just get back into football plays when her cell phone chimes again. And again. Four texts later and I unzip her purse to look for her phone. It could be Thaddeus with urgent news on Brenda and if that's the case, I want to let Makayla know ASAP.

The shimmery-pink device is peeking out from an inside pocket. Another text comes in as I slip it free. I press the home button and the device prompts me for the passcode.

"What is your code, Kay?" I wonder aloud.

I try a wide array of four-digit numbers to no avail and have timed out the device twice. One more wrong number and it will time out again. If these texts are from Thaddeus about their mother, I really want to get this to Makayla, so she can head to that division of the building.

"Thaddeus." The name suddenly hits me. Those two are twins and as close as two people can get. Glancing down at the number pad, I search for the letters THAD.

Eight, four, two, and three are the magic numbers.

Pressing the green message button, I check to see who the texts are from.

Not Thaddeus, it's an unfamiliar number with no name attached. Satisfied that it's not an emergency from Thaddeus, I press the off button. Just before the screen shuts off, a preview of the text catches my eye.

It's been too long since I hit that...

I unlock the phone, again, and open the text message. Scrolling up, I read the string of messages from the beginning.

> UNKNOWN
>
> Mickey, it's Brandt.

Mickey? Seriously?

Makayla hates that name, which he would know if he had bothered to get to know her. Every message after that is a guilt trip of sorts.

> UNKNOWN
>
> I need you.
>
> UNKNOWN
>
> It's been a crappy week and I need you to make me feel better.
>
> UNKNOWN
>
> You're the only one that understands me.
>
> UNKNOWN
>
> I'm depressed.

UNKNOWN

You're the only one that can ease my
pain.

What a load horseshit. Finally, I get to the last few
messages.

UNKNOWN

Parents are gone tonight.

UNKNOWN

Come over.

UNKNOWN

It's been too long since I hit that.

Heat rises in my neck and trails to the tips of my ears.
How dare he contact her after all the hell he put her
through. What if this isn't the first time that he has
contacted her. Does she endure this on a weekly, or a daily
basis? My blood begins to boil which causes my heartrate
to accelerate. If ever there was a time that I wanted to
choke the life out of someone, it's now. The more I look at
these messages, the angrier I become. Pain radiates
through my palm where my nails are digging into my skin.

In my rage, I don't hear the footsteps outside the door,
so I jump when the door opens, and my aunt walks in.
"Eryc, what are you doing?" She glances down at the pink
cell phone in my hand.

"Nothing." I turn the screen of the device toward my
body to hide the written words.

Aunt Rene furrows her brows. She can tell I'm lying, I'm a lousy liar. Instead of pursing her lips and condemning me for fibbing to her, like my mother would, she smiles. Closing the distance between us, she kisses my forehead as she reaches for my hand, turning the screen so she can see what is bothering me.

Air hisses through her teeth as she reads the last message.

That must have been enough for her because she doesn't even bother scrolling up to see the others. "Eryc," she squeezes my hand. "Makayla doesn't need to see this. She's a mess as it is."

"I know."

Releasing my hand, she turns toward the door. "You need to get rid of those."

I nod.

"We haven't started the exam yet. She's preparing for that now. In the meantime, delete that garbage."

"Yes, ma'am." I watch my aunt walk out the door and glance back down at the cell phone. I don't think about what Makayla will say when she finds out I messed with her cell phone. What she doesn't know won't hurt her. First, I block the number and then I delete the entire conversation. She does not need this kind of garbage in her life.

Shutting off the screen, I place the pink device back in the pocket of her purse where she had left it.

29

Makayla

Picking up the paper gown Rene gave me, I strip out of my clothes and tie the gown around my neck. Cool air caresses my back where the material gaps open. The flimsy material does very little to keep my body covered, but I suppose it does hide all the important areas. My fingers play with the rim of my socks as fear makes an appearance and twists my insides like a washing machine.

This is the first time in my life I have seen a gynecologist and I have no idea what this exam is or what to expect.

Will it hurt? I certainly hope not.

A soft knock on the door echoes in the silent room. "Honey, are you ready?" Rene's loving voice brings a little peace to my panic.

Honestly, I am nowhere close to being ready. I would rather donate a kidney than endure this exam and confirm what I already know. This is a nightmarish ordeal that I wish I could go back in time to avoid.

Being pregnant by a sick, twisted, and mentally abusive prick is not a reality I want to live.

No, I'm not ready.

"Yeah, I'm ready."

The hinges on the door creek as she opens it. Rene offers me a kind smile, one I return. If there is anyone on this planet that I trust to see me in all my glory, it's Rene. Just when I think I can do this, a petite nurse in a light pink uniform walks in.

My smile fades and my stomach goes back to doing backflips. I glance from the nurse to Rene. "Do we have to do this with an audience?"

Rene sits on a stool, rolls over to me, and pats my hand. "Honey, this is Nurse Shelly. She's here to assist me."

Nurse Shelly grabs a pair of gloves from the box on the wall and smiles at me with understanding as she puts them on her hands. "Don't worry, sweetie, I'm only here to assist and be a witness." She hands a pair of gloves to Rene.

The vinyl gloves stretch over Rene's hands like a second skin. With each passing second, fear coils around my heart, constricting the pumping organ until I grow lightheaded. If only a hole would form under me so I could fall into oblivion, that would be great. Tears blur my vision and when I blink, they trail down my face. Salty wetness seeps between my lips and I wipe my mouth with the back of my hand.

Nurse Shelly pulls a small tube out of the cabinet. After arranging several items on the tall metal tray, she comes to stand at my side. "Go ahead and lie back." She hands me a tissue to dry the tears from my face. "Relax, you're going to be just fine."

Relax?

I never would have thought there would be a time when that word was foreign to me. I can't remember the last time I was able to truly relax. Everything makes my skin crawl. Every noise startles me. Some days I wonder if I will ever be normal again.

The wheels of Rene's stool grind against the tile when she stands. "Okay, Makayla, the first thing I'm going to do is check your breasts." Sliding her hands under my gown, her fingers press on either side of my right breast, moving in circular motions. In less than a minute she is done and switches to the left side to repeat the action. It feels weird to have someone else touching this part of my body.

Once she finishes examining my breasts, she walks to the foot of the exam table that I'm lying on and adjusts these metal foot things. The metal contraptions are kind of scary looking and I'm uncertain about this next part of the exam.

Adjusting a large lamp, she points to the metal foot things. "You're doing great, Makayla. Now I want you to put your feet in these stirrups."

I do as she instructs. The metal is cold and uninviting.

Rene sits on her stool and says, "Slide as close to the edge as you can. I'll make this as quick and painless as possible."

I scoot down until my backside feels as if it will fall off the table. Rene lifts the cheap paper that is coving my most private parts and flips the switch to the gigantic lamp, shining the bright light right between my legs.

Shutting my eyes tight, I pray she hurries. This is the most humiliating thing I have ever had to endure.

The sound of paper ripping draws my attention to my right. Nurse Shelly hands Rene a long Q-tip then pats my hand with her gloved one. "We're almost done, hun." A few short minutes later and Rene hands the Q-tip back to Nurse Shelly, who puts it in a plastic tube.

Flipping the light off, Rene stands. "Shelly, can you run and get that ultrasound machine for me?"

"Sure thing." Nurse Shelly squeezes my hand before walking to the far corner of the room to fetch the portable machine.

The wheels rattle as she rolls it over toward me. Once she has it situated, she begins turning knobs and pushing buttons. The screen on the machine lights up and a black and white image appears.

"It's ready." Nurse Shelly slips a cover on the wand-like device and hands it to Rene.

"Okay, sweetie, this is an ultrasound." Rene points to the black and white screen. "It will show us the baby."

All air whooshes from my lungs when I realize what is about to happen. This baby will be showcased on that screen. Tilting my head back, I stare up at the ceiling. The last thing I want to do is look at this tiny creation. I know that makes me sound like a heartless witch, but I can't look. My heart might be comprised if I even glance at it, and the last thing I want is to feel anything for a baby created out of manipulation and pain.

The wand is cold and unwelcoming when Rene inserts it. Embarrassment tints my cheeks. A few clicks of the buttons and Rene talks to the nurse about the baby and how it looks great. Then she rearranges the wand and taps a few more buttons on the machine. "Ah ha."

Ah ha? What does she mean, ah ha?

Maybe it's not a baby, maybe I have a massive tumor.

Terror freezes the blood in my veins. I can feel all color drain from my face.

"What is it?" I glance down at Rene, but she is focusing on the screen, still moving the wand from side to side. "What's wrong with me?"

The silence is killing me. Glancing over at the machine, I look at what has alarmed Rene. Or rather, I try to look at what has alarmed her. All I see is a blurry black and white image. There is nothing on that screen that makes any sense to me.

Adjusting the wand and pressing a couple more buttons, Rene points to the screen. After she removes the wand and disposes of the sleeve, she says, "Do you see these two small round spots?"

Two small round spots?

Oh, God, it is a tumor. Squinting, I try to locate the baby amongst the tumor but this mess on the screen is Greek to me. My heart is hammering in my chest and sweat is beading on my upper lip.

"This," Rene points to one of the two spots, "is baby A." Moving her finger to the second darkened spot, she says, "And this is baby B."

"Baby A and baby B?" I shake my head, not fully understanding. "What about the tumor?"

A look of confusion comes over Rene. "Who said anything about a tumor?"

"But I—"

"I think you misunderstood what I was trying to say." She points to both dark spots. "Here you have baby A and baby B." When she says baby, she draws out the word.

It takes my mind a minute to process what she is saying but like a light switch, the bulb in my brain turns on. "Are you saying that those two little blobs are babies, as in twins?"

Twins. Not one but two little reminders of Brandt and the abuse I endured.

Great, this is not what I need right now.

"That's exactly what I'm saying." Pure joy is lighting up Rene's face, bringing out a wondrous glow in her cheeks. You would think she was the expecting mother-to-be with the glow she is sporting. She tugs on the end of her gloves, and they release with a pop.

Nurse Shelly tears a piece of paper from the ultrasound machine and then hands it to me. I take it. It's a printout of the image on the screen. I'm not sure what these two women think I want with this picture. Just the thought of *two* babies twists my stomach into mammoth-sized knots.

"Rene, can I speak to you?" I look over at the nurse. "Alone?"

"Of course." She nods to the nurse and in less than a minute we are alone.

I wait for the door to click shut before I open my mouth. "Look, Rene, I...I can't...I don't want—" Great, now

I'm all flustered and can't even speak a coherent sentence. Inhaling through the nose, I hold in the oxygen for a count of three before releasing the breath.

Rene strokes my hand. "It's okay, sweetie, take your time."

Deciding to just spit it out and get it over with, I say, "I don't want these babies."

Hurt registers in her eyes and she bites her bottom lip, probably to keep from saying something that would hurt my feelings or anger me. After a minute, she releases her lip. "Are you saying what I think you're saying?"

I close my eyes, so I don't have to see the disappointment on her face when I nod.

Her breathing comes fast, and she squeezes my hand. "I don't want you making any rash decisions here. Let's talk about what you're considering, and the risks involved."

There is no way she will ever understand. To her this is a blessing. To me, this is a curse. "I don't want to talk about the risks. There is no way I can raise these children. I just can't love them."

"Sweetie, there are other options. For starters, there's adoption."

I love this woman like she was my own aunt, but right now she is irking my nerves something fierce. So much so that I can feel my blood begin to boil.

Adoption is not on my radar. Why should I carry these

babies, nourish them, and push them out of my body when I cannot even stand the thought of them? Besides that, what if they turn out to be as selfish and evil as Brandt? "No. For one, I can't stand the thought of them. And two, I refuse to give birth to two creatures that could very well turn out just like their sperm donor."

A frown curves her mouth downward and a puff of air leaves her lips. There is a lecture coming and I am not in the mood to hear it. This is my decision. Mine and mine alone. I hand her the ultrasound picture and stand, holding my paper gown in place. When she opens her mouth to speak, I turn my back to her.

Conversation over.

Footfalls echo in the quiet room and soon the door opens and shuts.

Rene is gone, and I am all alone.

30

Eryc

S hadows move at my feet, and I look up. Aunt Rene is walking toward me with a sad, heart-broken expression.

Immediately my thoughts go to Makayla and the worst possible scenarios. "Oh, no. What's wrong? Is Makayla okay?"

"Physically, yes." Aunt Rene walks to her desk and sits with a humph. A piece of photo paper is in her hand. She stares intently at it. Several minutes pass before she glances up at me. "Makayla is fine." Passing the photo to me, I stare down at the image, unable to make out what it's supposed to be. "It's the ultrasound photo," she says in answer to my silent question.

Where in the world is the baby? All I see is a black and white image with two dark circles in it. Each dark circle has a small white peanut looking image within. I turn the photo sideways and back again, trying to see where the baby is located.

Rene takes the photo from my hands and lays it on the desktop, pointing to each little peanut shape. "Those are the babies."

"Oh." I pick up the photo and look again. Then her words hit me, and I realize what she just said. "Babies? You mean, more than one?"

Whoa.

At that moment, the door swings open and Makayla enters. A scowl quickly forms on her face when she sees the ultrasound picture in my hands. Plucking the paper from my hand, she tosses it on Rene's desk.

"I'm ready to go home." Retrieving her purse from the chair, she walks out of the room.

Stunned. That is what I am, I'm stunned at her behavior. What in the world is going on with that girl? Her behavior is baffling, this is not like her. She's not one to be rude.

Standing, I pick up the discarded photo.

Before I turn to leave, Rene speaks. "Be gentle with

her." She takes a deep breath. "I think she has decided to have an abortion."

What the hell?

I'm speechless.

Looking down at the photo, I shake my head. I can't imagine why she would decide such a thing but then again, I guess I can understand where she is coming from. She doesn't want a reminder of her traumatic past.

Crossing the threshold, I follow the path Makayla went. The hallway seems longer than it actually is, probably because I am trying to process the fact that Makayla wants to terminate these babies' lives.

The waiting room is void of her when I open the door and enter. Mel says bye when I walk past the check-in window, and I wave without looking in her direction.

Makayla is standing next to my car when I get to the parking lot. Her back is to me, and her shoulders are slumped. "Kay?" I call out to gain her attention.

She shakes her head. "I just want to go home."

"Okay." Pulling the keys from my jeans pocket, I press the unlock button. Sliding into my seat, I crank the engine.

Makayla is avoiding eye contact. I'm not sure why. Reaching over her, I slip the image of her babies into the glovebox.

A puff of air leaves her lips. "I gave that to Rene."

"And she gave it to me." I back out of my parking spot.

This time, she turns to look at me. "Why? It's not hers to give." Anger is starting to lace her tone and her nostrils flare with each breath she takes.

Wow, I had no idea she would get so wound up over that picture. "Relax, Kay. She just wanted to make sure you had it."

"Don't tell me what to do." Her voice pierces my ears and I wince at the shrillness of it. "I'll relax when I'm good and ready."

This girl is downright scary when she is angry. Remind me to never get on her bad side again. I turn onto I44 East and head toward home. The tension in the car is so thick I can hardly breathe. Makayla needs comfort and support. Sadly, I'm not sure I know how to offer either of those at this time.

We sit in silence for a few minutes because I just don't know what to say to her. She is angry for whatever reason. I didn't even do anything to her, yet her anger is aimed at me. Go figure. Green eyes turn toward me, and I chance a peek at her. Tears are pooling in her green orbs. It's clear to see that she is doing her best to keep them from spilling over. "She told you, didn't she?"

I don't need to ask what she is talking about. Yet I do anyway. "Told me what?"

Using the heels of her hands, she wipes at the tears that have fallen. "Don't play dumb with me, Eryc. I may have been born at night, but it wasn't last night. Your face gives you away, you're a terrible liar."

"Yes, she told me that you wanted to terminate the pregnancy."

"She had no right to share that with you." Her voice has lost some of its volume. Thank God. "Just because we're all close doesn't mean she can share what is being said behind closed doors at her office."

"You're absolutely right. It was unprofessional for her to tell me, and it was certainly unfair to you. But, Kay, she's just worried about you."

"I understand that, but this is hard enough for me. I don't need to deal with the two of you hovering over me like I'm a fragile China doll." She unzips her purse and starts rummaging around.

Glancing over, I see snot forming at the tip of her nose. Leaning over, I open the glovebox. I'm always tossing napkins in there when I order fast food.

Pulling a napkin free, I hand it to her. "Here."

"Thanks." She takes the napkin from my hand and blows her nose.

I cringe at the sound. When she is finished, she looks around for a place to dispose of the used napkin. I'm about to tell her to just leave it on the floorboard, but then she opens her purse and tucks it inside.

"Look, I can see the wheels turning in your head and I don't want a lecture. Not from you."

I take the 11th street exit. We are just a couple minutes away now. "Kay, just think about this before you jump to a decision."

"Why, preacher's boy, because I'll be damning my soul to hell?" The anger in her tone raises my blood pressure and I want to yell at her for saying *preacher's boy* as an insult.

Preacher's boy? Did she really just call me that?

That is the same name she called me when she was trying to fit in with the popular crowd at school. Is she seriously trying to push me away, again? Well, guess what? It's not going to happen. I refuse to leave her alone when she needs me the most.

I take a second to calm myself before I speak to her. "First off, do not call me preacher's boy. We are far too familiar for that crap. Secondly, I just want you to think about this before you do something you'll regret."

Pulling into her driveway, I shut off the engine and exit the car.

Makayla slams the car door. "You and Rene are not hearing me. I do not want a reminder of Brandt. Ever." She points to her stomach. "I don't want these. Period."

"But—"

"No." She walks around the car to stand in front of me, jamming her finger in my chest. "We're done. This conversation is over. Am I understood?"

I hold my hands up in surrender. "Okay," I say calmly.

Giving me a shove, she turns on her heel and storms off toward the house. She retrieves the keys from her purse and tries repeatedly to get the key into the keyhole, but her hand is too shaky to succeed.

"Kay." I wait a second before touching her because I know unexpected touches freak her out. Taking the keys from her, I say, "Let me open that for you."

Makayla enters the house and stops to look at me over her shoulder. "Listen, if you stay, and believe me, I enjoy having you here, then leave the baby topic alone. That is not a request, it is a demand. This is my body and my decision, not yours and not Rene's."

I bite my lip before answering her. Is there a chance I will bring this up for discussion in the future? Yes, absolutely. But for now, I'm willing to leave this topic on the back burner. "Fine. For now, I'll leave it alone."

She nods and heads toward the kitchen where she opens the refrigerator.

"Are you hungry? I can fix you a sandwich or cook something if you'd like." I peer over her shoulder to study the contents of the fridge.

She turns around to face me. "Can you make lasagna? I'm dying for some good lasagna."

I take a step back and look at her. She worries her bottom lip and wrings her hands together. This girl has never liked lasagna because she thinks it is too greasy. That and she hates cottage cheese.

"Yes, I can make lasagna," I say. "But I thought you hated lasagna."

"I do but that's what I want. Can you make it so it's not so greasy? Oh, and please skip the cottage cheese."

"Yes, ba—" I stop myself when I realize I was going to call her baby. Wow, I don't think either of us are ready for that step yet. "Yes, Kay, I can substitute with ground turkey or forgo the meat altogether."

Her brows furrow. "How do you make lasagna without meat?"

She is so cute when she wears the face of confusion. "I make my lasagna with squash, carrots, mushrooms, and zucchini in place of the meat...and I use ricotta cheese instead of cottage cheese. Trust me, it'll be good."

She scrunches her nose while she thinks it over. Shrugging a shoulder, she says, "Okay. I like the sound of your meat alternative, but please skip the mushrooms." She leans her elbows on the kitchen island and watches me with wild curiosity.

I sift through the contents of the fridge. It's lacking the necessary ingredients, so I'll have to go shopping if I'm going to make this for her. Pulling out the basket of straw-berries, I set them in front of her. "Snack on these, I have to run to the store for the ingredients. I won't be long, and I'll start dinner as soon as I return."

Makayla picks up the carton of strawberries. "Okay." Picking up a strawberry, she bites the tip and licks the red juice from her lips. "Don't forget to leave the mushrooms at the store."

"Yes, ma'am."

She wrinkles her nose at me. "What? Do I look like a thirty-year-old woman with a librarian's bun and glasses? I'm not a ma'am." Taking another bite of her strawberry, she goes to the living room to watch television.

I smile and shake my head as I get back in my car and head to the store.

31

Makayla

E ryc moves about my kitchen like he has lived here his whole life. Which I guess is kind of true, he spent more time here as a kid than he did at his own house. Noodles are boiling in a large pot, homemade sauce is simmering in another, and he is slicing the vegetables. I offered to help but he poured a glass of orange juice, handed it to me, and told me to sit and relax. So that is exactly what I'm doing.

The front door opens and closes with a loud bang.

"Sis?" Thaddeus's heavy boots thud against the hardwood floor as he walks toward the kitchen.

Fear of mom's health declining has me standing and rushing to meet my brother at the entry to the kitchen.

Thaddeus looks over my shoulder where Eryc is standing at the stove. He raises his brow then turns his ice-blue eyes back to me. "I'm glad you're here." Making his way to the dining room table, he sits and rolls his neck.

"Thad, is mom okay?"

In response to my question, Eryc comes to stand beside me. Clutching his arm, I silently beg God for good news. Mom seemed to be doing so much better last night and I just assumed she was on the mend.

Thaddeus looks from my face down to where I'm holding onto Eryc. Seconds pass by like hours and I can feel panic creeping in.

My brother steeples his fingers before meeting my worried gaze. "Yes, mom is fine. I spoke with the doctor in charge of mom's care, as well as the surgeon. They said she's recovering faster than they expected. Vitals look good and they will be moving her to rehab in a few days."

Relief surges through me, releasing the fear and tension from my body. Tremors fill me from the sudden release, and I squeeze Eryc's arm. "Thank God." My mom is going to be okay. Yes, she will be in rehab until she is strong enough to come home, but she is alive and well.

This is exactly the miracle I prayed for the night of her accident.

Turning, I release Eryc's arm and wrap my arms

around him in a hug. His arms slowly come around me. I know he moves slowly because he is afraid of startling me or setting off memories and causing a panic attack. I'm thankful for that. Without thinking, I stand on my tiptoes and lean forward to kiss his cheek.

Unfortunately, I miss his cheek. I miss because when I pull away from him, he turns to look at me, so when my lips land, they touchdown right smack on his mouth.

That small contact with his soft, warm lips ignites a spark in the pit of my stomach. Unlike the icky feeling I got when Brandt would kiss me, this little mouth-to-mouth contact warms me like a thick comfy blanket in the dead of winter.

Then I remember that Thaddeus is in the room and embarrassment heats my face.

I release Eryc and step back as far as I can with his arms still around me. "I'm so sorry, Eryc. I didn't mean to —" Casting my gaze downward, I stare at the spot between our feet.

Eryc's arms loosen around me, his hand comes to rest on my shoulder. Using his other hand, he tips my chin up. "It's fine, Kay." A smile appears on his face and his eyes seem to stare into the depths of my soul.

There is something in his brown pools. Kindness, compassion, and something else I can't quite decipher. When Thaddeus coughs, Eryc drops his hands and goes back to cutting vegetables.

Thaddeus stands and crosses his arms, a smirk set on his face. Leaning close to me and lowering his voice, he says, "Something has changed between you two. Serious vibes are coming off you both, in massive waves." He winks and then walks away.

I rush to follow him down the hallway. "What are you talking about?"

He stops next to the staircase. "What I'm saying, sis, is that it looks as though love is in the air."

Love? What in the world would make my brother think love is in the air? My accidental kiss with Eryc?

"Oh, my word!" I glace back to make sure Eryc isn't lurking around in hearing distance. "There is nothing romantic going on between the two of us. Do I love him? Well, yeah, just like I love you and mom and Rene." There is no way I am going to admit that that accidental kiss warmed me in ways I have never felt with another guy. In ways I look forward to feeling again.

His brow raises. "Mmhmm. Keep telling yourself that."

"Oh, my word, brother. I think you've fallen off your rocker."

"You know, no one would think differently of you if the two of you did have a thing for each other." He points toward the kitchen where Eryc is still cooking. "I mean, the two of you have been best friends since forever, right?"

"Well, yeah."

Leaning on the staircase post, Thaddeus crosses his

feet. "All I'm saying is that it's natural that you guys would eventually fall in love."

"Would you shut up, Thad?" I put my finger to my lips as an illustration for him to zip his lip. "And keep your voice down." I take a step back and glance down the hallway, toward the kitchen, to make sure Eryc hasn't overheard.

It doesn't appear that he has. He's standing at the island layering the lasagna in a casserole dish.

Thaddeus chuckles. "Sure, whatever you say, sis. Mark my words though, I can smell love a brewin'." Then he releases the post and moseys up the stairs.

He can smell love a brewin'?

What the ever-loving frack?

HAS it really only been one week since my mom transferred to the rehab facility? It feels like it has been years. The house isn't the same without her here. I miss her fresh baked muffins and the weekend movie marathons. Yes, Eryc has spent every minute of his free time here keeping me company, and I will be eternally grateful for that, but sometimes a girl just needs her momma.

Being home alone sucks. Thaddeus practically lives at the rehab center with mom, when he is not drinking himself into a coma that is. Eryc is a gem. He drives me to see mom every day after school.

Instead of attending classes at EC High, our teachers are continuing to email us the power points and assignments. As long as Thaddeus and I turn in all assignments by Friday each week, we are free to complete our classes online. Mr. Wilson, our principal, even went as far as to find a tutor to stop by the house every evening to help us.

My favorite daytime soap is playing on the television. I glance up from my laptop to see the return of my favorite character, Jason Morgan. It's about time they brought him back on the show. He is the classic bad boy, mobster hitman that everyone loves.

Returning my attention back to my laptop, I type into the search engine. I'm glad no one is home. It gives me time to do my research. Scrolling through my searches, I see what I'm looking for. *Women's RS Clinic.* This is the only clinic in Tulsa that performs abortions.

Punching the phone number into my cell phone, I give them a call.

Ring.

My heartbeat accelerates a notch.

Ring.

A lump grows in my throat, and I swallow it down.

Ring.

Sweat coats my hands and I'm starting to panic. This is the scariest thing I have ever done.

Ring.

"Women's RS Clinic, how may I help you?"

I pull the cell phone away from my ear, my finger hovering over the end call button. This is scary business. Before I end the call, I gather my nerve and put the phone back to my ear to answer her. "Hello. I'd like to make an appointment."

"I'm assuming that since you're calling this clinic, you're pregnant and looking to terminate?" The woman's voice is neither friendly nor hateful, she sounds more unemotional than anything.

"Yes, ma'am." I wipe my sweaty hands on my jeans. The stickiness on my palms grosses me out.

"Have you been here before?" Her robotic voice causes sweat to coat my hands again.

"No, ma'am."

I can hear her typing before she speaks. "I have an opening for a consultation in an hour, would you like to schedule that?"

"Yes, please."

"We'll see you at two o'clock." She hangs up before I can say bye.

My half-eaten sandwich is lying on a napkin on the coffee table. I should finish it, but I no longer hold an appetite. Fear of the unknown has my nerves on edge and my stomach in knots. Closing my laptop, I set it on the coffee table and gather my sandwich to throw away. It's early enough that if I leave now, I will miss Eryc and the lecture he is sure to give me.

The last thing I want to hear is how selfish this makes me, or how I will regret doing it, or how I will be disappointing God. This is my life and my body, not his. Besides he has no clue how having Brandt's baby, or babies, rather, would be a living nightmare for me. One I would never be able to escape.

The sound of a car door shutting draws my attention to the window and I pull the curtain back. Eryc is in front of his car, head down and pacing. His lips are moving, and I look for a cell phone or a headset but don't see any. Maybe he is talking to himself. As if he can sense me watching, he lifts his head and looks right at me. A bright smile curves his lips. Pushing away from the car, he heads toward the front door.

What is he doing here? I was hoping to leave before school got out so I could avoid him and his lecturing. "Well, crap."

Knock, knock.

Not waiting for me to answer, he opens the door and lets himself in like he owns the place. "Hey, Kay. How are you feeling?" He shuts the door and looks me over from head to toe.

How am I feeling?

Confusion causes me to furrow my brows. "I'm fine.

Other than this wretched morning sickness I'm doing all right. Why are you here? Shouldn't you be in school?"

He raises his hand ever so slowly. His knuckles brush along my cheek and rest on my jaw. "I just felt like you needed me, so I left and came straight here. Are you sure you're okay?"

"You shouldn't have skipped school to come check on me." I twirl a lock of hair around my finger, one of my many nervous habits. "I'm fine, Eryc. I promise."

Now please leave so I can go to this damn appointment without your knowledge.

"I couldn't stay there with this nagging dread that you needed me." He rests his forehead against mine.

Being this close to Eryc, I want to stand on my toes and press my lips to his. I want that warm fuzzy feeling that I got last time I accidentally kissed him. He doesn't know this but all these small affectionate touches, and him constantly taking care of me, are only deepening my feelings for him.

Thaddeus may have been right about love being in the air, except I doubt Eryc will ever return my love. Who in their right mind would love me after everything that happened with Brandt and now this pregnancy? I am doomed to be lonely for the rest of my life.

Cupping his face in both hands, I lean back, breaking the connection between our foreheads. The temptation to kiss him is strong. Closing my eyes, I inhale a cleansing breath and let it out before speaking softly. "I need to leave." Avoiding his gaze, I focus on his lips. Of its own accord, my thumb traces his bottom lip. "Promise me that you'll still be here when I get back."

"Of course, Kay." His gaze sweeps over me, studying me. "I'll be here when you get back."

During the time that Eryc and I have been rebuilding our friendship, I realize that I am falling in love with this guy. So much so that my heart will never belong to another. "I won't be long."

Releasing his face, I turn and leave before I chicken out and stay here with the only man who will ever hold my heart.

THE CONSULTATION with the nurse was confusing as all could be. I didn't understand half of what she said. But that is what I have come to understand about nurses and doctors, they speak their own language and forget that the rest of the world has no clue what they are talking about. Before I left the office, we set up an appointment for next week.

The appointment.

Exiting from highway 169 onto 11th street, I stop at Quik-Trip to fill my gas tank. The gas pumps are all occupied so I park behind a truck at the last pump. I dig through my purse and discover I have zero cash. My gaslight is on E and I'm not sure I have enough gas in the tank to make it home. It would be my luck to get a block from my house and then my car would die. Reaching over the console, I open the glovebox. Sometimes I will throw cash in there.

As I dig through the contents, I discover a five-dollar bill. "Yes." This will definitely get me home. Once I pull it free, a knock on the window draws my attention. Looking over, I see a young man standing there with a smile on his face.

I crack my window open just enough to hear. You never know what strangers are up to. "Can I help you?"

He shuffles from side to side. "I was wondering if you had a couple bucks to spare? I just need enough gas to make it home."

"No, I'm sorry." Thoroughly weirded out, I roll up the window and wait for him to walk away.

The truck in front of me leaves and I pull forward, shut off the engine, and exit the car. I glance up at the number on the pump then go inside to prepay. QuikTrip is busy but the employees are quick and efficient at getting the customers taken care of. On my way to the car, the hairs on the back of my neck stand on end and dread fills me.

Scanning the area, I don't see anything out of place and that creepy guy is nowhere in sight. Pushing the paranoia down, I twist the cap off the gas tank and fill the car with my measly five dollars' worth of gas.

It doesn't take long for the gas to reach the limit and shut off. Capping the tank, I shut the little metal cover and crawl back into my car. As I place the key into the ignition, the passenger door opens and that creepy guy slides into the seat with a gun aimed at my side.

Oh, God, please help me.

"Do what I say, and you won't get hurt. You got me?" Terror overwhelms me and my stomach knots up. The cold metal of the gun presses into my side. "Ya got me?"

Fear for my life has me nodding like a frantic fool. Who would have thought my life could get any worse than it already was?

"Put it in gear and drive normally."

Doing as I am told I pull onto 11th street and drive as normally as I can with the gun biting into my side.

"Turn left on Garnett." Flipping the blinker to signal my turn, I stop at the red light. A cop car stops next to us, and he leans back in his seat but keeps the gun pressed into my side. "Don't even think about getting his attention. I'll shoot you dead."

Tears are free flowing down my face. I make no move to gain the attention of the police officer. Silently, I pray for the officer to look over and see the gun, but he doesn't so much as glance in our direction. The light turns green, and I merge onto Garnett with no sign of the police following me.

Fear ripples through me at the thought of this crazy lunatic doing ungodly things to my body. As horrid images flick through my mind, a thought occurs to me. I can ram my car into another vehicle. Up ahead is a large diesel truck. Opportunity knocks when the guy beside me turns in his seat to look out the back window.

Pressing down on the accelerator, I ram my car into the back of the truck ahead of me. We hit with a bang and the crazy loon, who is not wearing a seatbelt, flies forward. His head hits my windshield with a crack, and I collide with the airbag. Time is ticking, I need to get out of here before this guy gathers himself and shoots me.

The airbag takes forever to deflate, and moaning meets my ears as Mr. Crazy stirs.

Hurry up, already.

This airbag is taking its sweet time deflating. It isn't long before my door opens, and a baritone voice asks if I'm alright.

"Yes, get me out of here."

Shoving the now deflated airbag out of the way, the burly man pulls me out of the car and inspects me. "Are you sure you're alright?"

As I open my mouth to answer and beg him to get me to safety, a loud bang resonates in the air and an object hisses next to my ear. Not understanding what is happening, I clutch my rescuer and urge him away from here.

His eyes meet mine for a brief second and then he collapses. It's now that I spot the crimson seeping from his chest and staining the pavement. He has been shot. Panic sets in and I jump over the body and run for the truck in front of me.

Just as I reach the rear of the truck, an arm snakes around my waist and cold metal presses against my temple. "I told you to do as I say, and you wouldn't get hurt. Maybe now you'll listen to what you're told." His voice is menacing and fear ripples through me in massive waves. "Say your prayers, brat."

Closing my eyes, something unexpected happens. The image of my ultrasound photo is crystal clear in my mind's eye. Those two little peanut size babies stare back at me, seizing my soul. For the first time, I fear for their safety. When this man pulls the trigger, it's not only my life that will end. Theirs will end as well.

For a moment, I wonder what they will look like. Will they have my auburn hair and green eyes, will they have Thaddeus's blonde hair and blues eyes, or will they look like a good mix of Brandt and me? Are they boys, girls, or one of each?

It is in this moment that something inside me changes. My heart begins to warm and my soul cries out for more. I begin to picture a life with these two babies, one boy and one girl, just like Thaddeus and me, who love life and love each other.

Two children that will grow up together with the same bond that I share with my twin. Their first day of school, first dances, first kisses, weddings. In the blink of an eye, this man is about to take that away from me, from us.

A gunshot rings out and I squeeze my eyes tighter. No pain comes and there is no bright light welcoming me into glory. The arm around my waist loosens and the metal drops to the ground with a clang.

Opening my eyes, I watch as my kidnapper falls to the ground with wide, blank eyes.

A tap to my shoulder causes me to jump and I let out a blood curdling scream.

"It's okay. You're safe now."

Those three words, *you're safe now*, repeat over and over in my head and I finally cease screaming.

Shock settles in and I collapse in the officer's arms.

I'm not sure how much time has passed but I wake to the sound of sirens and voices shouting above the noise.

Opening my eyes, I take in my surroundings. I am lying in the back of an ambulance, and a paramedic is pumping the bulb of the contraption connected to my arm.

"Good, you're awake." The paramedic pulls the stethoscope from his ears and smiles down at me. "You're going to be just fine."

I hear his words, but my brain is frozen on the horrors of gunshots and pools of blood.

32

Eryc

Deep into calculus homework, my concentration is broken by the ringing of my cell phone. Picking the device up from the coffee table, I glimpse the caller ID.

Unknown.

I never answer unknown numbers, they are usually those pesky salespeople wanting to sell you everything under the sun. Ignoring the call, I toss the cell phone back onto the coffee table.

Two seconds later, the ringing starts again. Unease settles over me at the thought it could be Makayla calling about a broken-down car or something. Answering the unknown call, I hold my breath as I wait for the caller to respond.

"Hello, is this Eryc Delmonte?"

Here it goes. Some salesman is going to try and rope me into purchasing siding, roofing, some cruise package, or offer me a free weekend vacation if I sit through a time-share presentation. Ugh, I really despise these types of calls. "Yes, this is he."

"Sir, this is Officer Kirkpatrick." Okay, so this isn't a sales call. The hairs on my arms stand on end. "I have a Makayla—" he pauses, most likely to look at his notepad for her last name, "Yasmeen."

My heart drops to the pit of my stomach. She has only been gone for a couple of hours. What in the world could have happened in that short amount of time?

"Is she okay?" Jumping up from the sofa, I rush out the door and to my car.

"She's fine but I'm going to need you to come down to the station on 11th street, near 169."

That's not far from here, I can make it in five minutes or less. "I'll be there shortly."

Disconnecting the call, I drive to the police station. Nerves has me chewing on my bottom lip with worry. Makayla is in a fragile state right now. The last thing she needs is additional stress. So, what the hell happened?

The parking lot is semi-deserted when I arrive.

Cutting the engine, I jerk the keys from the ignition and run toward the building. A woman in uniform greets me when I walk in. Her smile is genuine as she gazes up at me.

"I'm here for Makayla Yasmeen."

"Of course." Standing from her desk she motions for me to follow her.

We trek down a hallway to the only open door. Makayla is sitting in a chair with a blanket wrapped around her. Her knees are pulled up and she is hugging her legs. A tall and muscular officer is sitting at the desk across from her. He glances up when we step into the room.

When his eyes land on me he stands. "Are you Eryc?"

"Yes, sir." I reach out to shake his offered hand.

Makayla whimpers and we both turn our attention to her. She is rocking back and forth but her face is still hidden behind her knees.

"Have a seat, Eryc." The officer points to a chair in front of his desk.

My body yearns to go to Makayla, to wrap her in the protection and comfort of my arms, but the frown on the officer's face has me obeying his orders. Officer Kirkpatrick recaps the events involving Makayla and the details has my stomach recoiling. My heart aches to walk across this small office, to take her in my arms and carry her out of here.

"The department received a call for a domestic dispute. Upon arrival, the suspect fled. Officers chased him on foot. I'm not sure when or how he came across Makayla, but when we found them, he had her at gun point."

Gun point? Oh, God, no.

What is wrong with people? You have to be one sick SOB to kidnap a young girl and hold her at gun point. Anger creeps into my heart and I suddenly want to stomp to this creep's jail cell and pound his face until there is nothing left to pound.

"Eryc?" The sound of Makayla's weak voice brings me out of my murderous thoughts. She stands, drops the blanket, and runs to me. I stand and embrace her in a tight hug. "I thought I was going to die. He was going to blow my brains out in the middle of the street."

Jeez, my girl has been traumatized. If I thought she needed counseling before, I sure as hell think she does now. "It's okay, I'm right here."

"Miss Yasmeen, can you tell us what happened?" Officer Kirkpatrick picks up a pen and opens a small notebook.

She rests her head on my shoulder, fisting my shirt in her hands. The officer is kind enough to give her the time she needs to collect herself, which I'm thankful for. Blowing out a breath, she releases my shirt and turns to face Officer Kirkpatrick. "Yes, I'll tell you everything."

The officer nods and readies his pen. "Whenever you're ready."

Sitting in the seat I vacated, she grips my hand with crushing force and tells the horrid events. "I was on my home when my gas light came on. I pulled into the Quik-Trip on 11th, just off 169. This guy knocked on my window, so I cracked it enough to talk. He asked for a couple of dollars and when I told him I didn't have it, he left."

Officer Kirkpatrick nods his head and writes notes on his paper.

"I prepaid and pumped my gas. There was no sign of him anywhere. When I got in the car to leave, he slipped in and pointed his gun at my side and told me that if I did what I was told then I wouldn't get hurt. I didn't want to get shot so I followed his directions and drove down 11th toward Garnett where he told me to take a left-hand turn." Her grip on my hand tightens and her leg starts to bounce wildly.

"What else happened?" The officer quickly gazes at her while his hand continues making notes.

"While I was waiting for the light to turn green, a police car stopped next to us, and he told me not to gain the officer's attention. With that gun piercing my side there was no way I was going to get on his bad side."

Officer Kirkpatrick nods his head. "Good, you did the right thing. Then what happened? We found you not too far from there."

"I made the left-hand turn and while he was looking out the back window, I pressed down on the gas pedal and rammed my car into the back of a big diesel truck."

Oh, my God, Makayla could have seriously injured herself by purposely crashing her car. On the other hand, she was already in danger. Talk about a rock and a hard place.

"Okay, and then what?" the officer asks.

"The driver of the truck came to check on me. He pulled me out of the car and that's when the crazy guy shot my rescuer. I jumped over the dead body and ran but he was faster. He caught up to me and pressed the gun to my head and told me to say a prayer. When that shot was fired, I thought for sure I was dead...but it wasn't me that was shot, it was him."

My gut twists in knots over this information. This is the stuff you see in movies, not experience in real life.

Makayla was just making progress with her depression and trauma. This will only set her back about fifteen steps.

Come on universe, give my girl a break.

Closing his notebook, Officer Kirkpatrick meets Makayla's gaze. "I want to thank you for your cooperation. We'll be in touch if we need any further information, but I think you've given us enough." He is quiet for a few beats, his eyes scrutinizing her. "Makayla, I highly recommend therapy. We can give you a list of therapists if you're interested."

Tension causes her hand to stiffen in mine. "Is that really necessary?"

I balk at her question. Of course, this is necessary. Why can't she see that? Experiencing trauma such as this, messes with people. Therapy is nothing to be ashamed of.

The officer steeples his fingers. "It will help you greatly. As officers, we see therapists after we've been in dangerous situations. Trust me, it will be the best decision and it will help you."

"I'll think about it."

Officer Kirkpatrick's lips pull into a thin line. His gaze lifts to mine, silently pleading with me to make her see reason. *I'll do my best.* Tugging Makayla up from the chair, I wrap my arm around her protectively. "We'll take that list and consider our options."

"Great." The officer pulls a sheet of paper out of a folder and hands it over. There is a list of ten therapists on this recommendation sheet. "And thank you again for your cooperation," he directs at Makayla.

THE ENTIRE RIDE back to Makayla's, she holds my arm in a death grip, her head is down, and she is refusing to even look out the window. I can only imagine what she went through and how she is feeling.

Her sniffling is the only sound in this tiny space and that sound shatters me. I don't know how I can help her through this. Pulling into the driveway, I cut the engine and pull out my cell phone, sending a group text to my aunt and Thaddeus.

> Makayla needs everyone ASAP.

Aunt Rene is working so I know she may not see my message for a couple of hours, but hopefully Thaddeus isn't drunk already and reads his damn message. Makayla needs her brother right now. Hopefully this incident will not cause him to slip further into the bottle.

Why do bad things happen to good people? I just don't get it.

Opening the garage door, I walk her into the house. She settles in at the dining room table. Pulling down a coffee mug and the cocoa, I set about making her a cup of hot chocolate. Adding a dollop of whipped cream and a peppermint stick, I hand her the steaming mug.

She plays with the stick of peppermint, twirling it around in her drink.

Her body trembles and tears flow steadily down her face. Scooting a chair next to hers, I wrap my arm around her and hold her close. Whimpers escape her and the mug hits the table with a thud. Burying her face into my neck, she sobs with everything in her. Loud heartbroken cries echo in the room and her hands fist my shirt.

My own tears fall but I do my best to keep strong for her. Keeping my cries silent, I allow my tears to fall noiselessly. Clutching me tightly, her cries turn to wails and it's enough to do me in. My heart has officially shattered like fine China hitting concrete.

The front door opens and shuts with a soft click, and I almost don't hear it.

Thaddeus jogs into the kitchen and falls to his knees next to us. "Sis?"

Seeing his sister in agony sets him off and he sobs right along with her.

33

Makayla

Thaddeus rests his head on my shoulder. I angle my body so I can clutch him as well. Here I sit with Eryc's arm around me, holding me tight while I rest my head in the crook of his neck and fist his shirt with my left hand, and then Thaddeus is hugging my other side while I fist his shirt with my right hand.

My guys. The only two men in this world that matter to me.

My brother's sobs mirror mine, though it's not a surprise, we are twins. Our souls are linked in a way only a twin can understand. When one of us hurts, we both hurt.

When there is nothing left to cry, I release both men from my clutches and lean back.

Eryc keeps his arm around me, and Thaddeus takes my hand in his. My brother's eyes are bloodshot, and I can only imagine what mine must look like. "What happened, Makayla?"

The last thing I want to do is relive the events from earlier, but my brother needs to know. I just pray this will not drive him to drink any more than he already is. My heart cannot handle him slipping further into the bottle, not with my own mess to deal with.

Eryc hands me a tissue and I dry my eyes then blow my nose.

I give my brother a play-by-play of my encounter with that creep. His face blanches at the mention of a gun being pressed into my side.

"Oh, God," his voice is just above a whisper. When I mention my kidnapper pressing the gun to my head and telling me to say a prayer, Thaddeus jumps to his feet. "I'm going to kill him."

Tugging on my brother's hand, I urge him to sit. "Thad, sit down and listen."

Shaking his head, he crosses his arms. "Forget that. Where is he? I will find a way in his jail cell and strangle him with my bare hands."

Eryc eyes my brother. "My thoughts exactly but it's too late, the cops shot him before he could pull the trigger on her."

Thaddeus slumps back down. "Good." Meeting my stare, my brother says, "I cannot lose you. Not to a crazed maniac and definitely not to suicide."

"I know," I choke out.

"You have to get better, sis. For me, for Eryc, and for mom."

Eryc squeezes my hand, letting me know that he agrees with my brother.

I nod.

As much as I hate the idea of seeing a therapist, I know it is necessary in order for me to get better. My depression has lifted some since Eryc has been in my life, but I still struggle. There are moments when the urge to slit my wrists is strong. The last thing I need is for this incident to add to that and push me over the edge.

Sometimes life just sucks donkey butt.

AFTER MY MELTDOWN, which was embarrassing by the way, I made myself comfortable on the sofa with a fuzzy blanket and my reheated hot chocolate. Thaddeus is upstairs filing the claim with our insurance company about my wrecked car. My little Nissan is totaled, and I have no vehicle until I can afford to purchase a new one.

Rene is sitting on the coffee table, knee-to-knee with me, and talking but I'm not hearing a word coming out of her mouth. My thoughts are a mix of what Brandt did to me over the summer and the kidnapper that tried to kill me. My skin is crawling, and I want nothing more than to peel away my flesh to rid myself of this demonic fear swimming under the surface.

Standing, I start walking toward the staircase. I think I mention that I will be back down but honestly, I'm not sure if I said anything at all. My mind is a scattered mess and I feel like I am slowly drowning. Voices are floating around me like the static on a radio station that isn't getting a signal.

Closing the door behind me, I go to the bathroom adjoined to my bedroom. Automatically, I reach for the box of razors I keep in the medicine cabinet, but the shelves are empty where the razors and pain killers are normally kept.

Oh, that's right, Thaddeus confiscated those the other night.

Pulling the drawer open, I reach to the very back and retrieve my compact mirror. Opening the tiny contraption, I tilt it and let the cold metal razor slip into my palm. Unfastening my jeans, I slide them down mid-thigh and lean against the counter. Gripping the razor between my thumb and index finger, I slit the tender flesh on my upper thigh.

One, two, three thin lines bead with crimson.

The pain sears through me like hot lava and I let out a sigh of relief. Relief because this is a pain that I can control and one that will push the pain in my heart away, even if just for a little while.

Some people inject heroin to forget their pain. I inflict pain with a razor to forget mine. Deep down I know this is wrong. It will not fix my problems or take away what has happened to me, but just for a few blissful moments I can focus on something other than those horrid things that plague me.

Cutting myself was never something that I intended to get mixed up in. In fact, I used to call those girls who cut themselves, attention seekers. But July 4th I learned the truth. Cutters do not cut themselves for attention. The truth is, they don't want anyone to know that they inflict pain on themselves.

No, it's not attention that I seek but rather the relief of the pain that constantly crawls under my skin like a thousand maggots eating away at me. A gasp sounds next to me and echoes off the tile in the all-too-quiet bathroom. I open my eyes to find Eryc standing in the doorway with large round eyes.

"Kay?" He advances slowly like he is afraid I might jab his eye out with the razor I hold in my hand.

Embarrassment warms my face. I never wanted him to see this side of me. This was a secret I had hoped to take to my grave. Releasing the razor, it drops to the tile floor and bounces before landing next to my foot.

The fact that my jeans are down mid-thigh, and my pink panties are on display seems to have slipped my mind. Not once does it dawn on me to pull them up and cover myself. Eryc is still staring at me with wide, frightened eyes. The scene he has walked in on has stunned him and he looks as though he may break down and cry.

Embarrassment, anger, and fear all simmer on the surface, choking me. At this very moment, I want nothing more than to die so I don't have to see the disappointment on Eryc's face. Using the heels of my hands, I press on my temples to relieve the building pressure in my head.

No amount of wishing will rewind time. My secret is out and now I have to deal with the fallout. I never used to be this weak. There was a time when I was bold and brave, but that girl is long gone. Now I am exactly the kind of girl that I used to frown upon.

Covering my face with my hands, I lower myself down to the floor, my back sliding along the cabinets. Once I'm sitting on the floor, I pull my knees up to my chest and hug my legs.

Eryc squats next to me, snatching the razor off the floor and tossing it in the trash. He blows out a breath. "Kay, how long has this been going on?"

Squeezing my eyes shut, tears fall. It seems that is all I have done here lately is cry like a crazy loon. I have become *that* girl, the one who sits around and constantly cries. Eryc leans forward and swipes away my tears with his thumbs.

I can't bear to look at him and see pity or even loathing. Epic failure, that's me. God, what he must think of me. I have screwed up my life in so many ways. The course I have allowed for myself has left me in so many shattered pieces. Now it seems that Eryc is the one who has resigned himself to picking them up. He will never be able to fix me, I'm not sure why he is trying.

Eryc pinches my chin and lifts my gaze to his. "Look at me, Kay."

I shake my head because I can't bear to see what expression he is wearing.

Keeping my chin pinched between his fingers, he repeats, "Look at me, Kay." When I finally open my eyes, he asks, "How long have you been cutting yourself?"

I try to shake my head, but he has a good grip on my chin. The last thing I want to do is admit how long I have been cutting myself. It is like admitting out loud how big of a failure I am.

This was a secret that he was never supposed to discover. The preacher's son, a boy so pure and sin free, he never should have seen this. Now he knows beyond a shadow of a doubt that I am not innocent. I am nothing but a sinner, a big fat sinner.

Now he knows that I enjoy the white-hot pain that occurs when I slit my skin, not because it brings me joy but because of the reprieve it offers.

"How long, Kay?" The tone of his voice is still kind, but it also holds a warning. He wants an answer, and he wants it now.

I swallow down the lump that has formed in my throat. "Since July."

"Oh God, Kay." His words are whispered and pained.

When I burst into tears and a strangled cry erupts from my throat, he slips his arm under my knees and lifts me effortlessly from the floor. Cradling me against his chest, he carries me to my room and sits on the bed with me still in his arms.

Burying my face in his shirt, I continue to cry. The tighter he holds me, the less I care about what he thinks of me. I am broken, nothing but fragments of what I once was. Wrapped up in his embrace, I let it all out.

"I can't do this anymore." My voice is muffled by the fabric of his shirt.

Eryc is definitely seeing me at my worst. I guess if we can get through this, we can get through anything. Stroking my hair, he hums a familiar tune and starts rocking me like a mother rocks her infant. The tenderness he shows me hits me straight in the gut and causes me to fall apart even further in his arms.

As I cry, I realize one thing. Regardless of how terrifying it may be, I need to confide in my longtime friend. Eryc has proven himself over, and over again. He is the one person that I can lean on and entrust my life to.

I'm scared. No, I'm terrified, but he has to know. I have been drowning for far too long and if I don't get help now, my life will just spiral further out of control.

If I don't get the help I so desperately need, I will end up committing suicide.

34

Eryc

An hour. That's how long Makayla sat in my arms and cried. I thought for sure that either Thaddeus or my aunt would come barging in to see what all the ruckus was about, but they didn't.

No one even knocked on the door.

Now Makayla is sitting next to me on the edge of her bed and is confiding all of her deepest, darkest secrets. Though I read her journal, she fills me in on her depression due to the sexual abuse and how that depression soon led to her cutting herself. "I never once sliced my skin in visible places. You know, like on the wrists or forearms. I didn't want anyone to know there was anything wrong with me. I've always cut my upper thighs."

I have to admit, when I spied her in the bathroom with her pants down to her mid-thighs, I noticed all the scarring and fresh wounds. There were so many of them. She must have been cutting herself every day.

"God." I rub my hand down my mouth as I absorb her pain filled words. "I wish you would have come to me. I wish you had trusted me enough to let me in." Blowing out a breath, I look into her eyes. "You should have never gone through that alone."

"I didn't want people to think I was messed up. Do you have any idea how embarrassing it is to admit that you're broken? I didn't want to be viewed as less than human."

Less than human?

That's how she felt? Fear of being seen as *less than human* is the reason why she didn't come to any of us for help?

She is so loved by so many people. I wish she would have understood that none of us would have judged her.

Who am I to judge, anyway. I'm damn sure not perfect, I have my own downfalls.

"Anyway, the longer I allowed Brandt to abuse me, the worse my depression became. The deeper the depression, the more often the cutting. There finally came a point, the night Brandt shared me with Lee, that I couldn't take anymore. That was the night that I began to crave the one thing that promised me freedom from my shackles." She lowers her head as if she is ashamed of the words exiting her mouth.

I sit back and wait for her to explain further.

"Suicide. I wanted to end my life so the pain would go away. No more life, no more pain. You know?"

Listening to her retell her suffering is hard. Bile rises in my throat, and I have to swallow it down. No girl, no matter who she is, should ever have to endure even a fraction of the abuse that Makayla has. To top it all off, she kept it all bottled up and allowed it to consume her.

No more. I will not sit back and let her go through any more suffering without the proper support.

"Jeez, Kay. Just hearing you say that word kills me." Lifting her hand, I kiss her knuckles. "You are not alone. Never again do I want you handling this kind of crap on your own." Her bottom lip quivers and I know she is on the verge of more tears. "Promise me that you'll let us in. Let me in."

"I promise." She reaches over and takes hold of my hand. "When my world is falling apart and I can't find my way, I'll come to you. Always."

Progress.

This next phase in her life is not going to be easy. It will take courage and patience. She needs help from professionals that can dissect her turmoil and show her how to deal with it in a healthy manner.

Brushing a lock of hair away from her face, I ask, "You know what the next step is, don't you?"

"Yeah." She lets out a sigh. "It's time to admit that I'm in trouble and accept help."

I nod my head and wrap my arm around her. "That's my girl."

We sit in comfortable silence. I know she isn't ready to talk to Rene and Thaddeus about her addiction, at least not yet. So, we are sitting on the edge of her bed, staring at her wall of posters. Next to her bedroom door is the only movie poster, *Divergent*. The other posters are a good mix of genres, but I see more Justin Timberland than I do any other artist.

Time drags by at a snail's pace and when I dart my eyes to the clock on her nightstand, I realize that thirty minutes have passed since I carried her from the bathroom. Makayla follows my line of sight and sighs heavily when she sees how much time we have spent up here. "We should head down before they come searching for us," she says.

Yes, we should. I'm surprised that my aunt hasn't come up here yet, demanding that we join them downstairs. And I thank God that she didn't follow me up here, because Makayla would not have been able to handle that during her moment of weakness.

I stand from the bed and offer my hand out to her. Placing her hand in mine, she allows me to pull her up from the bed. Those sad eyes lock with mine and hatred swims in my veins. Hatred for Brandt and his two loser friends. Hatred for the idiot that kidnapped her. Hatred for the hand she has been dealt in life.

I just want to rewind time and prevent evil from coming after her.

Keeping hold of her hand, we descend the stairs. Aunt Rene is where I left her, sitting on the coffee table with her hands covering her eyes. Those hands drop when the toe of my shoe squeaks on the hardwood floor.

My aunt stands and crosses the distance to us. "I didn't mean to upset you, Makayla."

Makayla's fingers tighten around mine and I can hear her quick breaths. She is nervous, I can feel it in the way she is clinging to me like a lifeline.

Instead of speaking to my aunt, Makayla motions toward the living room. "Is Thad still here?"

"In here," Thaddeus yells from the living room.

Makayla takes a deep breath, holds it for five seconds and then blows it out. Those sad, green eyes lock with mine and she swallows loudly. "Here goes nothing." Tugging on my hand, she leads us to the living room.

My sweet girl doesn't sit. She stands in the center of the living room, so she can look her brother and my aunt in the eye. Thaddeus is leaning forward with his elbows resting on his knees and his fingers steepled at his mouth. Neither of them says a word while Makayla confesses her struggle with wanting to end her life and finally confessing her battle with cutting.

Thaddeus hops up from the sofa when she stops talking. "You told me—" He points his finger in her face. "That you were not cutting. What in the ever-loving blazes, sis? You lied to me." Jamming his finger into his own chest, he repeats, "You lied to me. Me. Your freakin' twin. Why? I love you." He pauses and inhales a deep breath. "We are twins. I share a connection with you that no one else will ever have." After yelling he storms out of the room.

Seconds later, the backdoor slams with enough force to rattle the pictures hanging on the wall. Then his motorcycle races from the driveway.

Watching him storm away in a fit of anger, breaks Makayla just a little more. Her entire body trembles and she is doing everything in her power to keep from crying out but it's futile. The sobs come, and they come hard. Screaming out in pain, she falls to her knees and buries her face in her hands.

I can't handle seeing her in this much pain. Witnessing this is shattering my heart further. My nose burns with the onset of my own tears, but I choke down my emotions because she needs me to be her rock. She needs me to help her pick herself back up and piece her broken heart back together.

Aunt Rene stands but I wave her off. This is my girl

and I want to be the one to console her. A piece of my heart is with her, and I need to be the one comforting and healing her. No one else. Kneeling beside her, I wrap my arms around Makayla.

Angling her body, she wraps her arms around me and buries her face in the crook of my neck and continues to sob. Tears soak my shirt and run down the collar, leaving a wet trail along my chest. I don't care. I'll take those tears and anything else she is willing to give me.

"I'll make a phone call to one of my colleagues. We'll get her the help she needs." Aunt Rene leaves the room with her cell phone in hand.

Makayla's sobs are loud and heartbreaking.

Scooping her up, I carry her to the recliner and sit. I wrap my arms around her tightly and tuck her head under my chin. "I'm here. I'm not going anywhere." I repeat those words to her over and over until she drifts off to sleep.

Resting is damn near impossible. Makayla wakes every half hour or so screaming at the top of her lungs with nightmares. At one point, I was afraid my aunt would have to give her a sedative to calm her enough to get some sleep.

Nightmares of being held at gun point plague her dreams, she wakes constantly, begging for him not to shoot her. I know these nightmares terrify her to the point that she is too afraid to be alone. So here I am, sleeping upright on the recliner while she lays on my lap, clinging to me for dear life.

Tomorrow morning, I am taking Makayla to see my aunt's friend and colleague, Dr. Fuentez. This is the next step to Makayla's recovery. Dr. Fuentez specializes in depression and suicidal tendencies.

35

Makayla
Four weeks later

I have been in counseling for four weeks now, two days a week. Things are starting to look up for a change. My nightmares are still there but not nearly as bad as before. At least now, I am able to get five solid hours of sleep verses next to none.

Dr. Fuentez is amazing. She not only sees me for private sessions, but she meets me for group therapy as well.

At first, I hated group therapy. Who in their right mind wants to air their dirty laundry in front of a room full of people? Not me, that's for sure, but I'm glad Rene made me go. Surrounding myself with other people that struggle with the same battles I struggle with gives me hope. I am not alone and there are others out there that understand and are willing to help.

I wave to Dr. Fuentez on my way out the door. Alesandra wraps her arm around mine as we exit the building.

Alesandra is a girl I met here in group therapy. She has been in the group for six months. I was shocked that this beautiful young woman with a heart of gold used to cut herself. After my first group meeting, she took to me like a mother hen. I am so glad that she did. Having her to talk to, no matter the time of day, has been my saving grace.

Eryc is still hanging around. As promised, he has not left me to deal with life by myself. He listens to me vent and offers advice, but Alesandra has been in my shoes and understands exactly what I am going through.

No offense to Eryc, but he will never be able to help me the way Alesandra can.

"Okay, girlfriend, I have a surprise for you." Alesandra leans into me with a silly giggle.

This girl always has a surprise for me. Some days its pizza, other days she takes me to the spa for a day of pampering. She is forever doing things for me. I think this is her way of keeping my mind occupied so I don't slip back into that dark place. One thing I love about her, she is not shy to grab Eryc by the hand and drag him along on our girly outings.

I pop a piece of gum in my mouth. "What kind of surprise?"

"Uh, uh." Pressing the key fob, she unlocks the doors to her Mazda. "Just text boyfriend and let him know you'll be home in an hour."

Rolling my eyes is a natural response. Eryc is not my boyfriend. "Al, you know he isn't my boyfriend, we're just really good friends."

"Uh, huh." She looks at me over the top of the car. "You keep telling yourself that."

Pulling out my cell phone, I shoot Eryc a text.

> Hey, I'm hanging out with Al for a bit. Be home in an hour.

His response is almost immediate.

> ERYC
> Okay. I'll be here.

A month ago, I had given him a key to my house. I figured since he spends all of his free time there keeping me company then he should at least have a key.

"Did you text boyfriend?"

"Yes." I don't even bother to correct her, again. There is no arguing with this girl. Believe me, I have tried. She is dead set on Eryc and I being a couple. We're not. I wish we were, but he has shown me no signs that he is interested in me as anything other than his best friend.

Can't Stop the Feeling blasts from the speakers and we are both singing along as loud as our voices will allow. This feeling of freedom and peace is wonderful. Now days, I am smiling and having fun. I didn't think I would ever be able to have fun again. I am so very thankful that Rene pushed me toward counseling and didn't take no for an answer.

Turning onto Mingo, I continue to sing as we pass building after building, wondering where we are going. When the car slows, I sit up and watch as we pull into a shopping center. It is after lunch, maybe we are going to eat sandwiches at the sub shop or burgers at the hamburger joint.

"Come on, girlfriend." Alesandra cuts the engine and exits the car, locking it when I follow suit.

Confusion causes me to furrow my brows and purse my lips. We aren't heading to either restaurant, we are headed to the shop directly between the two. Jaded Spades.

"What are we doing here?" Jaded Spades is a tattoo shop and last time I checked, I wasn't tattooed or looking to get a tattoo.

"Just trust me, yeah?" Alesandra takes me by the hand and drags me behind her.

The door opens with a jingle and a beautiful young woman greets us with a smile. "Hey, what can I do for ya?"

Alesandra tugs me next to her hip once we reach the counter. "I came by yesterday with a sketch, the infinity and semicolon with the word hope scripted in."

The young woman's face brightens, and a huge smile upturns her mouth. Which sparkles in her beautiful brown eyes. "Yeah, I remember that one. I frickin' love it."

"Thanks. It's for my friend," Alesandra nods her head toward me, "Makayla."

My eyes widen and I take a step back. "No. I don't want a tattoo." Finally noticing the tattoo sleeve on the young woman's arm, I say, "No offense."

"Oh, none taken." She looks between the two of us. "So, I assume this is a meaningful tattoo?" she asks Alesandra while tilting her head toward me in a silent question.

"Yes." Alesandra leans her hip on the counter and faces me. "Girlfriend, I sketched a design for you." She lifts her left arm. On her wrist is a beautiful light blue tattoo of an infinity with the word hope scripted within the lines, and right smack in the center of the infinity is a semicolon. "The sketch I did for you is identical except yours is purple because I know how you love your purple."

It's a beautiful tattoo but I don't understand why she

would think I would come in here and get a matching one. "I'm not sure why you thought I needed a tattoo."

The young woman leans forward and shows me her wrist. In the very center of her wrist is a plain black semi-colon. "Honey, the semicolon carries a significant message. In grammar, they are used to continue a sentence that otherwise could have ended but was given an extension. For those of us who suffer with depression, it symbolizes just that. We could end our lives, but we have chosen not to."

Now I get it. For weeks, I have wondered why Alesandra had the semicolon in her infinity tattoo and now I understand.

With the newfound understanding, I love this idea. "Okay, let's do this."

The young woman pulls a sketch out from under the counter and smiles at me. "Awesome, follow me."

ERYC'S CAR is in the driveway when we pull up. Just like he promised, he is here waiting for me. I say goodbye to Alesandra and make my way to the front door. When I get it open, I hear nothing but silence. No television, no sounds from the kitchen, nothing. I ease the door shut as quietly as I can and tiptoe across the foyer.

I am about to pass the living room when Eryc's socked

feet catch my eye. He is lying on the couch with his feet up on the armrest. Tiptoeing closer, I notice that he has a book open and its face-down on his chest. The cover of the book is eye-catching, and the title is one I have not heard of. *Devada.*

I will need to borrow this book when he is finished with it.

Eryc's eyes are closed in slumber, and he looks so peaceful laying there. Since my mom's accident, Eryc has gone through great lengths to take care of me. More so since I was kidnapped, and he discovered how deep my depression actually ran.

No wonder the guy is exhausted.

Now it's time that I do something for him. Maybe I will cook dinner tonight. I ease out of the room but halt when he speaks. It startles me because I thought for sure he was sound asleep. "That was the longest hour I have ever seen in my life. Thought you said you wouldn't be gone long?" He glances at his watch. "It's been two and a half hours already."

A giggle leaves my lips, a sound that is happening more and more now that Eryc and Alesandra are in my life. I really didn't mean to be gone so long but the tattoo took longer than I thought. Not because of the tattoo, but the tattooist, Courtney, got to talking to me and shared her own story with me.

Leaning my hip on the back of the sofa, I apologize. "Sorry, I just lost track of time. Has Thad been home yet?"

Eryc shakes his head. Knowing my brother, he won't be home until he is thrown out of whatever bar he goes to at night. Placing the book on the coffee table, Eryc stands. His brown eyes search my face, looking for something.

After a moment, he smiles and asks, "Kay, would you like to go out for dinner tonight?" I open my mouth to answer but he holds up a hand to halt my words. "I'm buying. I thought it would be a nice change to go to a restaurant."

He's buying? I'm not sure if this is part of the hormonal thing that pregnant women go through, but for some reason his offer to buy me dinner tugs at my heart and tears fill my eyes. It's stupid, I know, but I can't help the ball of emotions that coil in the pit of my stomach. Tremors run through my limbs, and I bite the inside of my cheek to hold in the sob that is trying to break free.

Jeez, he is going to think I'm an idiot.

To keep from looking like a bigger fool, I nod my head and smile. Though I'm sure my smile comes out looking like a crocodile bit me rather than looking grateful.

"You okay?" Eryc takes four massive steps toward me with concern in his eyes.

I nod, again, to appease his concern.

"Good." He tips my chin so that his gaze settles

perfectly on mine. "You pick the place and let me know when you're ready."

At his touch, a flutter stirs in the pit of my stomach. Following that flutter is a whole new wave of emotions. Emotions like I have never felt before. The kind that makes your toes curl and your fingertips tingle. With this rush of emotions, I feel a warmness come over my neck, cheeks, and ears. Because of the heat on my skin, I know that I'm turning a light shade of pink.

Eryc notices the tint to my skin. His eyes dart to my cheeks, then to my ears, and finally his gaze travels to my neck. It takes several seconds before he tears his gaze away from my neck.

I pull in a breath and wonder what is going through his mind. With my hair in a messy bun, I know I must look like a disaster. To keep from embarrassing myself further, I smile at Eryc and then rush up the stairs to change my clothes and get ready for dinner.

It doesn't take me long to change my outfit. After freeing my hair and giving it a quick run-through with the straightener, I sit on the edge of my bed and think about those little flutters that Eryc caused in the pit of my stomach.

I am not sure why those pesky butterflies have decided to show up now and wreak havoc in my tummy. Why not last week or last month? Why now? And why after I have made the decision to keep my babies and raise them on my own?

A fact I haven't shared with anyone else yet.

Then I catch my reflection in the mirror and wonder if he will ever reciprocate my feelings. The eyes looking back at me still hold a tiny bit of sorrow. Am I happier now? Of course, but I am also broken. I may be on the mend and enjoying life now, but I am not fully healed yet.

Even if there is a chance that Eryc might think I'm beautiful, could he actually love someone like me?

Someone who is broken. Who will always remain fractured long after I have healed.

A single mother of two unborn babies that were conceived through dirty deeds.

36

S adness still haunts my girl deep within her soul. I can see it in the green pools of her eyes. Yes, she is beginning to heal, and I am so thankful for this new friend of hers, Alesandra. In the past week, I have seen a major change in Makayla. Slowly, she is learning how to live again and be happy.

Though she is healing, she is still broken.

She doesn't know her worth, but I will do everything in my power to help her overcome this and recognize that worth. It pains me to see my once happy-go-lucky girl be this timid shell of herself. One who sits upstairs and cries when she thinks no one can hear.

Those cries haunt me in my sleep.

Like an idiot, I am still standing in the living room, staring up at the stairs, where Makayla had disappeared fifteen minutes ago.

The last thing I want is for her to see me standing here like a love-struck fool, so I turn around to retrieve my shoes from where they lay next to the sofa. As I do, I see Makayla's purse on the floor where she dropped it when she came in. The zipper is open, and her wallet and keys are spilling out onto the floor.

Bending down, I pick them up and stuff them back inside her purse. As I do, her cell phone beeps with an incoming message. I am getting ready to zip up her purse when the screen of her phone lights up. The light emanating from her cell phone illuminates a pamphlet and the printed words catch my eye before I can zip the tiny purse.

In big bold letters, it says *Abortion.*

Pulling the pamphlet free, I stare at the piece of paper. The woman on the front cover looks contemplative and the bright blue font churns the contents of my stomach.

Abortion? Why does she have this in her purse and where did she get it? I know my aunt didn't give this to her.

Our conversation the day she had the ultrasound

suddenly comes to mind and I feel a little nauseous. The realization that she is prepared to end their lives hits me like a ton of bricks and the pamphlet becomes like lead in my hand. Never in a million years would I have thought she would want to end those tiny lives growing in her belly.

Wanting this threatening piece of paper out of my hand, I stuff it back into her purse with more force than necessary. I know I need to zip her purse and put it back where I found it, but I can't bring myself to depart with it yet.

A vise closes over my beating heart and squeezes the life out of me. The air in the room thickens and oxygen is suddenly too heavy to pull into my lungs. Anger slithers through my veins and the urge to hit something, anything, is overwhelming me.

Yes, I know these feelings are uncalled for. Makayla is not my girlfriend, nor are those babies mine. As much as I try not to feel betrayed, I can't stop the feeling. In my heart, I have already claimed the three of them as mine. In my heart, Makayla has been mine for most of our lives.

I am so lost in the rantings in my head that I don't hear Makayla approaching until she speaks. "Hey, how does Chinese sound?" She is standing behind me, but I can't turn to look at her. If I do, I may say something I will regret. "Eryc, is everything okay?"

Is everything okay?

This girl is delusional. I bite the inside of my cheek to

try and control this anger building up inside me, but then she places her hand on my shoulder and sparks fly. With a move as fast as lightning, I spin on my heel, jerking the pamphlet out of her purse and then I throw it at her.

Glancing down at the pamphlet, she presses her fingers over her mouth and shakes her head. "You went through my purse?"

I don't answer her because if I open my mouth, my words will carry so much anger.

"You had no right, that is my personal property." Her eyes meet mine and they look shocked but also angry.

She's angry?

She has no right to be angry at me. "Don't you dare give me crap about your stupid purse. I didn't snoop through your purse. It was on the floor, open and spilling your junk everywhere. I was simply putting that stuff back inside your purse and *that* pamphlet was visible." I take a deep breath.

Breathe, don't do, or say, something stupid.

Then she bends down and picks up the pamphlet and that action is the rock that hits my dam.

Pointing my finger in her face, just a fraction of a space away from her nose, I let my angry words loose. "You are nothing but a heartless shell of the girl I once knew." Dropping my hand, I take a step back. "How could you?"

"How could I what, Eryc?" Fisting the piece of paper in

her hand, she turns her angry glare at me. "Have an abortion?"

I can't even look at her right now, so I stare at a spot over her shoulder.

Throwing the waded-up piece of paper at me, she says, "You don't know anything. You have no idea why I went there. I went there to—"

I don't let her finish that sentence. Her reasoning for doing this doesn't mean squat to me. Cutting my eyes to hers, I return that glare. Judging by the gasp and look of shock on her face, my glare pierced her to the bone. "I don't give a flip why you did it." Great, now I'm yelling at her. I never yell. Pulling in a breath to calm some of this anger, I mentally count to five before I speak. "These babies may have been an inconvenience to you, but to kill them before they've even lived—" I look away and continue in an exasperated breath. "I'm deeply disappointed in you, Makayla."

"Eryc, you're not even listening to what I'm trying to say."

"Because I don't want to hear your selfish reasoning," I growl.

"My selfish reasoning?" Now she's yelling.

"Yeah, Makayla, you're selfish." I speak through clenched teeth.

"Oh my gosh, Eryc. After everything we have been through these last couple of months, *this* is the one thing that is going to break us apart? Seriously?" She throws her hands up in the air then marches toward me, shoving me in the chest. "And I am not selfish."

"Yes, you are. Did you even consider how wrong this is on so many levels?"

"Listen here, preacher's boy."

I hate when she calls me preacher's boy.

"Don't you dare go bringing God into this conversation. You hear me? I understand your faith and I respect it, but this is my body, my pregnancy, and my choice."

"Your body, pregnancy, and choice be damned. You're being a selfish wench."

"I hate you!" She screams at the top of her lungs.

"Yeah, well, I'm not so fond of you right now either!" I scream back which causes her bottom lip to tremble.

Wiping the tears from her face, she snatches her purse from my hand and throws it across the room. "You don't know a damn thing."

All this screaming isn't doing either one of us any good. What I need is some fresh air and time alone. Holding my hands up in the air to indicate this conversation is over, I step around her and walk out the front door without a backward glance.

No explanations, no goodbyes, nothing.

As I descend the porch steps, I can hear her heartbroken sobs through the wooden door. The need to rush back inside and wrap her in the comfort of my arms wars with the desire to strangle her for killing those two inno-cent lives.

Those cries follow me across the lawn to my own house, but I continue to ignore them. If I don't, I will find myself back in her living room.

Though I'm now in my own home, and can no longer hear her wailing, my heart breaks for her. She has been through hell, and I did the one thing I swore to her I would never do. I walked away and left her alone.

Wonderful. I am now a liar.

Flopping down onto the sofa, I exhale a long breath.

Those tortured cries of hers will haunt me all night. This I'm sure of.

37

Makayla

Two days. That's how many days have passed since my argument with Eryc. Two days of pure hell. He hasn't stopped by to check on me or returned any of my phone calls. Nothing. Hell, I haven't even seen him in his front yard. I know he has been going to school because his car is gone in the mornings when I wake up, but it doesn't return until late in the evening. I think he's picking up extra hoursmore than his regular two hours a dayat the café he works at.

He's avoiding me, I just know it.

Had he given me a moment the other night to explain

things, he would have known that I didn't terminate this pregnancy. He would have understood that I do not want to be the douchebag of a parent my own father had turned out to be.

I didn't terminate this pregnancy because I have fallen in love with these two babies.

In fact, the night I was held at gun point was my crossroads. That was the night everything changed for me. Staring death in the face made me realize that though these babies were conceived by an evil prick, they are still a part of me. They are my flesh and blood.

But instead of listening to me, Eryc shoved his religious beliefs and opinions down my throat, and then walked away without a single glance in my direction. Watching him walk out that door broke me worse than Brandt ever did. It was like Eryc took my heart and put it through a meat grinder then smooshed it under his foot on his way out.

These past two days have been a hell worse than the hell I lived over the summer. I sit by the window, hoping to catch a glimpse of him so I can talk to him. To make him listen to the truth.

Heavy footfalls on the hardwood floor grow louder as my brother walks toward the kitchen. "Hey, sis."

Pulling the lunch meat and cheese out of the refrigerator, I toss them on the island.

Thaddeus takes one look at me and furrows his brows. "Are you feeling okay? You look like crap."

Oh, wow. Thanks Thad.

Opening the bag of bread, I pull out two slices and smear mayonnaise on them before answering my twin. "A, thank you so much for the wonderful compliment. Girls absolutely love being told that we look like crap." I add Doritos to my ham and cheese sandwich, pressing down in the bread so that the chips crunch nicely on top of the ham. "And B, Eryc is mad at me."

Thaddeus reaches around me to grab a Coke from the refrigerator. "Sis, the guy is in love with you, I doubt he's mad."

"I don't know about him being in love with me." I take a large bite of my sandwich, wiping mayonnaise from my mouth. "He found something in my purse that he didn't like and...well, now he's mad at me."

"He's mad over something that was in your purse? What did you have, a picture of him that you drew devil horns on or something?"

My brother is joking around but I can't feel the humor behind that comment. Not when my heart is in a million pieces and crying out for Eryc. "No, dipstick. It was an abortion pamphlet."

Thaddeus's eyes bug out and he chokes on the Coke he's sipping. "Well, it's not like you went and did it. Did you?"

"No, Thad. I went in for a consultation, last month before being held at gun point." I take another bite before continuing. "But Eryc wouldn't hear me out. He just jumped to conclusions, yelled, and then left."

My brother shrugs his shoulders like it's no big deal. "So, when he cools down, he'll be back."

"I don't think he will, Thad, that was a couple days ago."

Eyes growing wide, I see red tinting his neck. Thaddeus sets his can of Coke on the island hard enough the brown liquid splashes onto the countertop. "You mean he hasn't spoken to you in two days?"

Shaking my head, I answer my brother. "Not a word, he was angry with me because he thought I terminated the pregnancy."

"That shouldn't have made a difference." My brother is now shouting. He takes a second to collect himself. "It shouldn't matter what you did or didn't do. You are in the process of healing, and he promised to stand by your side."

"I know." Thaddeus's reaction is kind of scaring me. Why is he this upset over Eryc not visiting me? I mean, I have Dr. Fuentez, Rene, and Alesandra. It's not like I don't have a support group to help keep me from drowning.

No longer hungry, I lay my sandwich down on the counter.

"This makes me angry, sis." Thaddeus wipes the

spilled Coke with his hand, then wipes that hand on his jeans. "Knowing the hell that you went through with Brandt, and dealing with mom's accident, then you were kidnapped for heaven's sake. Knowing all of that, he just stops checking on you?" His breathing is coming faster now.

"He was upset," I whisper, glancing down at my uneaten sandwich.

"I don't give a flying flip if he was upset. You have been home all alone the last two days." His voice grows louder with each word.

I don't understand why he is getting this upset. Yes, I have been home alone the last two days, but Alesandra has been here to check on me. Frequently after I told her about my fight with Eryc.

Looking up at my brother, I flinch at the feral look in his eyes. There is only one other time my brother has had this look in his eye, that was when he found my journal and learned what that dipstick, Brandt, had done to me.

Thaddeus's eyes do not stray from mine, he keeps eye contact as he backs out of the kitchen and down the hallway. Curious what he is up to, I follow him down the hall to the living room, where Thaddeus moves the curtain to peer out. Following his gaze, I see Eryc walking to the curb to check the mail.

When my brother's gaze meets mine again, he looks

like a madman. His nostrils flare and his shoulders move with his rapid breaths. "Thad?"

A wicked smile curves his lips, and he bolts out the front door. I run to the open door and watch my brother descend the steps, his hands balling into fists at his sides as he walks toward Eryc.

"Thaddeus, what are you doing?"

Thaddeus isn't listening to me. I have to stop him from doing something boneheaded, like smashing Eryc's face in. Jogging out of the house, I call out to my brother again. He doesn't turn to look at me, he is completely fixated on Eryc. On the second step, my toe catches on a gap in the wood and I lose my balance. I reach out to brace for the impact.

In that moment, everything slows, and I feel as though I am moving in slow motion. Eryc's gaze moves from Thaddeus to where I am falling. His eyes grow wide, and he drops his mail to run toward me. My brother has no idea that I'm falling because his back is to me. Thaddeus stops Eryc with a hand to his chest.

Eryc shoves my brother out of his way and runs toward me.

Crack.

Pain radiates through my arm when it hits the pavement. The impact causes my arm to give out. The weight of my body causes me to fall forward, hitting my forehead on the concrete sidewalk. How embarrassing. Now, not only do I have a possibly broken wrist, but I will have a giant knot on my forehead as well.

Rolling onto my side, I try to focus on my brother and Eryc, but my vision is quickly growing blurry. As if that wasn't annoying, now there is a loud buzzing sound ringing in my ears which is blanketing the noises surrounding me. A shadow moves over me, and I blink several times to try to clear my vision, but it's still just as blurry as looking through water.

"Eryc?" I can't be sure who is standing next to me but since Eryc was running this way, I can only assume its him. One would think that this fall would be nothing more than a minor mishap, I mean kids fall all time and end up with goose eggs on their heads. Why do I get the special idiot treatment?

"Shhh—" Strong arms slide under my body and lift me. "I've got you, baby."

Eryc's voice is the last thing I hear before I allow the darkness to overtake me.

38

Eryc

"You stupid—" I look up in time to see Thaddeus marching toward me with his fists half raised. He is upset, that's easy to see. "Inconsiderate little—" His words no longer penetrate my ears when I see Makayla over his shoulder.

In her pursuit of her brother, she trips on the steps and falls, hitting her head on the sidewalk.

Dropping my mail, I start toward her but Thaddeus halts me with his hand on my chest. "No, you will not run away from me, you dumb moronic jerk wad."

Dumb moronic jerk wad?

What?

I shake my head at his nonsense. "You idiot, yell at me later. Kay just fell and hit her head." I shove Makayla's brother with enough force that he falls on his backside in the grass.

Thaddeus's eyes grow wide at my words and actions.

Ignoring him, I rush across the yard and to her side. Her breathing is labored, and she is blinking like she can't get her vision into focus. All color is swiftly draining from her face and the cut on her forehead is bleeding profusely.

Screw calling an ambulance, they will take forever to get here. I'll be able to rush her to the hospital before they even hop in their vehicle.

"Eryc?" Her voice is weak and pained. Seems like bad luck is attacking this beautiful girl right and left. God, why did I have to be such a shellfish prick these last two days?

"Shhh—" Gently sliding my arms under her, I lift her and cradle her against my chest. "I've got you, baby."

A sigh expels from her lips and her body goes limp. Great, looks as though she has passed out. Not good, not good at all. I move toward my car as quickly as my legs will carry me, while trying not to jar her around too much.

Thaddeus is standing where I left him, his mouth agape. "Did she fall on the babies?"

What is he talking about? I suppose Makayla hasn't told her brother yet. "Babies?"

Thaddeus follows me to the car. "Yes, you blathering idiot. If you had just listened to her the other day then you'd know that she did not *kill*, as you so kindly put it, the babies."

My steps falter at that confession. Makayla hadn't gone through with the procedure? For reasons beyond my comprehension, my heart soars and I rejoice internally. Those babies are alive, and I'm the happiest guy in the world. Or I will be as soon as I know that Makayla will be fine.

Thaddeus jogs around me to open the backdoor of my car. Getting Makayla into the backseat proves to be tricky. I put her in head first. From the other side, Thaddeus grabs her under the arms, dragging her until her body is stretched out along the backseat.

For fear of her rolling off the seat and onto the floor, I decide to sit back here with her. Digging in my front pocket, I toss the keys to Thaddeus. "Here, you drive. I'll sit back here with her to make sure she doesn't fall off the seat and injure herself further."

Truthfully, I should probably be the one driving, there is no telling whether there is alcohol in his system. But my heart is speaking over my rational thoughts. More than anything, I want to be the one holding Makayla. I want to be the one keeping her safe. Truth be told, I'm responsible for her predicament. If I hadn't run off the other day and ignored her calls and texts, then Thaddeus would have never been coming to confront me, and she would have never tripped trying to come to my rescue.

I'm such an idiot.

The drive to Tulsa Memorial feels like it is taking an eternity. Makayla isn't opening her eyes, at all. This is concerning me. Pulling my cell phone out of my back pocket, I send my aunt a text.

> On our way to the hospital with Kay. She fell and hit her head and is currently passed out.

Aunt Rene's reply comes almost immediately.

> AUNT RENE
>
> OMG. I'm packing my lunch away and I'll meet you guys upstairs. Keep an eye on her and call me if anything seems off. How much longer?

No worries there. My eyes haven't left Makayla's face this entire time. I glance out the window to see where we are and how much longer it will be before we get to the hospital. The Yale exit is in sight and Thaddeus is turning on his blinker, preparing for the turn.

I type my one-handed response.

> Turning off on Yale, be there in about four minutes.

"It's okay, baby girl, we're almost there." I brush hair out of Makayla's face as I speak to her. The car bounces when Thaddeus hits a pothole and Makayla lets out a faint grunt. My eyes search her face, hoping to see her eyelids crack open.

No such luck.

Glancing up at her brother, I say through gritted teeth, "Jerk, be careful."

Thaddeus ignores me, which is fine by me.

Other than the ugly gash on Makayla's forehead, she looks like she is sleeping. Guilt for her injury is eating me alive. I understand I'm not the one that tripped her, but I feel the responsibility all the same. Bending down to whisper in her ear, because I don't want Thaddeus to overhear, I confess, "I love you, Kay. Please be alright."

This confession is easy with her unconscious. With her in this state of unawareness, at least I hope she is unaware of what I say, I don't have to fear her look of disgust and face rejection.

Truth is, I love this girl more than life itself. These past two days without her were pure hell. I couldn't function at school, I'm pretty sure I failed my Calculus test yesterday, and I haven't been able to eat. I have been nothing more than a walking, talking zombie.

The stillness of the car draws my attention toward the front window. We are parked in front of the ER doors and two nurses in pale pink scrubs rush toward the car. I recognize one of them from my aunt's clinic. They are here to get Makayla and take her upstairs.

Thaddeus rushes to open the back door and gently lifts Makayla's head so I can slip out from under her. The two nurses maneuver their way around me and get Makayla on a gurney.

As they rush toward the sliding glass doors, one of them calls over her shoulder. "Fourth floor. Follow the signs for maternity and wait in the waiting room. Your aunt will find you after she's examined your friend."

The waiting room. That is the last place I want to be. I want to be by Makayla's side, holding her hand, and making sure she and those precious babies are safe. A nudge on my shoulder pulls me from my rambling thoughts. Thaddeus is looking at me with haunted tear-filled eyes. I have never seen him like this.

"Will they be okay?" He is blaming himself for his sister's accident.

Looks like we are both carrying that guilt.

"It's a bump to the head. Surely the three of them will be just fine." Even though those words leave my lips, I'm having a hard time finding any comfort in them.

I'm like Thaddeus, I'm worrying and fighting thoughts of the worst possible outcome.

He nods, crawls back into the driver's seat, and I take my place in the back. We park in the closest spot available, which happens to be at the very back of the lot, then we jog toward the entrance.

39

Makayla

My head feels like it has been run over by a Mac truck. The pressure building behind my eyeballs is excruciating. I hear movement next to me and open my eyes.

Big mistake.

If I thought the pressure behind my eyeballs was excruciating before, the light in the room triples that pain. A groan is the only sound I make as I turn my head to the side.

"Hey, sweetie." That familiar voice calms my anxiety and soothes away some of my worry.

"Rene." Dryness in my throat causes me to choke and I cough. I can't believe how raspy my voice sounds.

"Yes, sweet girl, I'm right here."

Blinking several times to adjust my eyes to the light- which I'm sure isn't very bright at all, but it sure does hurt, and it feels like I'm staring up into the sunI finally focus on Rene. She is sitting next to me with a laptop in her hand.

"Where am I?" It's a stupid question because as I glance around, I know exactly where I am. I'm in the hospital.

Those brown orbs gaze softly at me. "Sweetheart, you're in the hospital. Do you know why you're here?"

"I, uh, I remember that Eryc is mad at me." The events prior to being in the hospital are a little fuzzy.

"Eryc and Thaddeus rushed you here after you tripped and fell."

I fell?

Rene spins her stool around to read the numbers on the machine. This machine is currently connected to my arm and cutting off the circulation. Once the pressure from the cuff on my upper arm releases, she types on the laptop and then continues our conversation. "Your blood pressure is slightly elevated. It could just be a result from your injuries so I'm not going to stress over it right now, but I will be keeping a close eye on it."

The fall. I remember now.

Thaddeus was so angry at Eryc for not checking in on me and was on his way over to punch him in the face. I fell off the porch steps trying to chase him down and stop his foolishness. "Oh, God. The fall, did I hurt the babies?" My hands instantly clutch my stomach.

Leaning forward, I try to sit up, but my vision grows blurry, and the room begins to waver. Bile rises in the back of my throat.

I must show signs of being nauseous because Rene bends over to pick up the trashcan next to my bed and shoves it under my face. The nasty yellow demonic-like liquid burns my throat in its ascent. When the last of it exits my mouth, I fall back onto the pillows and breathe heavily through my nose.

Fear's tentacles wrap themselves around my heart and squeeze for dear life. Had someone told me last month that I would fear for the safety of my babies I would have thought they were crazy. But now I'm terrified. Since that day I was held at gun point, I started to fall in love with these tiny beings.

I never expected to love them as much as I do, but it has been a gradual love in the making and growing stronger every day. If anything were to happen to either of them, I think I would die a thousand deaths.

Rene sets her laptop on the bedside table and grips my hand in both of hers. "Hey, everything's okay. Stop fretting. Everything looks great. They both have very strong heartbeats." She gazes up at my forehead. "But you, my dear, have one hell of a head wound. I'm going to keep you here over night just to make sure it's nothing serious."

"Okay." Looking around the room, I notice that it is void of any visitors. There's not even a trace that anyone has been here. I don't know what hurts worse. Not seeing my brother, or not seeing Eryc. "Where is Thaddeus?"

Rene smiles. "He was here. He left a few minutes ago to check on your mom."

"Oh, okay." Disappointment overwhelms me, not because my brother isn't here, but because Eryc isn't. I was really hoping that once he found out about the babies he would stick around. What a foolish girl I am. Why would he care about a broken girl trying to overcome depression? I'm just a waste of his time.

Blinking tears out of my eyes, I look up at Rene when she pats my hand. "Eryc went down to the cafeteria to grab something to eat."

Knowing he hadn't left me all alone, I breathe a sigh of relief. "Thank you."

The tense muscles in my neck and shoulders release at the knowledge that Eryc is here and has been with me this entire time. Smiling back at Rene, I close my eyes, exhaustion overwhelming me, and drift off to sleep.

40

Eryc

Thaddeus and I carry our lunch trays to an empty table and sit down. The cafeteria is fairly empty, which is expected since it's three in the afternoon. Makayla's mishap happened shortly after noon. Her brother and I have spent this entire time up in her room. Each of us on either side of her bed, holding her hand.

When my aunt told us that Makayla would be fine and all her tests looked good, I had to work hard to prevent tears from pooling in my eyes. Thaddeus blew out a relieved breath, as did I. Now that we know her and the babies are fine, we are sitting here shoveling horrible hospital chicken and broccoli into our mouths.

"You know," Thaddeus licks his lips as he swallows the food in his mouth, "I still think you're stupid." I don't need him to tell me how stupid I have been. That is a fact I have been mulling over since Makayla's accident. I'm a total fool and this whole incident is my fault.

"I know, and I agree with you." There is nothing more to say. I agree, period. After today, I feel like the stupidest fool on the face of the planet.

The fact is, I love Makayla more than I do myself, and the other day I treated her like the dirt beneath my shoes. I'm such a jerk. I am nothing but a loser. A loser that will work extra hard to earn Makayla's trust once more.

"Hey sugar." Thaddeus and I both look up at the sound of the familiar voice. Standing in pale pink scrubs, the nurse sets her tray on a table across from us and walks over to our table. I recognize her right away. She was part of Brenda's healthcare team. Leaning over, she wraps Thaddeus up in a hug. "I heard about your sister, I'm so sorry."

"Thank you." Thaddeus is still holding onto this nurse like she is his lifeline.

"How are you doin'?" She doesn't seem to mind that Thaddeus is clinging to her like a frightened child. When he doesn't answer her question, she slips out of his hold to cup his cheek. "You listen to me, sugar, you're gonna be okay. You hear me? Ain't nothing gonna happen to that beautiful sister of yours. And the good Lord has your momma in his hands. Now you keep your head up and remember that." Placing her hands on her back, she stretches. "I hear your momma is givin' them nurses and doctors a run for their money."

This makes Thaddeus smile. I set my fork down and watch the exchange between the two of them. They have a familiar, easy-going demeanor toward one another. Good. Thaddeus needs someone in his life to offer him some sound counsel.

"Yes, she is. She would rather be home though." Thaddeus smiles at the nurse. "She's getting stronger every day."

"That's good. You let me know if I can do anything for you, okay?"

"I will. Thanks." After the nurse sits down to eat her meal, Thaddeus turns his sad eyes to me. "What happened to Makayla never should have happened. I'm failing her time and time again."

The pressure this guy puts on himself is unreal and will be his downfall if he doesn't relieve himself of it. For whatever reason, Thaddeus blames himself for his mother's accident, which is bogus because that was the fault of a drunk driver. Then there is his sister. He blames himself for what happened between her and Brandt. Not his fault, that blame belongs to none other than Brandt. Placing blame on himself for her being kidnapped is also bogus since he was nowhere near her when it happened. On top of that, now he blames himself for Makayla's fall.

"Hey." I cross my feet at the ankles and lean forward to rest my weight on my elbows. "You are not failing anyone here." Wetness pools in Thaddeus's eyes and he opens his mouth to speak but I hold up a hand to halt his words. "What happened to your mother was an accident that you nor Kay had control over."

Thaddeus pinches the bridge of his nose, like he is trying to prevent the tears that threaten to flood his eyes.

"As for Kay, there is nothing you could have done. Brandt is a douche that cares about no one. That jerk that tried to kill her was a loser that got what he deserved." I bite the inside of my cheek to keep from saying hateful things about Brandt and that criminal. "Her fall was something you couldn't have predicted either. She tripped, plain and simple." Though I know I am not to blame either, I still feel guilty for her fall. "But I feel ya on that one, I'm feeling guilt for her fall too. If I had just put my feelings aside the other day and just been there for her, without judgement, then she would have never been chasing you down those steps to stop you from confronting me."

Thaddeus nods but doesn't say anything. Instead, he picks up his bottle of Coke and takes a long drink. After several minutes of silence, Thaddeus glances at his watch.

"Mom is due for her next round of therapy in a few and I promised her I'd be there." He picks up his now empty tray. "Tell Makayla I'll be back. Let her know that I'm with mom."

I nod. "Of course."

Thaddeus stands and furrows his brows as if he has something to say but is too nervous to say it. It takes him a little while, but he finally spits out what he wants to say. "Will you stay with Makayla until I can get back?"

Why the guy feels the need to ask me to stay with her is beyond me. Does he not know that I will be by her side? Okay, yes, I did ignore her for two days, but I have no intentions of leaving Makayla ever again. "Yes, of course."

"You know, for a moron, you're a pretty decent guy." Tapping his fingers on the edge of the tray, he smirks. "And I happen to think you're good for my sister." Thaddeus doesn't stick around long enough for me to even reply with a thank you. With a nod, he spins around and leaves.

I drink the last of my tea and head back up to Makayla's room. When I reach her door, I ease it open, so I don't disturb her. She's lying in bed sound asleep. Her rosy lips are set in a relaxed smile and her hands are resting protectively on her stomach.

She is so beautiful.

Very, very gently, I drag a chair close to her bedside

and sit. Picking up her hand, I sandwich it between my own and watch her sleep.

Mine.

Whether she holds the same feelings for me as I do for her, she is, and will always be, my heart. Honestly, she has always held my heart in her hands. Even when we were dorky kids riding the streets on skateboards.

I have always been hers and hers alone.

41

Makayla

Little auburn-haired toddlers running around with ice cream cones fill my dreaming mind. I am happy and content until a vice squeezes my upper arm, cutting of the circulation. Not ready for the two toddlers to leave, I beg them to stay. My begging goes unheard as they giggle and continue playing until my dream fades.

Opening my eyes, I see a petite blonde-haired nurse standing next to my bed. She is glancing at the monitor, then she types notes on the computer. At the sound of my bedsheets moving, she lifts her gaze from the screen.

Her blue eyes sparkle with kindness when she sees me watching her. "Hey there, sweetie. I'm just checking on your blood pressure. It's back down where it should be. You and those babies are looking good." Nodding to the other side of the room, she says, "He's been here all day."

I glance over, fully expecting to see my brother. Instead, I find Eryc sitting in a chair with his hands folded together in his lap and his head dangling forward at a breaking angle. It amazes me how he can even sleep in that position. Talk about a major crick. The one guy who has become my rock, the one who brings me joy in my hurting world, is here with me instead of at home.

My nose stings with the onset of tears and I breathe deeply to stop them from forming. "He's been here the entire time."

I didn't phrase that as a question but the nurse answers anyway. "Yes, he's only left this room to grab food. He refuses to leave your side. That's quite the boyfriend you got there."

Quite the boyfriend?

Eryc isn't my boyfriend but hearing this nurse refer to him as such brings a smile to my face. I could totally see myself as Eryc's girlfriend. This guy has been healing me from my dark thoughts for over a month now. Because of him, I am slowly returning to the fun and happy girl I once was.

Eryc is the other half of my heart.

The nurse points to a red button on the railing of my bed. "Push this call button if you need anything."

"I will, thanks."

"You're welcome." The nurse pats my leg before gathering her little clipboard from where it lay next to the computer, and leaves.

From the long hours in this bed, my muscles are achy. I stretch to relieve some of the tension. When I do, a sharp pain shoots from my calf, up my leg and to my hip. The jolt surprises me and I let out a small yelp.

That little noise startles Eryc out of sleep and he immediately jumps out of his chair, rubbing sleep from his eyes. "You okay? Do I need to find the nurse?" He takes a step and I reach out to hook a finger through his belt loop. He glances down at where my hand is resting on his hip and places his on top of mine. "I can get a nurse if you need pain meds or something."

The concern on his face pierces my soul and I let him know that I'm okay. "I don't need pain meds. I just stretched wrong, I'm not in pain. I promise."

He scrutinizes my face, probably looking for signs that I really am in pain. I wasn't lying, I'm not in pain. It was just a small jolt that was most likely caused from my muscles being so stiff. "Okay." He runs his fingers through his hair then unhooks my finger from his belt loop.

One question is weighing heavily on my mind. Until I get an answer, I will not be able to relax. I inhale two deep breaths before jumping in head first. "Eryc, are you still mad at me?"

His face is unreadable, and his mouth is set in a firm line. Knots form in the pit of my stomach at the possibility that he hates me. "Kay, I'm not mad at you." Lowering his head, he casts his gaze downward. "When I discovered that pamphlet, it shocked me. You know where I stand on that issue."

"I know." Disappointment causes my voice to come out in a whisper.

"But regardless, I should have never been hateful toward you. And for that, I will be eternally sorry." Gathering my bedsheet in his hands, he twists it around his fingers.

I'm not sure what to say so I stay silent and wait for him to lead this conversation. Minutes pass, which feel like an eternity, then he lifts his gaze to mine. Unshed tears shine in his brown pools and the instant he blinks, they fall, leaving a wet trail down his cheeks.

Seeing the evidence of his sorrow, I sit up, ignoring the pain that radiates through my thigh and settles in my hip. Turning so my body faces his, I swipe my thumbs across his cheeks to wipe away the tears.

His hands come up and gently grip my wrists, being extra careful with my left hand which is in a cast. "Please don't feel sorry for me, Kay." Tugging my hands down to my knees, he scoots his chair closer and sits. Lifting my right hand in his, he says, "I was a jerk."

"No—"

Shaking his head, he cuts me off. "I was." Tears are now flowing freely down his face, and his body begins trembling. I can see that he is struggling to keep his sobs silent. I keep quiet and allow him the time he needs to collect himself. Eryc's breathing is long and slow, but his tears are not slowing down.

Finally, he leans forward until our foreheads are touching. "I'm so sorry, baby," he chokes out with a sob.

Baby?

That word freezes me. My whole body locks up on me and all I can do is stare into his eyes. Those brown orbs glisten with his tears and they seem to gaze all the way to my soul. That one word has nervous butterflies stirring in my belly and twisting in my gut. *Baby* is a word that Eryc has never used toward anyone older than three.

Was it a slip? A mistake?

"Eryc?"

Cupping my face, he tilts my head and brings his lips to mine in the softest of kisses. A kiss like I have never experienced before. Those warm lips linger in the most tender way and hold so much promise in them. Running his fingers through my hair, he gives a slight tug before pulling away to look into my eyes.

"Look, I'm not gonna lie to you. I understand that you

don't want ties to Brandt, I get that. Thaddeus told me you didn't do it, but I know you want to. It breaks my heart and goes against everything I believe in." Fingers still tangled in my hair, Eryc presses his nose to mine. "But you matter to me, and I will never turn my back on you again."

So many emotions pass over his features but the one that shines like a beacon is love. So much love. I tell him what I've wanted to tell him since he found that pamphlet. "That option is no longer on the table."

Confusion shines on his face and his brows furrow questioningly.

Gripping the loose fabric at his sides, I twist the material between my fingers. "When I was held at gunpoint, something in me clicked. I was suddenly afraid to lose the babies. I feared for their safety." Emotion thickens my voice, the threat of tears stinging my nostrils. "I...I don't know how, but when I stared down the barrel of that gun, my heart filled with love. Being a mom is not something I planned on, especially not with a guy I don't love. But it is what it is."

"So, you" He pauses. "You're not terminating the pregnancy?" Hope flashes in his brown eyes and they glisten with new tears.

To affirm, I shake my head. His hands drop from my face, and he leans back in his chair, silent. I wish he would speak so I could know what he's thinking. Biting my bottom lip, I wait for him to say something, anything, but he just sits there with an unreadable expression.

The silence is eating away at me, so I decide to break it. "I've decided that not only am I going to carry them to term, but I'm also going to raise these babies and give them what my deadbeat of a father never gave Thad and me."

42

Eryc

Wow. She is not only going to give birth to them, but she is going to keep them. This is amazing news. Joy fills my heart, not just because of the fact that they will have a chance at life, but because I will have them in my life. If Makayla allows me to, I will raise them as my own. The beating organ in my chest swells until I'm afraid it might burst from my body.

Are we too young to be parents? Probably. Should we be going to college and living out the rest of our teenage years. Yes, of course. But this is not the hand Makayla was dealt. Because I love her and want to spend my life with her, assuming she wants the same, this is also the hand I am being dealt.

I don't despise it. My love for her runs deep. I'll support her and the kids and be the kind of dad she never had. The kind of dad those kids deserve.

Her fingers start twisting in the ends of her gown and I know that this silence is making her nervous. Gripping my bottom lip between my teeth, I let it loose with a pop. Her gaze lingers on my lips, and I wonder if she can still feel them against hers. I know I can still feel hers along mine.

Not able to resist any longer, I stand from my chair and motion for her to scoot over. When she does, I climb in the bed next to her and gather her in my arms, leaning back against the mound of pillows. She sucks in a breath between her teeth.

She won't admit it, but I know she is in more pain than she wants me to believe. It worries me that she is in pain, but my aunt has assured me numerous times that Makayla and the babies are fine. Aunt Rene also told me that she will be sore from the fall, and it may take a couple of days for that soreness to go away.

Caressing her head where it rests on my chest, I take a deep breath and prepare to tell her exactly how I feel. I just hope she feels the same. "Kay?"

She tilts her head, so she can look me in the eyes.

"In case you haven't connected the dots and figured it out." I bite the inside of my cheek to calm my nerves. This will be the first time I have ever said these words to a girl before. Well, I have said them to my aunt and mom, but they don't count.

Her brows lift and she pulls back a little to see me better. "Eryc?"

Well, it's now or never. "I love you."

Her eyes grow wide, and her mouth falls open.

I have surprised her, that much I can see. What I can't decipher is whether those words surprised her in a good way, or if she is repulsed by them. "Kay? Please say something."

Tears build up in her eyes and fall when she blinks. I swipe my thumb over them but more fall to take their place. "Eryc." She shakes her head and my heart squeezes painfully. "As much as I want this, I can't ask you to love me."

I open my mouth to speak but she silences me with a finger to my lips.

"Eryc, I'm pregnant with someone else's children. You deserve so much more than me. You deserve your own family with your own children."

Selfless. That's what my girl is.

She is selfless for being willing to give up her own desires to ensure I get what I deserve. "You know what,

Kay? You are absolutely right. I do deserve to have my very own family."

I can see that my words have shocked her. She opens and closes her mouth several times, but no words come out.

This brings a chuckle out of me which causes her jaw to drop. "Kay, you are the family I want. I have never wanted another girl. It's always been you." Pointing to her belly, I say, "And these two precious babies are just a bonus."

This confession has the opposite effect from what I was hoping to accomplish. She sits up, holding the back of her gown closed, and scoots away from me. "Eryc, don't. You can't love me." Turning her back to me, she says, "You know what all happened this summer. I'm not worthy of your love."

"You are worth so much more than you know and can even imagine."

Now, she looks at me over her shoulder. "You're a preacher's kid and I'm just a sinner who drank and got high, then ended up with the wrong boy. Your parents would never approve because it would mess up their dreams of you going into ministry."

"A sinner? You're calling yourself a sinner?" I chuckle and she frowns at me. "Baby, we're all sinners. My parents included." She shakes her head, but I nod mine. "Trust me, there is nothing you've done that is a worse sin than mine. We all have a past. Some have a more colorful, or painful, past but we're all guilty of something. For instance, I've struggled with wanting to murder Brandt here lately."

At my confession, she turns around to face me, crossing her legs underneath her. "So, you want me, regardless of how bruised and damaged I am?"

I nod. "I do. You're it for me."

"Eryc, I'm a broken mess. Besides, I haven't even stepped foot in church in ages. Your parents will not accept me. Hell, there is no way that God himself will accept me."

"Kay, you have this all wrong. Yes, my parents are ministers, but they will accept you. They already have." I'm not sure where all of this is coming from.

"Eryc, I'm not worthy of your love."

Her negativity toward herself is slicing my heart in two. "You are worthy. Kay, this may sound ridiculous and stupid, but you need to forgive yourself for this past summer. Because until you forgive yourself and learn to love yourself again, that burden will not ease. You have come a long way since your therapy sessions, and I am so proud of you. But forgiving yourself is the key to fully moving on."

Tears spill down her cheeks and she chokes on a sob. "I don't know how."

Now we're starting to break through that tough exterior. "I'm here and I'm not going anywhere. We'll do this together. With the help of Dr. Fuentez, my aunt, Alesandra, and me, you will learn to forgive and love yourself again." Sliding my finger under her chin, I tilt her head up and lean in for another kiss.

This kiss is nothing like the first one.

The first kiss had been soft and tender. This kiss is possessive.

I claim her lips in a bruising kiss, declaring my love for her and claiming her as mine. Darting my tongue out to brush against her lips, I'm surprised when she opens her mouth and slides her tongue along mine.

Our tongues dance and glide together, desperate for more. She scoots close, wrapping her arms around my neck. Makayla is the first girl I have ever kissed, and damn, this feels amazing. I don't want this to end but I don't want a nurse to walk in and embarrass her either.

Breaking the kiss, I pull back.

We are both breathing heavily, and her lips are glistening from our kiss. She smiles and I caress her cheek with my knuckles. As she removes her arms from around my neck, I notice markings on her inner wrist. Gripping her hand, I tug her arm close and glance down at her wrist. It's a purple infinity with the word hope scripted within and a semicolon in the center.

I smile up at her. "You got a tattoo?"

"Oh, um." Sucking her bottom lip between her teeth,

she looks away. "Yeah, I did. Alesandra sketched it out and took me to have it done."

I know the meaning behind this tattoo, and I approve. "I love it."

"You do?"

"I do." I kiss her again and murmur against her lips. "I love you."

Makayla leans her forehead on mine and places her hand over my heart. "I love you too."

43

Eryc's admission terrifies me. I have never been in a relationship this serious. Hell, I haven't been in a relationship that lasted more than two weeks, let alone get to the *love* stage. And this guy says he will help me with the babies as if they were his own.

Say what?

I feel like I am living in the twilight zone. Tell me, what eighteen-year-old guy says that to a girl? None of them do. All the other guys our age would be running for the hills. No lie, they would be out of here before I could even say hello.

I glace over at Eryc. He is sleeping in that hard metal hospital chair with its minimal cushioning. This is the third or fourth time I have caught him sleeping like this and I wonder why he keeps putting himself in this position.

The angle his neck is bent in has to be causing him pain. Even though he could have gone home and slept in his own bed, he chose to stay here with me so I wouldn't be alone. That touches the very center of my heart.

A light knock on the door has me turning my attention from Eryc. Rene walks in with a nurse who is wearing those pale pink scrubs. The nurse smiles and introduces herself. "Hi, sweetie. My name is Marie. I'll be your nurse this morning." She heads over to the machine and presses a button. The cuff on my arm inflates, cutting off blood flow to my arm.

Rene watches the numbers on the machine and smiles once the air deflates from this stupid cuff. "Perfect." She glances over at her nephew and shakes her head with a smile. "That nephew of mine is as stubborn as they come."

I follow her line of sight and find Eryc beginning to stir. Blinking his eyes open as if he can sense our gazes on him, he smiles and leans forward with a wince. Rubbing the back of his neck, he stretches his head from side-to-side which results in two loud cracks.

Tucking my feet under me, I pat the mattress in front

of me. Eryc raises his brow but sits on the bed. "Turn," I say.

He does and I start to rub his shoulders and neck. It's a bit difficult doing this one handed, but I manage. Lowering his head, his whole body begins to relax, and he lets out a satisfied moan. Rene chuckles and then hands me a few papers. "Nurse Marie will get you ready to go home after you've had breakfast. Everything looks great and I don't foresee any complications."

"Okay." I cannot wait to get home. No offense to the staff here but I'm ready for my comfy bed and Netflix.

"Great. I need to get back to the clinic and attend to my patients, but I'll stop by tonight with dinner and check in on you." She pats me on the leg and waves to Eryc on her way out the door.

The nurse finishes typing on the computer and goes over the papers Rene gave me. Things to watch for like bleeding, persistent pain, sudden dizziness, and loss of balance. Eryc pays close attention and I have no doubt that he will be keeping a close eye on me. As she goes over the last page, another nurse walks in carrying a tray of food with a glass of orange juice and a carton of milk.

Eryc watches as I eat the eggs, bacon, and oatmeal. I try offering him a bite, but he refuses and urges me to eat it all. While I eat, he talks about football. Football is a sport I know nothing about. Yes, I go to all the home games, but I don't know the first thing about the sport. I do know what a touchdown is, so there is that.

I continue listening while I eat, nodding every now and then when he says something that sounds important. When the last of my food is consumed, Eryc grabs a bag from a nearby chair. Handing it to me he says, "I had Thaddeus bring you some clothes and proper soap and shampoo."

"Thank you." I take the bag and carry it to the bathroom. A nice hot shower is just what I need.

THE SHOWER indeed was what I needed, now I feel more like myself. Per my request, Eryc is driving me to the rehab center to see my mom. It has been a couple of days since I have been in to see her, and I miss her like crazy. Silence fills the car but it's not uncomfortable at all. Eryc's fingers are twined with mine and his thumb gently caresses the back of my hand. I'm on cloud nine and smiling like an idiot.

Walking into the rehab facility, hand-in-hand with Eryc, I wave at the nurses on my way to mom's room. Thaddeus is walking out of the room as we approach. "Hey, I was just on my way to see you."

Letting go of Eryc's hand, I wrap my arms around my

brother. Sadly, he smells like two-day old whiskey. "Thaddeus, you need to quit drinking. It's not healthy."

Planting a kiss to the top of my head, he says, "Don't worry about me." I wish he wouldn't shut down on me like this. "Mom just finished her morning therapy. She'll be happy to see you." Slipping his cell phone from his back pocket, he sends out a text and then walks away.

Mom is sitting in bed when we walk in. Smiling from ear-to-ear, she puts her magazine down and waves. "Hi, baby, I missed you."

"I missed you too, momma." I lean over and give her a gentle hug. She is a lot stronger now, but I can't help handling her with care.

She kisses me on the cheek and then motions for Eryc to come closer. "Come here, Eryc, and give me a hug." Eryc does and mom holds on to him for a good two minutes it seems. "I hear you've been taking good care of my Makayla."

"Yes, ma'am." Once mom releases him, Eryc stands behind me and wraps his arms around my waist, resting his chin on my shoulder.

Mom's eyes travel from Eryc to me and back again. When his hands press against my stomach protectively, mom raises a brow, but doesn't say anything.

Reaching out, I take hold of her hand. "Mom, we have something we'd like to talk to you about."

Eryc gives me a gentle squeeze, encouraging me to

continue. Mom doesn't speak, she gives me her full attention.

"Momma, I'm pregnant."

My mom smiles and pats my hand. "Oh, baby." Moisture builds in her eyes and wets her lashes. "This is not what I expected during your senior year of high school."

I frown at her words.

"But I know you will be the best mom in the world and I'm happy for you two."

My mom thinks Eryc is the father. Obviously, because she doesn't know about Brandt. That is a complication I will not burden her with until she is healthy and back at home. I will not comprise her recovery with that wicked truth.

"Thank you, Brenda," Eryc says. "We're very excited about them."

"Them?" my mom questions. After a second passes, she sucks in a breath and smiles big. "You're having twins?"

"Yes, momma."

The smile on her face grows even bigger and it lights up her eyes. "Oh, my little girl is having twins. I couldn't be more excited."

44
_____

Eryc
Five months later

The last several months have been hard on Makayla. She finally found the courage to go to the police with her journal. Brandt and Lee were charged. Vince got a slap on the wrist since he didn't physically touch her. But despite the stress of the trial, my girl was a trooper through the whole ordeal. And to our surprise, Brandt waved away his rights to the babies. He said he had no interest in being a father.

Brandt waving away his rights was music to my ears

and I rejoiced. I didn't want to share my kids with that sorry piece of garbage anyway.

In preparation for the babies, I took some extra classes and was able to graduate early. My parents were against it but I needed to free up my schedule so I could work full time in order to support my family. Those measly two hours a day were not cutting it.

Makayla is sitting on a barstool, sipping ice water when I walk in. She is a month away from her due date and miserable. The twins take up so much room, she has a hard time getting around. Hiding my surprise behind my back, I plant a kiss to the top of her head.

"And what are you hiding?" she asks.

Bending down, I kiss her lips as I slide the glass vase onto the counter in front of her. When I pull back, her eyes zone in on the dozen red roses.

"Those are so beautiful, Eryc."

"Not as beautiful as you, baby." I touch her swollen belly and one of the twins kicks my palm. "Somebody's happy to hear my voice." Another kick to my palm. I love feeling them kick and move beneath my touch. "Oh, I have something else for you." Bringing my other hand out from behind my back, I hand her the heart-shaped box of chocolates. "Happy Valentine's Day."

The wrapping crinkles loudly as she unwraps the box. Popping a chocolate in her mouth, her eyes roll back, and she moans. "Oh, my goodness, these are amazing." Once she swallows, she licks her lips and says, "Happy Valentine's Day to you too." Selecting a chocolate, she holds it up to my lips.

Opening my mouth, I bite into the creamy goodness. She's right, it is good. I watch my girl eat another chocolate and marvel at where we are. We have been a couple since October and are madly in love.

"I have one last surprise for you."

"What? Eryc, you didn't have to get me anything else."

"I know that." Footsteps sound in the hallway and Makayla turns to see her mother, Thaddeus, both of my parents, Rene, Chad, and Alesandra walk in.

While she is focusing on them, I slip down onto my knee and pull the soft velvet box from my pants pocket. "Makayla?" At the sound of my voice, she glances at me and gasps. "Baby, I love you more than I love the air I breathe. You are my entire world. Without you I am nothing."

Tears run down her face.

Opening the box, I pull the ring free. "Makayla, will you marry me?"

"Yes, of course." Cheers and clapping fill the room and Makayla giggles into our kiss. "I love you."

"I love you too." I help her when she starts to slide off the barstool.

She gives her mother a hug and then makes her way to everyone else. Just as Alesandra kisses her cheek,

Makayla doubles over, clutching her stomach. "Oh, that hurt."

I'm quickly at her side, supporting her under the arm.

Brenda reaches out to her daughter. "Makayla, honey, are you alright?" Just as Makayla straightens, she doubles over again. "That's it, we're going to the hospital," Brenda says.

I GAZE at my little auburn-haired babies, one boy and one girl. John and Irene. I have a feeling our little girl is going to give us a run for our money. Only minutes old and she already has an attitude.

Brenda is holding Irene, and my mom is holding John, each woman is cooing and babbling at the babies, and I can't help but smile at them. Joy swells in my heart.

This is my family.

EPILOGUE

Makayla

I couldn't be happier. The birth of my twins was the most amazing experience of my life, and I wouldn't trade them for the world. I am so glad I made the decision to keep them. They bring such joy to my life.

I'm still in group therapy and Dr. Fuentez is so much more than just my doctor, she has become part of my family. Alesandra is my best friend and has been a blessing to me and my babies. In fact, we refer to her as their Aunt Al. Eryc's best friend, Chad, has been given the title of Uncle. He has been around to help us every day. In fact, I think he has fallen in love with my kids.

Today is the day. The day that I become Makayla Delmonte. My mom is fussing over my hair and Janet, Eryc's mom, is fussing over my makeup. I just want time to fast forward so I can walk down the aisle and marry the love of my life.

Janet picks up Irene and mom picks up John. The two of them carry the babies from the room and Alesandra straightens my veil. "You ready?" I nod. "Good, because it's time to get this show started."

We walk out hand-in-hand and meet Thaddeus at the double doors. My father should be the one to give me away but unfortunately, he is a loser that gave me up before he got to know me. That's okay. I have my brother. Thaddeus holds his arm out and I loop mine through his. Alesandra opens the double doors, and the music starts the instant she steps foot in the sanctuary.

Thaddeus walks me down the aisle and gives me away then takes his place beside Chad as Eryc's groomsman. Handing my bouquet to Alesandra, I take Eryc's outstretched hands. Eryc's father is conducting the ceremony. When he gives Eryc the go ahead, Eryc recites his vows.

"Kay, you are my everything. You are my best friend. The woman that I love. I take you, not just as my best friend, but my lover, the mother of my children, and my wife. I will respect and love you in your successes and in your failures. I'll care for you in sickness and in health, until death do us part."

I swallow the tightness from my throat. His speech was so beautiful, there is no way mine will sound as good.

"Eryc, you are my world. I take you to be, not only my best friend, but my lover, the father of my children, and my husband. I will respect and love you in your successes and in your failures. I will care for you in sickness and in health, until death do us part."

Taking the ring from Thaddeus, Eryc slips it onto my finger. "With this ring, I thee wed. Wear it as a symbol of our love and commitment."

Alesandra hands me the matching band and I slip it onto Eryc's finger. "With this ring, I thee wed. Wear it as a symbol of our love and commitment."

Eryc's father, my father-in-law, smiles and says, "You may now kiss your bride."

Eryc cups my face and leans in ever-so-slowly. The anticipation of this kiss is almost more than I can bear.

When his lips finally touch mine, electricity sparks between us. This kiss is different from all the others we have shared. This one is a uniting of our hearts and our lives.

"Ladies and gentlemen, I present to you Mr. and Mrs. Eryc Delmonte."

PLAYLIST

Alter Bridge – Watch Over You

Bishop Briggs – Dark Side

Luke Bryan – Crash My Party

Luke Bryan – I Don't Want This Night to End

The Calling – Wherever You Will Go

Miley Cyrus – The Climb

Miley Cyrus – When I Look at You

Daughtry – It's Not Over

Five Finger Death Punch – Wrong Side of Heaven

The Fray – Look After You

The Fray – You Found Me

Chase Goehring – Hurt

Hozier – To Be Alone

Sam Hunt – Take Your Time

Imagine Dragons – It's Time

Lady Antebellum – I Run to You

Lady Antebellum – Just A Kiss

Lady Antebellum – Need You Now

Lifehouse – You and Me

Maroon 5 – She Will Be Loved

Tim McGraw, Faith Hill – Speak to A Girl

MUSE – Dig Down

NF – Let You Down

NF – Oh Lord

Christina Perri – Jar of Hearts

P.O.D. – Alive

Seether – Broken

Ed Sheeran – Thinking Out Loud

Shinedown – If You Only Knew

Shinedown – Simple Man

Justin Timberlake – Not A Bad Thing

Justin Timberlake – Say Something

Justin Timberlake – Until the End of Time

Twenty One Pilots – Heavydirtysoul

Keith Urban – The Fighter

NOTE FROM THE AUTHOR

Asking for help is nothing to be ashamed of. If you are struggling with depression, ask for help. Talk to your parents, a teacher, a counselor, a pastor, or call a hotline. There are people out there that want to help you.
You are not alone.

ABOUT THE AUTHOR

Tich is a born and raised Oklahoma resident and the mother of six. Her passion for reading started at an early age when her Aunt Vicky gave her the novel *Heidi* for Christmas. She didn't start writing until middle school, after being inspired by her best friend's short stories.

Being a mom of six is a huge blessing and she is extremely grateful to be able to stay home with the children. Other than books, she loves coffee and candles. There is nothing more relaxing than drinking coffee and reading a book while the aroma of a fruity candle fills the air.

Join the reader group on Facebook: Tich's Book Haven
You can also sign up for her newsletter via her website.

Connect with Tich Online
tichbrewster.com
Facebook: @TichBrewsterAuthor
Instagram, X, TikTok: @TichBrewster